Cranford Estate Siblings

*Wherever the siblings of Cranford Estate go,
scandal is sure to follow!*

As the future marquess, William must
marry appropriately, yet he's tempted by
his close friend's sister, Anna... A most
inconvenient attraction indeed!

Tilly flees London with her reputation in tatters!
And promptly meets Lucas, the Earl of Clifton,
and his adorable baby nephew. But with scandal
hot on her heels, will she make a suitable wife?

Eligible bachelor Charles is stunned when
strikingly unconventional Lucy goes out of her
way to avoid him. They have a connection,
but Lucy is hiding a heartbreaking secret...

Read William's story in
Lord Lancaster Courts a Scandal
Available now

And look out for Tilly's and Charles's stories
Coming soon

Author Note

After spending several years in India, Lord William Lancaster is returning to England to take up his position as the future Marquess of Elvington. When his close friend is killed, Lord Lancaster, wealthy and aristocratic, seems the answer to a young girl's prayers—but not so for Anna Harris, his friend's sister. Before his death, his friend appointed Lord Lancaster as her guardian for the time it takes them to reach England.

Anna is a resentful, smoldering young woman who proves to be quite a handful for the dark and rather sardonic Lord Lancaster, in spite of the unexpected passion that erupts between them on board the East Indiaman. Finding herself a wealthy young woman, nineteen, beautiful and impulsive, she wants to build a new life in England. It proves to be a turbulent voyage as she tries to fight her attraction to Lord Lancaster, but she is too vulnerable to his potent masculinity.

From India's shores to Regency London, their tempestuous romance is played out, a romance between two people destined for each other.

HELEN DICKSON

—

Lord Lancaster Courts a Scandal

HARLEQUIN
HISTORICAL

ISBN-13: 978-1-335-72374-1

Lord Lancaster Courts a Scandal

Copyright © 2023 by Helen Dickson

Harlequin Enterprises ULC
22 Adelaide St. West, 41st Floor
Toronto, Ontario M5H 4E3, Canada
www.Harlequin.com

Printed in U.S.A.

Helen Dickson was born and still lives in South Yorkshire, UK, with her retired farm manager husband. Having moved out of the busy farmhouse where she raised their two sons, she now has more time to indulge in her favorite pastimes. She enjoys being outdoors, traveling, reading and music. An incurable romantic, she writes for pleasure. It was a love of history that drove her to writing historical fiction.

Books by Helen Dickson

Harlequin Historical

Caught in Scandal's Storm
Lucy Lane and the Lieutenant
Lord Lansbury's Christmas Wedding
Royalist on the Run
The Foundling Bride
Carrying the Gentleman's Secret
A Vow for an Heiress
The Governess's Scandalous Marriage
Reunited at the King's Court
Wedded for His Secret Child
Resisting Her Enemy Lord
A Viscount to Save Her Reputation
Enthralled by Her Enemy's Kiss
To Catch a Runaway Bride
Conveniently Wed to a Spy

Cranford Estate Siblings

Lord Lancaster Courts a Scandal

Castonbury Park

The Housemaid's Scandalous Secret

Visit the Author Profile page
at Harlequin.com for more titles.

Chapter One

1810

The sun was high and a quiet wind blew the clouds slowly across the sky as William Lancaster, Lord Lancaster and future Marquess of Elvington, rode into the suburbs of Bombay, having travelled over many days from Agra in the north of India, stopping at established campsites along the way.

Slowing his horse to a gentle trot, he delighted in the scents and sounds all around him. The road was busy with all manner of traffic—bullocks and mules pulling carts piled high with wares of every description, wheels and hooves churning up clouds of dust in their wake. The whole of India was dry and exhausted as it awaited the longed-for downpours of the monsoons.

With amazement and interest William reined in his mount when a horse and rider drew his attention. The rider was a young woman and he paused to observe her as she rode over the vast landscape, as refreshingly cool as an invigorating wind. It was her sheer energy and vibrancy that drew him to her. She was seated with ease astride a spirited light grey mare, which she controlled superbly. He noticed her hands, the reins looped loosely through them, fine hands, light but strong, and he had no doubt that she knew how to handle even the most spirited horse.

She presented a lovely picture in her blue-sprigged dress, which spread over the flanks of her horse, outlining her long slim legs beneath her skirts and setting off to perfection her trim waist and firm breasts. A wide-brimmed hat sat on her head and a heavy plait as thick as his wrist and the colour of ripe corn bounced against her spine. With a gentle kick of her heels, she gave her mount its head with a graceful expertise, breaking into a gallop and scattering birds and a couple of grazing cows. She rode like the wind, leaping effortlessly over a low fence, horse and rider locked together as one entity.

It was most unusual for a young European lady to adopt the masculine form of riding—they usually chose to ride side-saddle, at least when in public, and with more decorum, although he suspected that here was no ordinary young lady, but one who cared little for convention. It was clear she had no regard for her safety. Why had she no groom to protect her from the dangers that lurked in every shadow? Not until she had disappeared from view did he continue on his journey.

Four inches over six feet tall, William Lancaster was a man diverse and complex and could be utterly ruthless when the need arose. He possessed a haughty reserve that was not inviting and set him apart from others in society. There was a hard set to his firm jaw and his wide, well-shaped mouth was often in a stern line. There was an aggressive confidence and strength of purpose in his features. His face was one of arrogant handsomeness and dark brows slashed his forehead. His hair was thick and ebony black. In the midst of so much darkness his eyes were brilliant blue, striking and piercing. Hidden deep in them was a cynicism, watching and mocking.

Eventually he found himself at the house he was looking for. The British civil population had established a settlement a couple of miles or so from the centre of the town. It was dotted with neat bungalows and houses built in the European style, with the addition of a veranda to shade the rooms from the hot sun. Tethering his horse to the gatepost of the one he wanted, he walked up the short gravel drive. The single-storey house was white with blue-painted shutters. The white walls had taken on a pinkish hue. Two neatly mown lawns were surrounded by banks of sweet-peas and roses, their scents mingling with the smell of warm earth.

The door was opened by a lady he realised must be Mrs Andrews, the wife of a civil servant in the East India Company currently stationed in Lucknow. She was expecting him and knew the purpose of his visit, which was to take her ward to England. Mrs Andrews was of medium height with light brown hair and soft grey eyes. In her late fifties, she was kind and amiable and she welcomed William into her home. Cold drinks were brought to them by a servant. For a while their conversation was formal and polite as she enquired about his journey from the north and told him how she was looking forward to joining her husband very soon in Lucknow.

'Is Miss Harris happy to be returning to England?' William asked.

'Sadly, no, she is not. I'm afraid she was most upset to learn of her brother's death—and especially so when she was informed that you would be arriving in Bombay to take her back to England. She knows there is nothing to keep her in India, but she has fallen in love with the vibrancy of the country—as most people do who come here and have no wish to return to the dull greyness of London. You must try to understand how she feels and her reluctance to leave India.'

'She's had a whole month to come to terms with it.' He raised a quizzical brow and shrugged impatiently. 'Heavens! It is not my intention to upset the girl.'

'No, of course not. You are to take her to her uncle, I believe.'

'That was what Johnathan wanted. Knowing he was dying, he wrote to his uncle informing him to expect his niece.'

'Was there nothing that could be done when he was wounded?'

'Unfortunately not. After the attack he lived just long enough to make arrangements for his sister.'

'Was the culprit apprehended?'

He shook his head, averting his eyes, the memory and the brutal manner of his friend's death too painful to think of just then. 'No—there were several involved in the skirmish. It could have been any one of them.' William was almost certain he knew who had killed his good friend Johnathan Harris, but proving it was another matter. Knowing William was to return to England, Johnathan had given him the task of taking his sister with him and to see her settled with his Uncle Robert in London. Unable to refuse a request from a man who had saved his live on two occasions, a man whose life William could have saved with forethought, with guilt eating away at him and wanting to ease his friend's last hours, William had agreed.

'It's a great pity her mother isn't going to be in London to take charge of her. From what I understand, she is a woman who concerns herself with her own pleasures and is only too happy to let her daughter fend for herself. That is all very well for her grown-up son, but a young girl, vulnerable and at the mercy of a harsh world, is another matter entirely. I believe Mrs Harris is in London at present—with her latest gentleman.'

'I know very little about her. Johnathan rarely spoke of his mother. What's Miss Harris like?'

'It hasn't always been easy over the three years she's been with us. At least her education has been taken care of. There are times when she can be stubborn and wilful, a streak that is tempered by an incredible gentleness and compassion, for she is inclined to let her heart rule her head—especially when she finds a stray or wounded animal in need of protecting. I have tried to curb her wilfulness...' She sighed, shaking her head. 'I suppose the fault is mostly mine for allowing her far too much freedom. My husband and I—never blessed with children of our own—have become very fond of her and we'll miss her terribly when she goes.'

'I expect you've done an admirable job, Mrs Andrews. It must be difficult at times taking charge of someone else's child.'

'She is no longer a child, but a grown-up young lady.

I can only hope that when she leaves here, she will have learned something to her advantage that will benefit her in her new life.'

'I am sure you have done whatever is necessary to prepare her for the journey.'

Irritated that his charge was not there to receive him, William got to his feet and walked towards the veranda. He stood looking out over the garden. Not enamoured of escorting an impressionable nineteen-year-old on a voyage of five to six months, depending on favourable winds and weather, he viewed the journey with a jaundiced eye.

William was an impressive-looking figure. At twenty-nine years old, the heir to a marquessate, he had been born at the magnificent Cranford Park estate in Berkshire. When he had come out to India almost ten years earlier, he had been in the employ of the East India Company before deciding to go it alone. And now he was returning to England to settle some urgent matters that had cropped up with his family.

When Miss Harris finally arrived, she did not so much as enter the house as make an entrance, coming in from the back of the house and pausing for a moment in the doorway before striding into the centre of the room and throwing her hat into the nearest chair. William was standing with his back to her. He felt her presence in the house before anything was said, having an odd, prickly feeling on the back of his neck. The sensation was so strong that he turned slowly and saw her.

Her stillness was like a positive force and there was something about her, something vibrant, and she held his attention by the perfect picture she made—a pale silhouette against the darkness of the open doorway behind her. Oddly enough, her incredible loveliness seemed enhanced by her dishevelment for her hair, having come loose from its plait, fell about her shoulders in glorious golden waves and framed a face that was untouched and ethereal. He stared at her, realising that this was the young woman he had seen earlier atop her horse, capturing all his attention then as she did now. He stared at her, her eyes flashing defiantly back at him. No humility for her!

William stepped forward, bowing his head slightly, but without taking his eyes from hers, returning her stare in a cool way. She was studying him closely. There was neither coldness nor hostility in her eyes. She was graceful, like a gazelle. When he looked into her large eyes which were surrounded by a thick fringe of dark lashes, he saw they were intense and of an unusual honey-gold colour—or was it amber?—and they gave her whole face a magical look. In them were gold flecks of light, reminding him of the tigers of India.

She had also acquired the lovely honey-gold skin from spending time in the sun without the protection of a parasol. In fact, she seemed to radiate a feminine perfection, with all the qualities he most admired. She was looking at him, silent and unblinking. Her eyes glowed with an inner light and hinted of the woman hidden beneath the soft innocence of her face.

William suspected this was no ordinary young woman. He sensed in her an adventuresome spirit, which had no room for convention or etiquette. There was nothing demure about her, as was the case with the usual young ladies who flitted in and out of his life, whose eyes would be ingeniously cast down, even among those they knew, which was proper. This young lady showed none of the restraint instilled into young girls of good family.

'So, fate has decreed that we meet again,' he said softly.

When he spoke his voice was well modulated and deep. The young woman continued to stare at him openly, which seemed to cause him some amusement.

'Fate? You have the advantage, sir. What are you talking about? I don't believe we have met.'

'I saw you on my way here—riding a rather beautiful horse.'

'Really! Yes, Bella is a beautiful mount—and I don't believe in fate.'

'Ah, but fate has a habit of playing strange tricks,' William replied softly. 'Do you make a habit of riding out alone?'

She threw back her shoulders and lifted her head, the action saying quite clearly that she was not ashamed. 'Yes—all the time. I was doing no wrong,' she stated firmly, as though her insistence would convince him of it.

'Come, Miss Harris. Do you seriously believe your brother would have approved of you riding out without some kind of protection?' Instantly he was appalled by his own words. Nothing had been further from his mind than to berate her for her recklessness of riding out alone. What the hell was wrong with him? He sounded petty and unpleasant—her expression told him so—and what had it to do with him?'

'I beg your pardon?'

'I am merely pointing out that it is not advisable for a young lady to ride so freely about the countryside un-accompanied. Your brother would not have approved.'

Miss Harris faltered then and William saw her fingers clench more firmly about the riding crop she still held. 'My brother, Johnathan, is dead, so whether or not he would approve is neither here nor there. There is nothing he can do about it now. I thank you for your concern, sir.' Her expression dared him to attempt control of her. 'It is kind of you to show concern for my safety, but I assure you I am capable of taking care of myself.'

Her eyes darkened and William felt the blood run warm in his veins and the heat of it move to his belly. Her small chin squared up to him and her eyes brightened in her proud challenge to his authority. She reminded him of a kitten showing its claws to a fully grown lion and William felt a surge of envy for the man whose task it would be to tame her.

He must never forget that she was the sister of his closest friend, a fine, well-respected man. She was not a woman to be tumbled, enjoyed and forgotten. Had he set eyes on her before he had promised to act as her guardian and before his friend's demise, he would have walked away, his emotions intact.

But that was no longer an option and he owed it to Johnathan to see that she reached London. At that moment Anna Harris presented more of a challenge to him than any skirmish he had faced. He watched as she turned away and walked quickly towards Mrs Andrews, her swaying skirts adding further impudence to her movements. A half-smile curved his lips as he slowly followed her.

'What time do you call this, Anna?' Mrs Andrews chided. 'You knew Lord Lancaster was due to arrive and what do you do? Disappear.'

'I'm so sorry, Mrs Andrews. I just wanted to say goodbye to Bella. She'll miss me when I'm gone.'

'Be that as it may, my dear, but Bella is just a horse, for goodness sake.'

'She's not just any horse. She's the best horse I've ever ridden, the best horse in the world, and I shall miss her sorely.'

'Of course you will, Anna, but there will be other horses for you to ride in England. Now say hello to Lord Lancaster properly, otherwise he will think you are completely devoid of manners.'

Miss Harris dutifully looked at William and said in a stilted, unconvincing voice, 'It is a great pleasure to meet you, Lord Lancaster. We have never met, but Johnathan mentioned you often in his letters.'

'Yes. Johnathan was my closest friend. As your brother he was deeply concerned about your welfare and responsible for seeing to your future. I am here because for personal reasons I, too, have to return to England—which could not have worked out better. Johnathan appointed me your guardian until I have delivered you to your uncle.'

'Goodness, you make me sound like a parcel you have to deliver, Lord Lancaster.'

'I apologise. We have passage on a vessel due to sail first thing tomorrow morning. The journey will be long and tedious—five or six months at the most. I have a letter stating your brother's wishes if you wish to see it. Johnathan realised you haven't seen your Uncle Robert in a long time. He gave due consideration to this fact and wanted to do all in his power to cement the natural ties of blood, to make sure you were taken care of. He has also left you a legacy to be administered by your uncle, which I know will be of immense help to you in the future. '

'I see. And if I refuse?'

'Don't be silly, Anna,' Mrs Andrews reproached. 'You cannot refuse. You have to go.'

Miss Harris looked at her, a soft pleading in her eyes. 'But why? Why must I go? When I recall my outward journey, I do not look forward to the voyage with much pleasure. I would so like to stay in India with you.'

'You know perfectly well that I am leaving Bombay, Anna, to go to my husband in Lucknow. He is spending more time there and wants me to be with him. Johnathan only did what he thought was the best for you. It is only right that you go to your family in England.'

'But I don't want to go,' she retorted petulantly. 'India is where I want to live, not England—and especially not with Uncle Robert—or Aunt Constance, who is a harridan.'

'I cannot imagine your aunt has done anything so bad as to warrant your harsh opinion of her,' Mrs Andrew's admonished.

'Mrs Andrews is right,' William said shortly. 'Your feelings regarding your aunt are not what I am here to discuss. Your uncle will do the right thing by you.'

Miss Harris looked at him sharply and her eyes

flashed. 'And you would know that, would you? Have you met Uncle Robert?'

'No, I have not. Until I know you are secure in your uncle's household you are under my guardianship, However, it is important that you have a female chaperon while on board, which is why I've made arrangements for you to travel in the company of a Mrs Preston and her maid. She is a widow and returning to England to be with her family. You will be ready to leave here no later than six o'clock in the morning.'

Miss Harris' eyes blazed. 'I see you have it all arranged.'

'Anna!' Mrs Andrews snapped reprovingly. 'Please remember your manners. Lord Lancaster is our guest and has gone to considerable trouble to arrange matters for you. Please excuse her, Lord Lancaster, but, as you see, Anna's social graces leave much to be desired.'

Giving Miss Harris a searching look, William tended to agree. Without any male influences in her life, it was all too clear that she had been allowed to go her own way unchecked for far too long. He was of the opinion that it would not have done Anna any harm to have remained at the academy she had been attending before Johnathan had taken her out and brought her to India.

Having fallen into a frowning silence, she glared at him. Her mouth was set in a mutinous line, her jaw tightly clenched. 'I have not been out in society often enough to obtain social graces,' she grumbled.

'Then it is time you started,' Mrs Andrews said, unusually sharp, 'and you will do so now by apologising to Lord Lancaster.'

Anna glanced at Mrs Andrews, noticing her look of

deep displeasure along with her polite, silent impatience as she waited for her to apologise to Lord Lancaster. Sighing audibly, she looked at him. 'Please forgive me. It was not my intention to be rude.'

He smiled. 'You are forgiven. And what do you find to do all day?'

'I have friends here—we do all manner of things to occupy our time, but most of all I like to ride. Due to a fall, Mr Berringer—who is old and frail anyway—lets me exercise Bella and, when one of the ladies in the cantonment acts as chaperon, we go into the town. I also help Mrs Andrews with her charity work. We are extremely busy—are we not, Mrs Andrews?'

'Yes, my dear, and I don't know what I am going to do without you.'

William nodded, wondering why he was going to the trouble of asking such banal questions of this quite innocent young woman. Why was it that her bright spirit, which was open and forceful and which would not be cast down, and the deep warm glow of her eyes, should irritate him so? He was to be in her company for months and she was certainly pretty enough to make the voyage more pleasant.

Then he caught himself up short, reproaching himself for his callous disregard for a young woman's feelings. As a mature male, not a callow youth to whom she was accustomed, but older and therefore wiser and more experienced, she was under his guardianship until such a time as he could relinquish her to her uncle's keeping.

'I have no desire to go to England to live with Uncle Robert,' Miss Harris said, as if to say it one more time would provide some kind of miracle to let her remain in India. 'I lived with him when not at the academy. We didn't get on—which I believe was the reason why Johnathan decided to bring me to India.'

William's voice softened when he next spoke and the atmosphere inside the room began to relax. 'Whatever his reasons, do this for Johnathan. It is what he wanted for you.'

Impatient to be on his way and taking his leave of Mrs Andrews, he strode to the door. 'I must go. I have to meet up with my valet, who went on ahead to the ship,' he said, his voice oddly gentle, capturing Miss Harris's eyes. 'I have much to do before we leave. I will have a carriage sent for you at six o'clock precisely.'

Anna followed him out of the room. 'Were you with Johnathan when he died?' she asked quietly.

The question appeared to take Lord Lancaster by surprise. He looked at her hard for a moment and something dark entered his eyes, but it was soon gone and he averted his eyes. 'Yes,' he said quietly. 'I was with him to the end.'

'Did—did he suffer? Having been hurt in a fight, or a skirmish, I expect he was in pain.'

'Yes—yes, he was, but be assured he had the best care possible at the time.'

'Poor Johnathan. I hate to think of his suffering. And the culprit? Was he caught?'

'No, I'm afraid not.'

Anna was silent, thinking about her brother and deeply saddened that she would never see him again. With a feeling that Lord Lancaster didn't want to talk about it—probably because he and Johnathan had been close and it pained him to do so, she said, 'Is it true that Johnathan has left everything to me?'

He nodded. 'It is true. You have become a very rich young lady.'

'I am sad that it has come about because of Johnathan's death. Are there conditions attached?'

'There may be one or two. I have the details, which I will produce for your uncle—who I have been told is a lawyer—to take care of. Johnathan did not hold your uncle in the highest regard, but he was in no doubt that he is an honest man and will do what is right by you.'

'Yes, Uncle Robert will do that.'

'I am sure he will. I will see you in the morning, Miss Harris.'

Anna stood on the veranda as Lord Lancaster mounted his horse and rode away. She stood watching him in thoughtful silence until he had disappeared down the road. She had already made up her mind that he was high-handed, domineering and arrogant, but if so, why was she drowning in a sea of mortification? Why had she felt the need to argue with him, which was what any well-brought-up, self-respecting young lady would not have done.

His appearance in her day had lasted for such a little while, but long enough for him to have made an impression on her. She was bewildered by the strength of her own feelings, whatever they were, and she wasn't at all sure what she was going to do about it—if anything. Right from the moment when he had taken his leave of her and he had turned his clear, far-seeing eyes on her, when he had merely looked at her and then turned away, there was a boredom about him, an impatience to be gone. She was no more than a silly young woman, his attitude seemed to say, knocking her confidence sideways.

She had been amazed by his obvious indifference to her, for was she not Anna Harris, the most sought-after young woman among the East India Company's raw recruits who passed through the cantonment? But Lord Lancaster was not like them. He was a mature, experienced male, a man of the world, and she was weak in her ignorance and must learn from it, for while she was under his guardianship it could be no other way. She had found herself defenceless against the strange magnetism of him, the masculine vitality of him. His eyes were the colour of the sapphires that came from the mines of Kashmir—cold and unyielding.

When she had first entered the house, her eyes had been caught by the handsome gentleman. In contrast to the bored languor of other gentlemen she had met since coming to India, he moved with the easy grace that expressed confidence, which sat on him lightly, but which belied a strength of steel. His manner was authoritative, his tall frame positively radiating raw power and the kind of unleashed sensuality one of her romantically disposed friends here in Bombay always talked about.

His charm was evident in his lazy smile and there was an aura about him of danger and excitement that stirred her young and impressionable heart. But what she didn't like was his proprietorial manner towards her. That she was to travel with him would be the major setback to the journey. The journey would be interminable until she could be free of his disturbing presence. She could only hope that once they reached London, she'd be able to put her future into perspective and to view Lord Lancaster in a more favourable light.

The death of her brother had been doubly tragic. Not only had she lost the only member of her family who cared for her, but his death meant she had to leave India and go and live with her Uncle Robert and Aunt Constance at their sufferance, at their mercy for the roof over her head.

But not for long, she hoped. Lord Lancaster had told her Johnathan's legacy was considerable. That would give her the means to control her own life. Marriage, which was all the females of her acquaintance seemed to think and talk about, was not for her—not yet anyway. She wanted more from life—excitement, and to help others less fortunate than herself. Perhaps one day she would come back to India. Her heart soared at the thought. Suddenly the future didn't seem so bleak.

The following morning the carriage Lord Lancaster had promised arrived at exactly six o'clock. Homesick already, for she would always consider India her home, there were tears in her eyes as she said goodbye to Mrs Andrews. Mrs Andrews also shed a few emotional tears and waved her off, promising that she would write to her in England.

The streets leading to the wharf were a riot of colour and teeming with people. The sound of canaries and other brightly coloured birds hanging in cages above the shops always caught Anna's eye. This always saddened her because she hated to see such beautiful birds so constrained. How she would like to set them free as they were meant to be. When the carriage reached the wharf, the sun was already blazing down out of a seamless blue sky. The huge East Indiaman, a merchant vessel and warship called the *Bengal* that Anna was to board, dominated the scene. It was a hive of activity, with wagons and carts of all sizes loading and unloading the ship before it prepared to cast off her mooring lines and set sail for England.

A mixture of different cultures thronged together—Hindus and devout Muslims and the more conservative Europeans all adding to the colour and vibrancy around her. A babble of conversation and shouts floated on the warm morning air. The arrival and departure of the massive East India vessels always attracted large interest as civilians and soldiers in scarlet coats going home on leave went aboard.

Anna tried not to think of the tales of shipwrecks, of pirates and interlopers which were omnipresent and rife in the Indian Ocean, and that many a servant of the Company, having survived his term in India, might die in a tropical storm by being flung overboard. She was relieved they would be sailing in a convoy of five vessels, which would assure them a safe arrival in their home port.

Lord Lancaster was there to meet her and to see her baggage was taken aboard.

'Come,' he said, placing his hand under her elbow, 'I'll take you aboard. We'll soon be under way.'

'I brought only what I thought I would need for the journey.'

'Resourceful of you,' he murmured, admiring her despite himself for attempting to come to terms with the ordeal of leaving India. Her eyes were sad, her heart-shaped face showing signs of strain. He spoke gravely. 'I know how difficult this is for you. I know how you feel.'

'How can you?'

'I, too, am leaving India—probably for good. That saddens me.'

'I see, then, yes, I empathise with you. I'm not looking forward to the long voyage, but there is nothing one can do about that.'

Gently, he said, 'You are being very brave. Not many women would want to face such a journey alone.'

Anna nodded, managing a slight smile. 'I realise how irritating it must be for you having to escort me, but since there is nothing to be done, I'm afraid you will have to learn to live with me.'

'That should be interesting,' he commented softly and watched in amusement as a pink flush of embarrassment flagged her cheeks.

'I see nothing funny,' she blurted.

'You don't? Perhaps you lack a sense of humour.' As Anna opened her mouth to rebut the charge, he gave her an arch look. 'Don't worry. I'm sure you'll soon settle down when we get underway. And as for me learning to live with you, Miss Harris—it works both ways.'

Momentarily Anna dismissed any grievances against him and gave him her first genuine smile. 'I quite agree. I know you think that what you are doing is in my best interests, and please don't think that I'm not grateful, but I will form my own friendships once I am on board and not bother you unduly.'

William was stunned by that smile. Something warm and powerful unfurled within him. He stared at her, bemused for a moment before suspecting the smile was feigned to appease him. 'I welcome that—and my name is William. Since we are to be together for the time it takes us to reach England, I think we can dispense of formalities. Besides, I find the use of titles cumbersome. Best we start as we mean to go on.'

'Yes, sir,' Anna said with a wide grin.

'Yes,' he repeated, chuckling as he turned away. A man came towards him.

'Shall I take the young lady's baggage?'

'Ah—Mac,' William said, handing over one of Anna's bags. 'Thank you. That would be a help. This is Mac,' he explained to Anna. 'My valet, manservant, call him what you like, but I really could not do without him and he knows it—and he never ceases to remind me,' he said, giving Anna a conspiratorial wink. 'Is that not so, Mac?'

'Aye—so it is,' Mac replied, proceeding towards the ship.

Of medium height and slim build, born in Scotland, his full name was Iain McKenzie. His heritage was etched into every hard plane of his face. More often than not he was dressed in black, his face set into an expression of stoic patience. He had an uncanny intelligence. His knowledge of India and the fact that he was conversant in Urdu and Bengali had recommended him to William. Mac had been with him since he had arrived in India, his previous employer having died of a seizure.

'Come,' William said, escorting her through the jostling crowd. 'I'll take you to Mrs Preston. You will find the accommodation not to your liking, but you will appreciate space is limited on board. Are you a good sailor by the way—not prone to sickness?'

'I managed the journey out without getting sick, but I will have to wait and see when we get under way.'

William glanced up at the ship's rails as he escorted Anna aboard, his heart sinking when he saw the familiar mocking face of James Ryder staring down at him. William knew the man was to return to London, but he had hoped he would be travelling on one of the other vessels in the convoy. As William decided how best to deal with this new turn of events his senses were heightened sharply by his growing awareness of the menace Ryder would pose for Anna.

He cursed Ryder. His hatred of the man was deep-rooted, with festering memories of what he considered to be his suspected murder of Johnathan. It was imperative that he was kept away from Anna, but it was a task that would prove virtually impossible when stuck on a ship together for months on end.

There was already a buzz of excitement gripping those on board as the ship prepared to cast off. Anna glanced about her. Men scurried purposefully over the polished decks, seeing to the provisions. She was standing beneath a confused tangle of ropes, cables and spars, while far above her head, in the forest of masts and canvas, sailors swung from yard to yard, checking lines and raising sails. The great masts swayed in gentle rhythm against the blue sky, while the ship creaked and groaned alarmingly at the motion. Anna was hard pressed to refrain from turning around and fleeing back to shore.

Mrs Preston was stout, cheerful and talkative. She also had a passion for cards and a fund of interesting stories about the years she had spent on the subcontinent. She was also a widow, her husband, who had been a District Officer for the East India Company, having died of heart problems six months ago. She was not yet fifty and had been in the east for twenty years, but the birth of six children and suffering the death of four of them, had left their mark on her. She was going home to be with her remaining children who were at school in England.

'My dear child,' she said when Lord Lancaster had left to take up his quarters and seeing the anxiety in Anna's eyes, 'I can see you are worried about making the journey, but you needn't be. I've made the journey back and forth twice without mishap—just the occasional tropical storm. Come, I will show you to your cabin. It is next door to mine, which I share with Celia—she looks after my personal needs. I am sure we will all get on and be friends in no time at all.'

Space was limited. The cabins were makeshift affairs with women and children herded together. Anna's cabin was very small, with the minimum of furniture and a canvas side separating her from Mrs Preston and her maid, which could be taken down in an emergency.

With the ship's timbers creaking all around her, feeling restless and eager to get out of the hot, airless cabin, on a sudden impulse she climbed a companionway. Moving towards the rail, she looked along the deck, which was seething with activity, and caught a glimpse of Lord Lancaster in conversation with a group of passengers. He looked her way, but made no move towards her. She turned her head away, but his extraordinary eyes drew her back.

When he turned and disappeared from sight, she could not believe how he had captured her reluctant imagination and fired her restless spirit. Never had a man looked so attractive or so distant. Although she was his social inferior in every way, there was something about him that evoked in her a wicked but exciting feeling. His manner towards her was not that of an inept, clumsy youth, but as a man, experienced, bold, dashing.

Yet he was so unsuitable for her in every way.

Chapter Two

The ship took its place in the convoy and began to glide beneath an azure sky into the open sea. The chances of a propitious passage for the slow-moving, heavily laden merchantmen were largely dependent on favourable winds. Seagulls screamed and wheeled above the frothing wake and the straining canvas overhead swelled and sighed to the rush of the wind, while a fine veil of mist and spray rose from the bow. Feeling the heat of the penetrating sun beating down on her, Anna leaned on the rail as the ship bucked and plunged through the white-capped waves.

She felt the sadness of standing on the deck, watching the familiar shores of India fade as the heavily armed vessel caught the offshore breeze and sailed out into the Arabian Sea to what was an uncertain future. When she had come to India she had been enchanted by the vibrancy of the country. She had loved Bombay and life in the cantonment, where she had often danced the night away.

She had been just one of a civilised society, if one

could ignore the heat and humidity of Bombay and the suffocating stuffiness of some of the English. Sporting their top hats and waistcoats and woollen suits as if they were in London, they would never dream of succumbing to the natural elements of the country. The wind carried the mingled scents of the city—of dust and the rich and spicy food of the bazaars, the rotting vegetation and sweet smells of frangipani and jasmine, far out to sea.

Tears pricked her eyes. Already she was homesick for India.

A hand fell lightly on her shoulder and she spun round.

'Oh—Lord Lancaster. You startled me.'

'William—I told you to call me William.'

'I forgot.'

'Are you taking a last look?' He looked down into her upturned face. 'Missing India already?' he said, correctly guessing the cause of her dejected attitude, the droop of her shoulders.

'It seems far away already,' she admitted, unsure whether she wanted his sympathy, but comforted by it nevertheless. His hand still rested on her shoulder and she moved slightly so that he had to remove it. The warm, strong grip disturbed her, making it more difficult for her to regard him as her guardian. 'How can one belong by blood to one country, yet feel most at home in another?'

He leaned on the rail next to her. 'I don't know, but many people I know feel that way. However, this has to be better than the heat and humidity of Bombay,' he said. 'You will see the sea in all its beauty and fury before we reach England. The air is fresh, which I appreciate.'

'Yes, I love it,' Anna said, dragging her gaze from him and looking at Bombay, which could be seen through a cloud of mist, giving a truly magical appearance with its gilded domes and towering minarets catching rays of the sun. 'The sea's so beautiful when it's calm like this—which, I suspect, will be a different matter when we reach the Cape.'

'True. It can be rough. It is not surprising that attempts are being made to open up new routes between India and Europe.'

'But how is that possible? What other route can there be without having to navigate the Cape?'

'It is possible, though scarcely advisable, for travellers to the east to take the overland route from Alexandria to the Red Sea. It is often dangerous and presents little competition to the sea route, which gives you some idea of the hardships. More adventurous pioneers employed by the East India Company are exploring potential routes through various countries, but for now we have no choice but to put up with the long sea route.'

'Will you ever return to India, do you think?'

'I doubt it. I have responsibilities at home that need my attention.'

Anna would have liked to ask what things, but thought better of it. It was none of her concern and she did not think he would appreciate her asking.

'You will have noticed there is a complement of troops aboard,' he said, casting a disapproving eye at a young soldier who was sauntering past, his eyes passing with appreciation over Anna. Already she was attracting the eye of some of the soldiers. Confined to the ship for such a long time, the presence of a young and lovely young woman on board was bound to stir temptation. 'It will be difficult, confined as we all are on board ship, but I ask you to distance yourself from forming any kind of alliance with any of them.'

Anna turned her head and looked at him. 'I have no intention of forming any kind of alliance with anyone, but I will not be discourteous and unfriendly to people—strangers or otherwise. Why are you telling me this?'

'Because there is one particular gentleman I want you to avoid. His name is James Ryder. If he tries to seek your company, you will have nothing to do with him.'

Feeling a surge of indignation at the possessive content of his words, Anna stared at him in amazement. 'I won't? Why ever not? This person you speak of is not familiar to me, but I gather you don't like him?'

'Does one like a rattlesnake?' His words were calmly spoken, but there was an edge to his voice. 'There is a dark side to Ryder that someone as innocent as you cannot possibly begin to conceive. There is enmity between us and it's more than a matter of not seeing eye to eye over a few difficult episodes in the past. You will have nothing to do with him. Do you understand?'

There was a warning underlying the lightness of his words and Anna knew he spoke in all seriousness. 'Your aversion towards James Ryder is your affair and nothing to do with me.'

'You may not think so, but Ryder is to be avoided. I feel you have a propensity to argue with me, which I did not expect. Perhaps the air at sea will be more conducive to your health and temper than it has been in Bombay.'

'There is nothing wrong with my health or my temper that some distance away from you would not cure,' she countered.

The blue eyes considered Anna without a hint of expression, then with slow deliberation. Had it not been for the coldness that came into them, his reply might have passed as a flippant remark. 'Then I shall have to take that into consideration and adjust my time accordingly to assist you in your cure.'

'That would be appreciated. This is just the start of the voyage home. I will not let you dictate my every move while we are on board ship. Should Mr Ryder speak to me, then it would be discourteous of me to ignore him.'

'I see you have a propensity to argue and defy me, Anna.'

Anna glowered at him with stubborn, unyielding pride, her chin pert, her hands bunched into fists by her sides. 'Not intentionally,' she replied with infuriating calm. 'I have a propensity to hate being dictated to.'

He looked at her hard. 'You are not in the least how Johnathan described you.'

'And how was that?'

'He assured me you are a charming, delightful and remarkably intelligent young woman. In short, you are an absolute treasure.'

Anna was stung by the irony of his words. 'And now you have met me you don't believe him.'

'Not if the past few minutes are anything to go by. I

am more astute than Johnathan was. I prefer to reserve judgement.'

Lifting her chin proudly, Anna met his gaze, not with defiance but with quiet resolve. 'You don't want to be my guardian, do you?'

'I loved and held your brother in the highest esteem. I may not be happy about his request for me to take you to your uncle, but whether I like it or not this is where we are.'

'I realise that my presence is an inconvenience, but taking everything into account, you must see that I have been more inconvenienced than you.'

'In which case, since we have no choice in the matter, the obvious solution is that we should both try to make the best of things and be cordial to each other. Don't you agree?'

'I will do my best.'

'I suppose that is the best I can hope for. In the meantime, you *will* do as I say, Anna,' he said with quiet authority. 'While you are on board this ship you are in my charge. You will do well to remember that and the sooner you accept it the better it will be for both of us. You are accountable to me for your actions. Is that understood?'

She didn't even recoil from the anger she saw simmering in his eyes. Her own anger rose up, licking like flames inside her, her face as uncompromisingly challenging as his. 'You can go to the devil, William Lancaster, and the sooner the better.'

'Oh, I will—in my own good time.'

'I own no man my superior and least of all you.'

'Stop it, Anna. I am not daunted by your defiance.'

'You wouldn't be daunted by a pit of cobras,' she fumed, thankful that everyone on board was too busy to take note of their heated altercation. 'Does everyone march to your orders?'

'Always.'

'Not me. I don't need protecting. I am perfectly capable of taking care of myself.'

William scowled down at her, but did not argue the subject further.

Focusing her eyes on India's distant shore as the great ship dipped and rose, tilted and sank in an endless sickening rhythm, Anna took a step back from the rail, feeling the blood drain from her face. she swallowed and looked at him. 'If you will excuse me, I will return to my cabin. I—I believe I am going to be...unwell.'

Without more ado she turned on her heel and left him staring after her. Mrs Preston waylaid her.

'How are you feeling, dear?' she said, looking at her with concern. 'Goodness! You are rather pale.'

'I hoped that because my stomach wasn't susceptible to the waves on my journey to India, this time would be no different, but I fear it is not to be.'

'I'm so sorry you don't feel well. If there is anything I can do to help, please don't be afraid to ask—although I have to say that I don't travel well either and will probably be prone myself before long. Hopefully Celia, who has a cast iron stomach, will remain unaffected.'

In the confines of her cabin, Anna immediately fell on to her berth, the angry words she had exchanged with William Lancaster forgotten as the ship dipped and rose beneath her. She eyed the small porthole with the sun filtering through with a jaundiced eye. Feeling the roll and pitch of the ship beneath her, it wasn't long before the pangs of seasickness overwhelmed her. Opening her eyes, she saw the small cabin rise and fall alarmingly. She shuddered and closed them again quickly.

She did consider returning to the deck for some fresh air, but quickly changed her mind when the ship sank to even lower depths and her stomach went with it. She found it impossible to do anything else other than grip the side of the berth with one hand and reach for a bowl with the other as she became racked with nausea.

For the next few hours, she lay in the grip of her seasickness, beginning to wish that when the ship went into one of the troughs it would take her with it. Celia came to see how she was faring and at some point Anna's brain registered her telling her that Mrs Preston was also suffering from seasickness.

Later she opened her eyes to find another figure bending over her.

'Go away. I fear I am extremely unwell and I don't want to see anybody.'

'I've seen much worse.'

'I feel—I feel—Oh, dear.' Again she reached for the bowl, which William held for her. 'Please don't,' she whispered, mortified that he should see her in such a dreadful condition, but when she again leaned over the basin she ceased to care if he was there or not.

The rest of the night and throughout the following day she was aware of Celia and her guardian coming and going. She ceased to care how she looked. Several

times she felt her face being wiped with a wet cloth and
her hair combed back from her brow.

After another full day of sickness, she began to feel
a little better. Opening her eyes, through a haze of acute
physical misery she struggled to sit up, but abandoned
the effort and was forced to rest her aching head on the
pillows. Remembering how deplorably ill she had been,
she lay and relived each moment she could recall with
horrified dismay.

She had a vague recollection of William bending
over her, of him sitting on the bunk and holding her
when she was struck with nausea. He had laid her
back on the pillows and covered her with the blankets,
washed her face and forced water and a little brandy
down her throat and tenderly brushed the hair from her
damp face with a matter-of-fact competence and lack
of embarrassment that she couldn't believe.

She was nonplussed about who had removed her
dress and loosened the laces on her petticoat, hoping
it was Celia. Clutching the blankets up to her chin, she
preferred not to think of the indignities of her sickness. It was far too embarrassing. One thing she was
conscious of was an unfamiliar and inexplicable feeling of being safe and protected. She didn't know why
the presence and the ministrations of this man, who
had been Johnathan's close friend, should give her this
warm feeling of safety and she was too physically exhausted to understand it.

Anna did not realise that for William Lancaster, who
had been involved in more than his fair share of skir-

mishes of one sort or another, had faced death on more occasions than he was comfortable with, had assisted with the wounded from those battles and performed a variety of actions that went beyond his official duties when employed by the Company, dealing with a young woman in the throes of seasickness was nothing out of the usual. But seeing her laid so low affected him deeply and he could not abandon her entirely to Mrs Preston's maid, who had enough to contend with caring for her mistress.

In truth, seeing Anna laid so low and without family and comfort, he had to do what he could for her. She looked so defenceless, so very young, curled up on the berth as she struggled with her sickness. Her head rested against the pillow, her hair tumbling around her and spilling on to the covers. With her shoulders slumped in her weakness, there was a sad vulnerable quality to her.

At one time when he had come to her cabin as she slept, with sunlight streaming through the small porthole dancing across her sleeping form, he had been aware of a quickening in the region of his heart. She was lovely as she slept. She had thrown back the covers and the slender shape of her body was revealed beneath the thin fabric of the chemise she wore, her shapely, slender legs exposed. A rosy flush stained her cheeks and her dark eyelashes cast shadows on her flesh.

As William stood there staring down at her, he was aware that she aroused emotions that were new to him. Thinking of the anger and defiance she had shown when he had asked her to avoid James Ryder, he had the unsettling knowledge that it was not going to be as easy as he had thought being with her day after day for God knew how long.

As memory smote him, for a moment he felt a heaviness in his heart. Of course she would want to know why she should avoid James Ryder, but he couldn't tell her—not yet. The wounds were too deep. The truth was still too raw, too hard to bear, of how James Ryder had in all probability wielded the knife that had killed Johnathan and how, if it hadn't been for him, William, Johnathan would still be alive. His grief was deep, his shame and the pain of it an all-consuming agony.

For his own sanity, if he was to reach London with his heart and his sanity intact, more often than not he was going to have to leave Anna in the care of Mrs Preston.

When the sickness began to leave her, he had left her to Celia's gentle ministrations. When he next returned, he knocked on her cabin door and went in. Sitting up on the bunk, she clutched the covers tight under her chin. The heart-shaped face was unusually pale and the shadows under the wide dark eyes made them appear even larger.

'I've come to see how you're feeling—and to bring you some food,' he said, indicating bread and butter and soup on a tray.

Anna turned her head away. 'It's very kind of you—but—but do you have to mention food?' she whispered in her wretchedness. 'It's the last thing I want just now.'

William gave her a tolerant smile. 'If you want to feel better and regain your strength, then you have to eat.'

'I can't. Please take it away.'

'Not just yet,' He sat down on the edge of the berth and faced her. 'Unless you want to go on being seasick, you must have something in your stomach.' Taking the bowl of soup from the tray, he dipped in the spoon and held it to her lips. When she turned her head to resist, he said firmly, 'Come, I insist.'

The soup was hot and nourishing and, unlikely though it seemed, she managed to swallow half of it and take a few bites of the bread before shoving it away and resting her head back on the pillow. William was relieved to see it had put some colour back in her cheeks and that her eyes had lost their dullness.

'It's just as well that almost every woman and child aboard are prostrated with sickness, or I am afraid that I should have damaged your reputation beyond repair. As it is, attention has been directed elsewhere, the ladies unable to spare a moment beyond their own sufferings, so I felt I could safely minister to your needs.'

'I know Mrs Preston has succumbed to the sickness—although she is beginning to feel a little better.'

'Yes, I believe she is.'

'I don't suppose you were afflicted,' she retorted, her expression implying that any kind of disability wouldn't dare approach him. She kept her voice low so as not to be heard on the other side of the curtain.

'No—which is a blessing. Someone had to take care of you and with most of Celia's time being taken up with her mistress…'

'Please don't go on,' Anna snapped. 'I—I suppose it was you who removed my dress—and loosened the laces of my chemise.'

She had spoken without thinking about something

she had never done before. Underclothes were considered an unmentionable subject, and she had done that—and to a strange man—a man who had had the incredible effrontery to act as her nursemaid when she had no defence.

Mrs Andrews would have swooned with horror. To a large extent the prudery of those in the academy she had attended in England as a girl, and then in the cantonment in Bombay, had enshrouded almost every aspect of domestic life in layers of taboo. William Lancaster, however, remained unmoved and unsympathetic.

He grinned in the light of her scarlet face. 'It was necessary. There are times when common sense always stands one in better stead than a slavish adherence to conventions and, had Celia not been on hand, I might have done so. However, to save your blushes you can rest assured that it was Celia who saw to that.'

The embarrassed colour faded from Anna's cheeks and the horror in her eyes replaced by interest. When he put it like that, common sense was preferable to convention, but she was glad it was Celia who had removed her dress and not His Lordship.

'I've never thought of it like that,' she murmured. 'I'm beginning to realise that your point of view is practical after all—but I'm glad Celia was on hand.' A dimple broke out in her cheek and her young face lost its gravity when she smiled.

'Had I known when your brother asked me to act as your escort and guardian that it would include playing nursemaid, then I might have declined. You'll soon be in fine fettle, Anna,' he said, standing up and gathering up the crockery. 'You should rest more easily now. I'll come and see you later.'

At the door he paused when she said his name. Turning, he looked back at her.

'Thank you,' she said softly, 'for taking care of me.' She gave him a wobbly smile.

William was deeply moved by her smile, which he returned. This pitiful young woman whom he had tended through her sickness had humbled him, which was not something he was familiar with. 'You're welcome.'

Alone, Anna closed her eyes and relaxed, relieved there'd been no mention of their altercation about James Ryder before she'd taken to her bed. The motion of the ship no longer affected her as it had before, or perhaps it was that the soup had benefited her. She felt so much better, but strangely disinclined to move.

As the ship sailed on into the Indian Ocean, with his hands behind his back William watched the shores of India recede into the distance. His mind was concentrated on his return to England and the changes, if any, he would find. He was the son of Stephen Lancaster and the grandson of the Marquess of Elvington. On the death of his father when William was five years old, he had gained the courtesy title of Lord Lancaster, his grandfather having no subsidiary title to give.

When his mother's year-long mourning for her husband was over, she had married a close friend, Sir Edward Anderson, a man far inferior to her first husband. With the power of his title and position and with strong objection to the marriage, his grandfather had forbidden her to take William with her when she had left Cranford to take up her new life. Feeling the wrenching loss of his parents and with little respect for his grandfather, who was an autocratic and exacting man, William had been educated at Eton and later at Oxford.

On finishing his education, he was angry and unable to forgive his grandfather for his treatment of his mother, so, risking the odds rather than accepting his noble heritage and all it entailed, he had set out to make his own fortune in India and create a future more to his liking, employed by the East India Company.

After four years, deciding to go it alone, along with Johnathan he had left the Company. They were fortunate. As young men with ambition and ability, fortune had done nothing but smile on them in India. Gambling on a series of investments and the mining of precious minerals, they had succeeded beyond anything they could have hoped for.

India had brought immense changes to his life. He was wealthy, a man of power. His life was orderly and run the way he liked it, yet, as time went by, he became restless. The excitement that had so captivated him in the beginning had begun to wane. There was something missing, something he couldn't find no matter how hard he tried, until the day in Kashmir when he had halted his horse on the banks of the Indus and turned his eyes to the east where the river ceased its flow in the Arabian Sea. That was the moment his heart told him it was Cranford he missed, that it was time to go home, that he had been away too long. He could no longer deny the fact that if he was to marry and raise a family, then Cranford was important to him.

His heart had swelled with longing to see again Cranford's rolling acres that stretched as far as the eye could see, Cranford that had been in the hands of the Lancasters for centuries. Each Marquess had done his bit to see that it was passed on to the next generation. All this would be in his hands on the demise of his grandfather. Quite suddenly he laughed, a deep rich laugh which seemed to capture the untamed spirit of the man.

He would marry, of course, a woman with an impeccable pedigree, a woman who would preside over Cranford with grace, a woman trained to manage the demanding responsibilities of such a large house. Through their children he would live on after his own death. Marriage had never been high on his list of priorities, but if he was to carry on the succession then he must put his mind to it as soon as he returned to Cranford.

He knew he would never be able to shake off the draw of India, how it felt to have the sun on his face and his horse beneath him as he rode into the northern hills with Johnathan by his side. But that belonged to his past. Now he must channel all his energies into Cranford. How could he have been so dismissive of his heritage?

He had been saddened to learn of the death of his mother several months before. Charles, twenty-two, and Tilly, sixteen, his half-siblings, resided in Chelsea village with a paternal widowed aunt, their father having died two years previously. On one occasion William had returned to England to see his half-siblings but had not made contact with his grandfather. He was anxious to see them again, to see how they fared, to get to know them and to do what he could to help them in the future.

* * *

Three days after being struck down with sea sickness Anna had recovered enough to leave the cabin and go on deck. She breathed in the salt tang of the ocean all around her and felt the restful warmth of the sun on her face.

Her fellow passengers included several other ladies, some with children. There was a large number of military men, all returning to England. She wondered if they were going on leave to visit their families or going home for good. Across a broad stretch of water, she observed over vessels in the convoy.

Each East Indiaman was like a floating village. There was a man for every trade on board, along with over seventy well-disciplined seamen. Passengers were issued with printed regulations to establish good order on board. Duties were performed by the crew—decks kept clean and clear and guns lined up behind their gun ports should they run into trouble. Captain Leighton was a strict man and permitted no relaxing of vigilance.

At night the ship became like a ghost ship, when candles were doused and noise kept to a minimum, these precautions being designed to hide a ship or fleet from an enemy's attention. The ships loaded with valuable cargoes—indigo, cotton, silks, exotic spices, tea and peppers—were coveted prizes for pirates and other sea wolves, including the French army, with whom the British had been at war for several years. It would be a welcome prize indeed to capture a fully laden East Indiaman.

Dinner was taken mid-afternoon. There was a plentiful supply of food and drink, which went some way to improving the general comfort of being cooped up together for the long voyage. It was inevitable that life would become tedious. With a dozen or so children on board it was important that they were kept occupied. Games were played along with lessons in reading and writing. Anna was always willing to help where she could.

Slowly the days slipped by. Anna saw little of William. She did not seek his company and he did not trouble her with his, but she felt he was forever watchful.

Arriving on deck one afternoon to take some exercise, she glanced over to where he was standing at the rail, his legs planted firmly under him, his hands clasped behind his back, his thoughts known only to himself as he stared towards the west, his eyes narrowed against the blinding glare of the water. Anna followed his gaze, wondering what he could see beyond the brilliant blue of the ocean.

Crossing the deck, she stopped beside him. His face was set in harsh lines and there was a tension in his manner that suggested some kind of inner struggle. That was when she realised that she knew absolutely nothing about him or his background.

'You look far away, William. Penny for your thoughts—which is what Mrs Andrews used to say to me.'

He looked down at her and smiled. 'I was thinking of nothing in particular. These long voyages have the habit of doing that to a person—with nothing to do but stare at the sea.'

A breeze rippled the plume in the brim of Anna's bonnet and she turned her face to better feel its coolness on her cheeks, offering some relief from the heat and humidity, finding as she did so that her eyes were drawn to her companion's irresistibly. His steadfast gaze held hers so she could not look away.

'Are you thinking of India?'

'Yes, I am. I remember when I first set eyes on Bombay. The comparison of the colour and vibrancy of the city and the dullness of London was startling.'

'It is something we shall all have to get used to. No doubt you will be relieved to get home again.'

His expression became grim. 'Yes, I will, although I have no doubt there will have been changes.'

When he didn't enlarge on this, although she was curious to know what awaited him in England, thinking he might have no wish to discuss something that was private and personal to him, she quelled her curiosity. 'Do you have brothers and sisters?' she asked.

Suddenly he looked at her and smiled. 'I do have siblings, Anna. Two, in fact.'

'Are they older than you or younger?'

'Younger—Charles and Tilly. They are my half-siblings, my mother remarried when my father died. Tilly is sixteen years old and dark haired like me.'

'You must miss them, being away for such long periods.'

He nodded, squinting into the sun. 'Yes—yes, I do, although circumstances always kept us apart. I was five years old when my father died. My mother remarried a year later and went to live with her husband in Chelsea. As my grandfather's heir, I was left at Cranford— that's the Lancasters' ancestral home in Berkshire—and raised by him. Hence, I saw very little of my mother and my half-siblings when they came along.'

Anna's sympathy was evident. 'That must have been awful for you.'

He nodded. 'When I last saw Tilly she was twelve years old—she writes frequently—long letters about the academy and our mother before she died almost a year ago. It's hard to realise that when I next see Tilly she will have passed her seventeenth birthday—no longer a leggy twelve-year-old—and will have completed her education at the academy.'

'Did you get on with your grandfather?'

'No—not one bit. He's a hard, exacting man—he treated my mother very badly when she left Cranford to marry someone else. School was a welcome relief away from the reach of his dark shadow.'

Anna was deeply affected to know this. For him to be separated from his mother at such a tender age must have been heartbreaking and difficult for him to deal with. 'Then when you get home I hope you find he has mellowed with age. What was it like for you—India?'

His expression softened, the sun glinting in his eyes. 'Exciting. As you know, before Johnathan and I decided to make our own way, I worked for the Company in the early years—which is where a great many Englishmen find employment. We made friends with Englishmen and Indians alike—we had contacts, which helped me in what I set out to achieve. We travelled huge distances, often to hostile territory, frequently risking our lives for each other.

'We learned a good deal about the country and about its people—dragging poor old Mac along with us. Having lived in Calcutta with his previous employer, he speaks Urdu, with a smattering of Bengali and other languages. He proved to be a great asset.' His expression became serious. 'You have not yet asked me about your brother's legacy. Are you not curious to know more about it?'

'Yes—of course I would. I never expected him to leave me anything.'

'You are now a wealthy young woman, Anna. You have something like forty thousand pounds at your disposal—maybe more. Do you understand what that means? You are rich. What do you say?'

She stared at him. She had received a shock and if her face was expressionless, it must have shown in the brilliance of her eyes.

'Well,' he said, 'what are you thinking?'

'Truth to tell, it is far more than I envisaged. All that money! But however much it is it will be most welcome. Will I have access to it as soon as I arrive in England?'

'Aware that your greed-inspiring fortune would make you prey to all manner of fortune hunters, Johnathan decided it would be more sensible for you to have a generous allowance. The bulk of your inheritance will be kept in trust until you are twenty-three—or if you marry before that—and excellently guarded from scheming individuals by your Uncle Robert.'

'I see.' This had come a huge disappointment to Anna. 'That won't do at all.'

'May I ask why not?'

'When I realised Johnathan had left me some money I made a pact with myself there and then. With his legacy I want to work, to build my own wealth—to use it in some way for the common good. I'm not sure how I will do that, but once I am in London and free of the womanly constraints that have suffocated me all my life, I thought I would seek advice.'

'You will have to speak to your uncle about that. He is a lawyer after all. He will be able to advise you. And—marriage?' He raised an enquiring brow. 'Isn't that what all young ladies aspire to? As a woman of means society will accept you in your own right.'

'I don't care about any of that and I don't want to marry anyone. There is too much I want to do. I will not tie myself down to a man who will see no further than my money and dictate my every move. I will not give any man the right to do that. That isn't what I want. What I don't understand is how Johnathan managed to amass such a fortune when he left the Company.'

'The Company prefers to pay its servants a set wage and ban them from private trading, but no one would brave the risks of life in the East as a mere salaryman. The subcontinent is not short of temptation for Englishmen who are far from home and thrown into an exotic and alien world. The Company did put an end to private trading before the end of the last century, but it still goes on.'

'And does the Company condone this?'

'Providing it does not jeopardise Company profits, they turn a blind eye. Although nominally acting on behalf of the Company, many individuals, Company servants or otherwise, trade on their own account and many become rich as a result.'

'Did you?'

'Did I what?'

'Become rich?'

He smiled, his eyes twinkling roguishly. 'I did all right—but as you are aware, Johnathan and I left the Company to make our own fortunes. Where you are concerned, I have letters of instruction from Johnathan and a copy of his will, so you can rest assured that, without loopholes, his will and his instructions are simply, yet concisely, drawn up. You are shocked, I see, which is not surprising. When Johnathan left you with Mr and Mrs Andrews in Bombay and dropped out of sight, you probably thought he had forgotten your existence, but that was not so.'

'No, I'm beginning to realise that. The extent of my suddenly acquired fortune has given me much to think about. Suddenly I am free, free to do as I want—an independent person.' She laughed. 'I like the sound of that—although,' she said, frowning, 'I will have to work out how to behave as an independent person.'

'Were you very close to Johnathan?'

'I like to think so. Being so much younger than he was we were rarely in each other's company—the longest time was the voyage to India. My mother always looked on me as more of a duty to be taken care of, whereas I was always aware of Johnathan's affectionate concern for me. I'm glad he decided to bring me out to India. I wouldn't have missed that for the world.'

'And now you are going home.'

She sighed. 'Home? I've never really had a home. My mother didn't want me. Uncle Robert didn't want me, not really—and Aunt Constance wanted me even less. I felt intimidated by her—by both of them. Constance is one of those dictatorial ladies who go successfully through life helped by an immense and unshakeable belief in their own infallibility, without intelligence or sensitivity. They are ignorant of all the rights or feelings of others and refuse to entertain another's point of view. She won't welcome me back. To say I was shocked to be taken out of the academy and told Johnathan was taking me to India was an understatement.'

'Did you not want to go with him?'

'Oh, yes. Going to India was the start of a great adventure, an exciting experience, and I welcomed it. While coping with the complex differences between east and west, I came to love the country.'

'And your father?'

Suddenly awkward, she bit her lip and averted her eyes, but not before William had seen the pain in their depths. 'I—I thought you and Johnathan were close friends. Did he not speak to you of his family—of my father?'

'For reasons of his own he was reluctant to do so. What I do know is that your father died in the Fleet prison—where his creditors had finally put him.'

Her face became downcast. 'Yes—that's true. It was an awful time. I loved my father—and to be taken like that—it was cruel.'

'I imagine it was. Where were you living at the time?'

'South of the Thames—in Richmond.'

'What was your father like—as a person?'

'Handsome, funny. He was a gentle man, a quiet, serious man, who lived for his books and took pleasure in the fine things in life. He loved looking at paintings and sculptures and enjoyed collecting things—worthless things, but he always found beauty in them. He would joke that had he been born with talent, he would have been an artist—which would have been his way of expressing himself. He always had a warm hug for me.'

'What happened to the things he collected?'

'Oh—my mother got rid of most of them. Too much clutter, she said. He was close to his mother—my grandmother. I remember her as being a lovely, gentle lady. She always petted and loved me—and I loved her dearly. I have some items of hers—books, mostly, and knick-knacks she was fond of. I even have her diaries, which I haven't read. There is something so intensely personal about a diary which speaks of feelings and emotions. I would feel as if I were spying on someone's most intimate, private feelings if I read them. My father gave these things to me when she died. He took after her and told me my resemblance to her was remarkable.'

'It would seem your father had an eye for beauty.'

'Yes, he did—which was what attracted him to my mother. Unfortunately he was not much good at keeping hold of his money. He would throw it around without a care—and especially on Mother, to whom he was devoted. He would buy her expensive jewellery and cloaks lined with fur and nobody had the slightest idea that he couldn't afford it until it was too late. He made some bad investments which resulted in him going to prison.' She sighed sadly. 'He was always drawn to some crazy scheme or other.'

Carefully William schooled his features as he took note of the pain showing naked on Anna's face upturned to his. 'And you?' he asked, placing a finger gently under her chin and tipping her face up to his, his eyes searching, probing, seeing something flicker in those dark, appealing depths—a secret grief, perhaps. 'How old were you when he died?'

There was a silence, inhabited by the living presence of the ocean. In spite of herself Anna found her eyes captured and held by William's blue gaze. Aware of his finger still placed beneath her chin, she suddenly recollected herself and took a step back, forcing him to drop his hand. 'Eight—I was eight years old.'

'Three years old than I was when my father died. And your mother?'

Anna shrugged. 'When my father died she was destitute. She was well born—her father was gentry—and her air of breeding was unmistakable.' Anna smiled when she remembered her mother. 'She hadn't been bred to work. Johnathan was working for the Company in India. An eight-year-old girl was obviously a hindrance so hoping Uncle Robert would do well by me she took me to live with him. He immediately packed me off to an academy for young ladies to be educated—and to get me out of the way.'

'And your mother? What happened to her?'

'Over the years she appeared occasionally—she sent money to the academy for my support—and we all knew where the money came from,' she said, her tone subdued, an embarrassed flush mounting her cheeks. 'Beautiful, amoral and widowed, she was perfectly delighted to become one of society's butterflies, who flitted about the London social scene. Not only was she very beautiful and vivacious, she was always laughing.

'When I last saw her in London before I left for India, she was clinging to the arm of her latest gentleman, looking like a lady dressed in silks and velvets and with pearls about her throat. Both Uncle Robert and Aunt Constance were disapproving of her mode of living. Johnathan told me the men in her life were rich and powerful. The last of her gentlemen—who she is probably still with—is an earl and very rich. He's bought her a fashionable house in town. The last letter I received was from a Curzon Street address.'

William watched her, filled with compassion, for she spoke in a tone of unutterable sadness. 'I'm sorry. It must have been difficult for you.'

After a moment she spoke again, her voice sorrowful, almost vague. A hint of tears brightened her translucent eyes, which were like windows laying bare the suffering and many hardships she had suffered in her younger life.

'Yes—yes, it was. There was some kind of fatalism about my mother. Contrary to popular belief, I have found the passing of time and the dulling of grief have little to do with one another—at least, that was the case where my mother was concerned. She never rejected me—she just didn't see me—only herself. She was always busy with her own life and when I was born I was viewed as an afterthought. I suppose I was too young to understand her.'

Fresh tears collected in her eyes and spilled hot moisture down her cheeks. 'Perhaps now you will understand why I am not over the moon to be going to Uncle Robert.'

Raising his hand, William brushed away her tears with his fingers. 'I do understand, Anna, and I can see that your mother—a woman with colossal aspirations, like many more women in her situation—would find it virtually impossible to go out into the world as men do to seek their fortunes. The unsavoury occupation she chose might well pose a danger of impacting on you when you reach London. I can see that your mother's neglect pains you.'

'Yes—yes, it pains me,' she uttered in a torrent of anguished words, angry that he should speak with such disrespect about her mother's way of life, a woman he had never met and had no right to judge. His cutting remark about her *unsavoury occupation* erupted inside her like a volcano and she longed to lash out at him. 'You cold-hearted, arrogant beast. How dare you? You insult my mother and I will not allow anyone to besmirch her name.' Gulping on her tears, drawing a deep, quivering breath, Anna tried to gain control of her rioting emotions.

'I think she does that very well herself,' William said drily.

'Despite her chosen lifestyle, she is still my mother and I will hear no wrong said about her.' Anna paused just long enough to take an infuriated breath. 'You have been born with blue blood in your veins and all the advantages that come with it, but you have a lot to learn. It isn't where a person comes from that matters. It's what a person is that counts. You are being vindictive without just cause.'

'Then I can see that some form of atonement for my ill-chosen words is in order. I ask your pardon.' William saw her eyes register an anguish he couldn't begin to comprehend and observed the gallant struggle she made to bring herself under control.

There was a silence, inhabited by the sound of the sea and the snapping of the canvas above. In spite of herself Anna found her eyes captured and held by William's sharp, probing gaze. Aware of his finger still poised on her cheek, she was not immune to his touch and an alarming, treacherous warmth was creeping through her body. It was impossible not to respond to this man as his masculine magnetism dominated the scene—there was a danger it would dominate her and she could not allow that to happen. When his heavy-lidded gaze dropped to the inviting fullness of her mouth, she recollected herself and recoiled with an instinctive fear that he might get too close.

'Please don't look at me like that.'

William's desire for this young woman was hard driven, but he couldn't overstep the mark. 'Then I think you'd better return to your cabin.'

Terrified of making an overestimation of her ability to carry out the course she had chosen for herself, somehow she managed to walk away. Halfway across the deck she turned and glanced back. He was looking at her hard. He smiled and his eyes were suddenly warm—warm with what? Understanding? Pity? She hoped not. She couldn't abide pity from anyone, least of all from William. Quickly she turned away.

Chapter Three

William felt a surge of reverent admiration for what Anna had achieved, for what she had overcome, and his admiration was reinforced by the pain and loneliness she had endured throughout her short life. Despite her loyal defence of her mother, he silently cursed the woman to hell for her despicable treatment of her daughter.

William had caught the flare of anger his words about her mother had caused. For a split second her face had looked defenceless and exposed. Already he was beginning to regret his words—he hadn't intended to give offence—which, being sensitive about her mother's occupation, she had misinterpreted—especially after the confidences they had shared a moment before, when he had thought that perhaps matters were improving between them.

His eyes continued to watch her as she walked along the deck to return to her cabin. Her step was one of confidence, as if she sensed hidden dangers ahead, but was determined, nevertheless, to enjoy them. She moved gracefully, with an added fluency that drew the eye to the elegance of her straight back and the proud tilt of her head.

In that dazzling moment when she had turned her head and met his gaze, he had not been prepared for the impact. The attraction had been instantaneous. The unexpectedness of it astounded him and Anna would have been surprised if she had known the depth of his feelings as she walked along the deck.

Suddenly the voyage had begun to take on a certain appeal and for a moment he was tempted. When a female looked at him as she had done, the signals—danger signals, signals of warning—alerted him. *Careful, William*, he said to himself. Because of who she was, she was out of bounds.

Young, original and fresh, unbeknown to her Anna Harris possessed an indescribable magnetism in abundance, with that unique quality of innocence and sexuality rarely come by. She possessed a youthful beauty and an untouched air of shy modesty, yet she had about her a primitive earthiness that sat strangely at odds with her gently bred gentility. When she smiled a small dimple appeared in her cheek and her rosy parted lips revealed perfect, small white teeth. William was enchanted. Women like her were as scarce as a rare jewel and must be treated as such.

Already she had become a popular figure on board. There was more than a hungry gleam in the eyes of the young men that followed her, but none approached her, for they knew she was in his charge. Only James Ryder had the daring to do that.

Ryder had come out to India as an employee of the

Company two years earlier. Having been dismissed for grave misconduct, he was returning to England. Much to William's disapproval, when Anna was in this particular young man's vicinity, his eyes were ever watchful. It was only a matter of time before he approached her.

Instead of returning to her cabin after dinner, finding the gloom below decks oppressive, Anna wandered along the deck. The crew were kept busy aloft, climbing masts and yards. It was rough today, the wind blowing strongly astern, the force of it taking hold of her hair and blowing it in wild confusion about her head.

The sun wasn't shining and the ocean wore the colours of the English Channel on a dull day in December. Feeling the cold and wishing she'd brought a wrap, when a slender young man with ash-blond hair, good looking in a sleepy kind of way, stumbled on to the deck, cursing as he was buffeted by the wind, she smiled.

'By Jove,' he exclaimed, 'but it's blowing a gale. I didn't expect to find a lady taking the air as fresh as this.'

'I think it's exciting when the sea's as rough as this. I like watching the waves.'

'Really? Well, I suppose it takes all sorts. I find it more interesting watching the fish and their antics in calmer waters.'

Anna looked at him with new interest. He was also regarding her with interest and as she gazed at him his mouth widened into a smile. He eyed her up and down quite openly as though he were enjoying a private joke. 'You will have made the voyage before, I expect.'

'When I came out here. It seems to be a long way to the Cape. It won't seem so bad when that is behind us. I was going to remain in India a tad longer—though I'm glad I didn't, since it has given me the opportunity to meet you.'

Anna felt the colour rise to her cheeks. 'Thank you, sir.'

He smiled slowly. It was a nice, winsome smile, which made his eyes crinkle at the corners. 'I've seen you before, but we haven't been properly introduced. I'm James Ryder.'

So, Anna thought, this was William's nemesis, the man he had warned her about and told her to avoid. She couldn't for the life of her think why. He appeared polite and charming. Glancing about the deck and seeing no sign of William, with a sense of satisfaction in defying him, she smiled, warming to the admiration in his glance. His aura was so magnetic that it was impossible to resist his advances. 'My name is Anna Harris'

'What lovely hair you have, Miss Harris—even though the wind is having fun with it. Where did Lord Lancaster find you?'

'He didn't—find me, I mean.'

'But you are travelling with him to England, aren't you? I've heard it mentioned.'

'Yes, but I don't know him very well.'

James nodded. His eyes gleamed. 'No—no one seems to know very much about our Lord Lancaster,' he drawled in silky tones. 'Man of mystery and all that. How old are you, Miss Harris?'

'Nineteen.'

She clutched the rail harder as a sudden squall buffeted the ship, sending a heavy shower of spray into the air around them. They both laughed and ducked instinctively. James Ryder put a firm hand on her elbow.

'I've heard somewhere that the salt water is rather good for the complexion, but I would be failing in my duty if I did not take you to safety,' he said, in no hurry to let her go. 'Come below. One of the crew has taken his violin out and is playing some lively jigs. Some of the passengers have even thrown away some of their inhibitions and are dancing—although it's proving to be more of a tumbling about with the ship being tossed about all over the place.'

Together they fought their way below, clinging to every handhold they could find. Many of the passengers were gathered in the saloon where a sailor was playing a merry tune. Children in good spirits were dancing about, some with their parents. James Ryder took Anna's arm and looked deep into her eyes. His face was lethargic and sleepy looking now he was in the warmth and he had stopped grinning for the moment.

'I think you are quite wonderful, Miss Harris. Do you know that every man on board is in love with you?'

One of Ryder's friends, seeing Anna looking about her helplessly, came to her aid. 'Steady on, Ryder. You'll end up making an ass of yourself as usual. As you can see, young lady, my friend isn't himself right now. I'm afraid he imbibed too much liquor during dinner.'

Anna gave him a smile of tolerant understanding as Ryder waved him away dismissively.

'Go away, Hugh,' he snorted. 'This charming young lady and I are going to dance. You do want to dance with me, don't you, Miss Harris?'

'No—really…' Anna laughed, resisting his arms, which seemed to be all over the place. 'If I dance with you in your present state, I fear we are both in danger of ending up in a heap on the floor…and then where will my dignity be?'

He refused to take no for an answer and the next thing Anna knew she was being propelled around the crowded floor as James Ryder flung himself into the spirit of things and was soon dancing as merrily as the rest, taking a laughing Anna with him.

Suddenly Anna was aware of a tall male presence. William Lancaster had moved across the floor with such speed that she had not seen him come. At a stroke, amusement fled from Ryder's florid face.

Anna observed how both men changed colour— James's countenance flushed even more, William's whitened beneath his tan and froze into a mask of pure hatred. He cast James a look that would have pulverised rock. Anna froze. Her eyes were wide open, her expression incredulous. Their eyes met, William's glacial, his mouth drawn into a ruthless, forbidding line.

He glared at Ryder. 'I think you, sir, forget yourself.' His voice was like steel.

Most of those enjoying themselves failed to notice the quiet altercation. Ryder's friends stood back with the wary disbelief of the innocent and uninvolved. Anna could feel the unnatural tension in the air. She glanced apprehensively between the two men, realising that she was witnessing their deep-seated enmity, that it went way back and that she was merely the catalyst for the present grievances.

William subjected James Ryder to a look of severe

distaste and chilling contempt. 'The drink has clouded your mind—or possibly some other substance. You're high as a kite. I advise you to go on deck and sober up— if you can avoid falling over the rail—which I doubt would happen to you. You'll stay alive, Ryder, no matter how the cards are stacked against you. The devil has a way of taking care of his own. If you intend to remain that way, then I suggest you stay away from me—and especially Miss Harris. So let that be an end to it.'

Struggling to stand up straight against the roll of the ship, his senses and his body too anaesthetised by drink to be concerned by the threatening menace emanating from the formidable Lord Lancaster, James Ryder grinned inanely, seemingly not in the least daunted by the other man's anger.

'An end to it?' he slurred, continuing to have great difficulty standing still as the ship dipped and swayed and whatever substance he had consumed earlier making it even more difficult. 'As far as I am concerned, there will never be an end to it. You, sir, have offended my honour—I have a mind to call you out. I want revenge and I will stop at nothing until I have obtained it.'

Anna gasped with horror at his words. 'No—please, you must not.'

Both men ignored her pleas and William looked at James Ryder with all the violence born of hatred.

'Honour,' William scorned. 'I dispute that. There isn't an honourable bone in your body. As I remember, you have the disgusting morals of a tom cat. Do as I say and keep away from Miss Harris.'

Anna's eyes passed from one to the other in puzzlement as she tried to comprehend what they were talking about. None of it made sense. That they felt prejudice towards each other was obvious, but William was talking of another matter which had nothing whatsoever to do with him finding her with James Ryder.

'William, why are you so angry?' she asked. 'What is he guilty of?'

'I shall not offend your ears by telling you.'

James Ryder stepped away from them. 'I think I'd better go to my cabin. Please excuse me, Miss Harris, and thank you for your delightful company. I'm sorry. It was not my intention to make a scene or to give offence.'

Casting about for something to say to diffuse the tension, but unable to do so, Anna watched the man leave the saloon, where he stood for a moment to light a cheroot, before disappearing.

Taking a deep breath and eager to cool her burning face, Anna marched out of the saloon and made her way back on deck. Only then did she turn on him, her eyes flashing with indignation. 'That was beastly of you,' she fumed. 'He may have over-imbibed, as you put it, but he has behaved like a perfect gentleman.'

William's look cut through her, his eyes ice cold. 'Ryder doesn't know the meaning of the word.'

'That is your opinion. I don't know what has happened between the two of you and if you won't tell me then I will make up my own mind. I would appreciate it if you did not embarrass me like that again. I know what I'm doing.'

'So do I. Getting into bad company. If you remember, I did warn you about Ryder.'

'He was perfectly polite. He did nothing wrong that I could see. I have already told you that I don't need you

to tell me what I should do all the time,' she retorted
crossly. 'I am able to do that for myself.'

'You think so? How quick you are to defend him,
Anna. Perhaps you are attracted to Ryder.'

'I don't know him well enough for that. Today is the
first time we've spoken to each other. Why are you being
like this? James says—'

'I don't care what *James* says. He knows nothing
about how to behave when he's in the presence of young
ladies.'

'And I suppose you do. Really, William, I cannot for
the life of me understand why you are making such a
fuss.'

As he towered over her, William's lean, hard face
bore no hint of humour. His lips curled with bitterness
and a coldness entered his eyes. 'Of course you can't,
but for God's sake don't go developing feelings for him.
It would not be wise—in fact, it would be a disaster.
Keep away from him. He's not to be trusted in any way.'

Anna felt the ire rising inside her because of his
highhandedness. It was wholly inexplicable, but she
suddenly felt as if the devil had got into her, giving
her an overwhelming urge to exasperate this arrogant
Lord as much as he had exasperated her. 'I would like
to make up my own mind about that. I like him. Besides, why should you care?'

'Because, strange though it may seem to you, I have
enough human feeling after ten years in India and meeting people like him to feel concerned when I see someone I know out of their depth. Trust me. It would be a
mistake. You should wait until you reach London and
find yourself someone decent and with more money

than you. Which shouldn't be difficult, given the fact that every male on board this ship is singing your praises and all of them are more than halfway to being in love with you.'

Anna did not flinch or look away. 'Have you forgotten that I have stressed that I have no intention of marrying?' she reminded him.

'No, but I dare say you will change your mind soon enough when you reach London and have every rake in town sniffing after you and you are tricked into marriage. Your uncle won't have long to wait before he has you off his hands,' he said unkindly, a steely glint in his eyes.

Anna's world tilted crazily. She found it difficult to meet his gaze, but she did. 'So you really think that, do you, William? That as soon as the rakes and fops in London begin paying me attention and whispering sweet nonsense in my ear, I am so silly and weak that I will be unable to resist them and reverse my decision not to wed?'

His voice was hard and his eyes gleamed dangerously beneath his fiercely swooping eyebrows. 'Why not? You may have more in kind with your mother than you realise.'

Horrified by his words, Anna drew herself up straight and met his gaze directly, defiance in every line of her body. His cutting tone and the injustice of his words increased her anger. But it was the way he retained his arrogant superiority that was hard for her to take.

There was a spot of colour on each cheekbone and her mouth was as thinly drawn with determination as her antagonist's. She held her head up in defiance and for a moment she saw a glimmer of something in William's eyes which, had she not known better, she might have called admiration.

'How dare you? Are you deliberately trying to be cruel? Your insult towards my mother, to which I take great exception, is unforgivable. If you must assassinate her character, then do so in a voice that cannot be heard the length and breadth of the ship.'

'I shouldn't have said that. I apologise,' William said on a note of contrition.

'For what? Insulting my mother and telling all and sundry?'

'Both. I spoke in a manner for which I am ashamed and regretful,' he said, his voice curt.

'You? Ashamed? Are you quite sure you know the meaning of the word?' she scoffed.

'Your determination to defy me at every turn draws me to it. You will give up this wild scheme you have to form a friendship with Ryder and spend more time with the ladies on board. Do you hear me, Anna?'

'I do. What I want to know is how you mean to make me?' she asked, her expression ready to tell him she would not be ordered about like a servant.

'There are ways and means. As your guardian I am entitled to obedience.'

Anna's eyes struck sparks of indignation. 'Is that so? Are you telling me that you would keep me a prisoner?'

'Not exactly, but I would make sure you did not appear on deck as often as you do.'

'You cannot expect me to cower below while I wait for you to allow me on deck. I am not ashamed of my friendship with James. How can I be when I do not know what he is guilty of?'

William looked away, his voice low when he spoke. 'I can't tell you—not yet.'

Anna stared at him, seeing something dark and mysterious enter his eyes. She seemed to have touched on a tender spot of his vulnerability. 'Why not? Why can't you tell me?'

'Because it's—difficult. All I ask is that you bear with me on this. Don't make the mistake of falling for Ryder. That would be a foolish thing to do. Whatever sentiment he has created, you have been deceived—although with his looks and that smooth charm, his success is not to be wondered at,' he mocked sarcastically.' Catching a glimpse of the fierce sparkle that had sprung to her eyes, he asked, 'What is it?'

'I won't be badgered, William. I happen to like James—and you are behaving like a heavy-handed jailer. Please don't.'

'Is that what you think? I am giving you this advice for your own good—and I am not your jailer.'

Bright colour surged inexplicably into her cheeks. 'You are certainly behaving like one.'

When Anna opened her mouth to argue further, William said, 'Drop it, Anna. The incident with Ryder should not have happened. I did warn you. I meant every word I said when I told you to avoid him. You will oblige me by refraining to have anything to do with him while on board this ship. Is that understood?'

'You are beginning to get on my nerves, William,' she flared, choosing to ignore his question, 'so if you have finished, I am going below.'

'A word before you do and then it will be an end to the matter,' he reproached curtly. 'I am not a man to start a quarrel with you, but I will give you this word of advice. If you persist in baiting me with your tongue, you will *want* to remain below deck.'

Anna's eyes were blazing as if they had a fire behind them. 'I will come on deck whenever I wish. Threaten me all you like, but do not think I am afraid of you.'

'Then you should be,' he mocked, his tone caustic. 'Where I have been for the past ten years has frayed my courtly manners and I often forget how to behave as a gentleman should. So, if you continue to argue every time we meet, you will learn to guard your tongue. Surely we can benefit from a surface friendship until we part company in London?'

The colour drained from Anna's face as his words sank in. A light blazed briefly in his eyes, then was quickly extinguished. She was deeply conscious that his easy, mocking exterior hid the inner man, and as she gazed into the fathomless depths of his eyes, some instinct warned her that his offer of a truce could make him more dangerous to her as a friend than he had been as her antagonist.

There was a withheld power to command in him that was as impressive as it was irritating. If she agreed to a truce, she was determined he would not get the better of her. She would not let him reach her, for by shielding her innermost self from the touch of another human being she would always be strong and complete and in control.

'I don't want to argue with you either. I will give it some thought.'

Afraid that she was going to crack completely and

make a fool of herself, to escape the vibrating tension between them, Anna raised her chin and turned. With all the dignity she could muster she walked away from him, her slender hips swaying graciously. She didn't see the admiring light in William's eyes, or the indefinable smile lurking at the corner of his lips as he observed her less than dignified progress when the ship lurched and she almost tumbled down the companion ladder.

William couldn't think of anyone, male or female, who would have stood up to him the way Anna had just done, verbally attack him and walk away as regal as any queen. She had spirit, a fiery spirit that challenged him. Her arrogance was tantamount to disrespect, yet in spite of himself he admired her style. Nor was she afraid of him. That was the intriguing part about her.

He was used to watching her graceful, slender form moving about the deck, used to hearing her soft laughter that could lift the spirits and used to the way her eyes would flash when she was angry. He couldn't bear to see her waste those wonderful assets on the likes of James Ryder. No matter how he argued, ordered and demanded her to avoid him, she would continue to defy him and there was not a thing he could do about it—unless he told her the truth, the whole sorry, sordid truth of how her brother had died and his own shameful part.

It was something he had never told a living soul, and he couldn't bring himself to do that now. The remembrance of it ate at him. The agony that he let Johnathan ride off into the night alone knowing of the threat that hung over him rose up inside him, nearly choking him.

That Ryder had been waiting for him, ready to play the assassin, he was certain of.

Afterwards he had thought, *My God, what have I done—letting him go off alone like that?* He missed his friend. His grief was deep. He had valued and enjoyed their time together, working with him, their travels. Johnathan had not deserved what had happened to him and he was full of remorse for it. He was also ashamed, ashamed that he and he alone had allowed it to happen. He was to blame. If it wasn't for him, Johnathan would still be alive.

Telling Anna wasn't an option just then. She would hate him for it and he couldn't bear that.

Bleakly he wondered if he'd ever be able to think of that night without this terrible ache, this savage urge to rip Ryder to shreds whenever he laid eyes on him, on his mocking face, his knowing eyes. Ryder held him and Johnathan responsible for his dismissal from the Company and he'd sworn vengeance. William didn't doubt for a moment that seducing Anna as he had Johnathan's Lucy, a woman his friend had been devoted to and intended to marry, was his way of paying him back.

Following their angry altercation, Anna decided the wisest course of action was to give William a wide berth until he'd calmed down. Avoiding James Ryder wasn't easy—and nor did she want to, despite being ordered to by William. When William was otherwise occupied in his cabin, James Ryder would make a beeline for her and his light and easy manner always cheered her. He had a natural refined elegance, which true-blooded aristocrats displayed in the way they walked and talked—a blend of generations of breeding and environment. He was classically handsome, yet there was an earnest boyishness in him that was appealing, direct and charming.

Being with William made her realise how different the two men were. James was all charm, weakness and decadence and so much fun to be with, whereas William was of a more serious and reserved disposition. Apart from being a vital, strong, compelling man, he was also the most private individual she had ever encountered.

William had thought he had solved the problem of his lovely young charge by refusing to go near her, but his plight somehow only became more difficult as the great ship carried them swiftly to the southern cape.

An East Indiaman was only so big. Since Anna, more often than not with Mrs Preston, chose to spend the greater part of each day on deck, he couldn't help but see her frequently. As so often happened when she wasn't within his sights, to his chagrin he found himself beset by visions of her, of how she'd looked when she'd ridden her horse over the Indian plain and how the sun picked out the lights in her softly curly hair.

Though he had once thought himself immune to the subtle ploys of women, even though he'd known her for such a short time, he had begun to think he would never be free of her. From the very beginning she had stirred his baser instincts. Yet much as she ensnared his thoughts, he found his dreams daunting to his manly pride whenever she flitted through them like some puckish sprite. Although he'd have greatly preferred to limit her constant assaults on his thoughts and his poorly depleted restraint, he was beginning to suspect that, in comparison, standing firm against Napoleon's forces would be child's play.

But for now he was furious that by his own behaviour he had driven a wedge between them. He had done her a great disservice and an even greater disservice to Johnathan. He had promised his friend that he would take care of his sister, but by his actions and her own determination to stand against him he was in danger of driving her into Ryder's arms. He didn't intend to give her the opportunity. The guilt he felt for his part in her brother's death continued to eat away at him and his conscience smote him. Whatever it cost he was determined to do right by Johnathan's sister. It was time to make amends.

Anna was alone on deck, leaning on the ship's rail and looking out to sea. She was thinking of William and the bitter words they had exchanged, which always invaded her thoughts when she was alone. It troubled her for she didn't like being at odds with anyone, least of all William who hadn't asked to be saddled with her for the entirety of their journey to London. Not that he was since they hadn't spoken since the day he had chastised her for being with James.

Her hurt and humiliating anger had not lessened, but this unpleasantness couldn't go on. In her opinion she had done nothing wrong. None of it was her doing, so surely it was up to him to break the ice. With a frown puckering her brow and chewing her lips, she was startled when he suddenly appeared beside her, towering over her, his broad shoulders blocking out anything but him.

'I can see,' he drawled in a deep, amused voice, 'that with an expression like that on your face you must be thinking of me.'

Anna tilted her head to look up at him in surprise. Her eyes and brain recognised his presence, but her emotions were bemused by anger and damaged pride and were slow to follow. He had crept up on her with the stealth of an animal with its eyes on its prey. Her scowl deepened.

'You're right. I was.'

'Don't tell me. You are plotting some new way to antagonise me or how best to murder me.'

'Yes. And with as much pain as possible.'

Unperturbed by her cross words, he moved closer to her, an infuriating smile on his handsome mouth, his black hair curling attractively over his head and into his nape. 'Come now, you don't mean that.'

'Yes, I do. I never say anything I don't mean.' She glanced up at him towering over her. There was an uncompromising authority and arrogance in his bold look and set of his jaw that she didn't like.

'I upset you when I berated you over your escapade with James Ryder, for which I apologise. I was angry and said things I should not have.'

Rendered almost speechless by his apology and change of attitude, she welcomed it, yet she was suspicious. 'Yes, you did.'

Sensing that she was wavering a little and that he was close to victory, William pressed home his advantage. 'It would be poor spirited of you not to accept my apology.'

'What are you saying?'

'Only that a truce would not go amiss between us. Come, what do you say? Why do you hesitate?'

'I don't, but a truce isn't friendship. It's only a halt in hostilities.'

William grinned. 'It's a start. I would like to enjoy your company better, Anna. I would like you to be more amiable towards me.'

'Why? Because you want to bring me to heel?'

He arched a brow, amused. 'No, but I would like you to be less hostile towards me, less stubborn.'

'I don't believe you. If it's your intention to gentle me, you will have to use brute force.'

In spite of himself William laughed outright.

Wounded by his reaction, Anna glared at him. 'You're enjoying this, aren't you?'

'Every minute of it,' he confessed, his eyes dancing with merriment. 'So, Anna, what do you say? Is it a truce?'

After thinking it over for a moment she gave him an impish grin, unable to stay angry with him when he was clearly contrite. 'Yes, all right. Truce it is.'

'That's a relief.'

'It is? Why?'

'Because you and I have been invited to dine with Captain Leighton later. Mrs Preston has also been invited.'

Taken completely by surprise and already wondering what she could possibly wear for such an auspicious occasion, she went to her cabin.

'Goodness, Mrs Preston,' she said when the lady came bustling in, expressing her absolute delight over their joint invitation. 'What on earth shall I wear? There is nothing in my scant wardrobe suitable for dining at the Captain's table.'

'You are to accompany Lord Lancaster?'

'Yes, I am. You know, Mrs Preston, Lord Lancaster is acting as my guardian until I reach England and yet I know absolutely nothing about him. How strange is that?'

Mrs Preston smiled knowingly. 'Now there's a tale. He's complicated, my dear, that I do know, which I am sure you have observed for yourself.'

'Do you know him well?'

'Not as well as my husband did, but I was in his company on many occasions. He is certainly a man of mystery—although in India I suppose he would be called a nabob—he's extremely rich, you see. He's a hard task master, a man who lives by his own rules and answers to no man.'

'And his family?'

'He is well connected—his grandfather is the Marquess of Elvington and I've heard his ancestral home, Cranford, is no less splendid than the Palace of Versailles. When he gets to London he will find himself under siege from every husband-hunting female and fathers curious to know how beneficial a son-in-law he might make.'

'I believe he was already acquainted with Mr Ryder when he boarded the *Bengal*.'

Mrs Preston looked thoughtful. 'Yes, he was. I heard there was an angry exchange between the two of them, but I didn't hear the cause of the altercation. It was all very secretive as I remember.'

'I wonder what it could have been. But whatever the answer to that question, it doesn't solve my problem of what I am going to wear to dine at Captain's table.'

After much deliberation Anna had chosen to wear a pale lemon muslin dress, modestly cut. Celia brushed her hair until it shone and arranged it in soft curls about her head.

On nearing the Captain's cabin, she heard the sounds of low laughter and tinkling glass. With trepidation she paused in the open doorway to find a few other passengers already present enjoying the social atmosphere. The cabin was built in the aft part of the quarter deck. Compared to the passengers' cabins it was quite luxurious, with dark blue velvet curtains and hangings and finely furnished. A clock ticked away the minutes with its brass hands. There was a desk with charts and navigational equipment and the mahogany furniture glowed warmly. An oriental carpet covered the highly polished surface of the floor.

Mrs Preston left her side to speak to an acquaintance. Standing in the doorway, Anna felt terribly self-conscious, conspicuous and strangely vulnerable.

From his vantage point opposite the door, William idly watched the guests arrive without consciously admitting to himself that he was watching specifically for Anna to appear…and then he saw her. In her dress of pale lemon muslin that clung to her small breasts and miniscule waist and complemented her tanned face, her stance was one of quiet, regal poise. She had an intriguing, indefinable presence that made her stand out, even in the moving kaleidoscope of movement and colour and animated voices. It was as if everything and everyone was in motion except Anna. Resplendent in a claret coat, William headed slowly but purposefully towards her.

'You look lovely,' he said with a smile of pure masculine appreciation.

She turned her head and her face broke into a smile. 'Thank you,' she replied, feeling like the dazzled young woman she was.

Taking her arm, he drew her further inside. 'You'll know everyone present—in particular the ladies. You meet the same people all the time, people who know all about each other since they're together all day and every day for the time it takes the ship to reach England. It does get rather tedious, I always think—however, tonight's an exception.'

Anna looked at him. 'Why? Surely you don't mean it's because I am present?'

He grinned. 'Of course. Who else?'

Her eyebrows rose. 'Are you telling me that I'm peculiar in some way—that I don't mix?' she asked defensively.

'On the contrary. I admire your courage. You've fitted in remarkably well. Are you always armed for battle, even when someone makes an innocent remark about you?'

'It wasn't innocent. You implied that I'm different.'

'You are different—and before you raise your defences, that was meant to be a compliment.'

A smile touched the corners of her mouth. 'I'm sorry. I'm just not used to getting compliments.'

His eyes moved leisurely over the fragile features, pausing at length on her soft pink lips. 'You'll soon get used to it. Let me introduce you to Captain Leighton. He's impatient to meet you.'

Anna had seen Captain Leighton many times as he went about his ship, but they had not yet been introduced. He was a tall, thin man with handsome features, several years older than William. There was an unmistakable look of admiration in his eyes as he gave her a gallant bow.

'Good evening, Miss Harris. It's a pleasure to be introduced to you at last.' He gave William a look of mock disapproval. 'Lord Lancaster has kept you secreted away far too long. Now let me get you a sherry—or perhaps you would prefer some wine?'

'A sherry would be lovely.'

When Captain Leighton had handed her a sherry, Willian bent his head and spoke quietly in her ear.

'Hungry?' he asked as she sipped her sherry.

'Yes, I am rather.'

With limited space in the cabin, people were beginning to take their seats at the table. Anna found herself seated across from William. The atmosphere was one of congeniality, but Anna felt awkward since everyone was much older than her. Glancing up and down the table, she saw how the other women were looking at William, in particular an extremely voluptuous lady seated next to him. Sitting straight-backed in her chair,

Anna avoided her companion's penetrating gaze, concentrating her attention on the food.

Anna didn't particularly enjoy the meal. A variety of meats was offered, but few vegetables and none of the fruits she had grown accustomed to in India. Little wonder, she thought, that there were outbreaks of scurvy on board. One of the ladies present informed her that when they reached the Cape and fresh provisions were brought on board, fruit would be a priority.

'Have you enjoyed the evening, Anna?' William asked as they left the cabin.

'Yes. It made a change.'

'I'm sure you'll be invited again before too long,' he said, glancing back at Mrs Preston, who was speaking to another lady who had been at the dinner. 'Allow me to congratulate you.' A lazy, devastating smile passed over his features. 'In the space of just a few hours you have endeared yourself to every one of those present—especially the gentlemen. I have no doubt when you reach London you will slay the lot of them.'

'Please don't exaggerate.'

'I don't. You will bowl them over and down they will fall like skittles. No doubt they will turn poets overnight to express their love for this bright new star in their heaven.'

'Really?' she said drily. 'And will you pen one yourself, My Lord?'

'You will break enough hearts among the *ton* without wanting mine.'

'And I think you must have imbibed too much wine, William.'

'And I think you were by far the most beautiful young lady present.'

'What? More so that Miss Chesterton?' she teased.

'The lady you were seated next to who fluttered her eyelashes constantly and hung on to your every word. The two of you certainly appeared to have plenty to talk about.' Turning from him, she began to walk on. *'She's an engaging and thoroughly charming woman.'*

William's brows rose and he was momentarily speechless as he followed after her. 'You may have thought so, Anna, but it is not the kind that passes for charm in the ladies of my acquaintance. Besides, it may have escaped your notice, but Miss Chesterton is travelling with her parents, their purpose of going to England to arrange her marriage to a personable gentleman who works for the Company in London.'

'Really?' she replied, continuing to walk on ahead. 'In which case her fiancé would not appreciate you flirting with her.'

Scowling, William continued to follow her, the passage too narrow for them to walk side by side. 'I did not flirt with her—and I don't think you need say more. I think we should revert to how we were before—silent—before my ego takes a battering,' he said coldly, all good will having gone from his voice.

'Oh, dear,' she threw back at him, her lips curving in a mischievous smile. 'Who am I to dent the ego of William Lancaster?'

Hearing the humour in her tone, William could hardly believe his ears. When she suddenly stopped and turned to him, his eyes darted to hers and he saw her puckish smile. His scowl relaxed into a reluctant

grin and he tried to negate it by chiding as sternly as
he could, 'Impertinent minx. I'll thank you not to poke
fun at me in future.'

Unchastened and unrepentant, Anna met his gaze
head on. 'Why? Because it is you who lacks a sense of
humour?' she remarked, accusing him of the very thing
he had accused her of earlier.

He nodded slowly in acknowledgement of her scor-
ing a hit. *'Touché.'* Reaching behind her, he opened
a door. 'Please—spare me a moment of your time,
Anna—you, too, Mrs Preston,' he said when she caught
up with them. 'This is my cabin—I think a little wine
is in order to round off the evening.'

Anna paused in the doorway, looking inside. Mrs
Preston had entered ahead of her. Mac was there. Anna
smiled at him. Laying aside the jacket he had been
brushing, he invited Mrs Preston to take a seat, whereby
the two of them retired to a comfortable sofa and began
engaging in conversation.

Seeing Anna's hesitation, William took her arm and
drew her inside before closing the door and proceeding to pour some red wine out of a crystal decanter.
Placing a glass before Mrs Preston, he gave his attention to Anna.

'Goodness,' she breathed, taking in the fine furniture and polished surfaces and the narrow berth with
silk hangings, taking particular note of the pile of books
on a desk. 'Your cabin is certainly an improvement on
mine. Do you have to pay for better accommodation?'

He nodded. 'It's well worth it considering the length
of the voyage. You weren't serious about Miss Chesterton, were you?' he asked, handing her a glass of wine.

'Not really,' she replied, sauntering around the cabin and casually picking up a magazine from a small table. 'She'd bore you to death within a week, but you rose to the bait like a trout for a fly. To be fair, I don't think you would care for her at all—but she is more your age.'

Astonishment registered in William's expression as he realised that at twenty-nine she evidently regarded him as long past the age to consider any woman younger than himself to wed. 'Now you make me sound like Methuselah.'

There was something about the innocent joke, something about her engaging smile and the laughter that caused an unexpected, uncontrollable and, under the circumstances, bizarre reaction from William. He started to laugh, a good, rich sound. He was laughing at her audacity, at her impertinence. After a moment he smoothed the laughter from his face and took a much-needed drink of brandy.

'I think you'd better drink your wine. Oh, and just for the record,' he said on a more serious note, 'I never flirt. Behaving like a lovesick, besotted idiot is not my style.'

'No, I don't imagine it is,' she said with a smile. Setting down her glass, she proceeded to flick through the magazine, a magazine about art. 'You have plenty of reading to occupy your time,' she commented, nodding at the books. 'I had absolutely no idea that so much knowledge existed in your cabin.'

'It helps pass the time. Feel free to borrow any you like. There are some on an India theme, with interesting illustrations.'

Anna's eyes narrowed when she mistook his meaning and bristled at what she considered an intended slight.

'I don't just look at the pictures. Contrary to what you might think, I am not illiterate.'

'I don't underestimate your intelligence.'

'That's a relief. I am quite accomplished at my letters. I read anything you care to name and am conversant in French and Urdu. Perhaps if I were to choose something by Voltaire or Socrates you would be more impressed. Usually I read for enlightenment, for knowledge, but I also like reading something light.'

'You speak French and Urdu?' William asked incredulously, with surprise and doubt.

Anna made a pretence of looking offended. 'You seem surprised.'

'I confess that I am. There are few ladies of my acquaintance who are familiar with the classics—and I am hard pressed to think of any one of them who is conversant in any language other than their own native English and perhaps a smattering of French.'

Now it was Anna's turn to be surprised. 'Then I can only assume that your experience with the female sex is somewhat limited, William.'

A gleam of suppressed laughter lit William's eyes and Anna could only assume, correctly, that her remark about his inexperience with women had been taken in the way she had intended.

'I imagine you can also outshoot most men and handle a horse better than any other female.'

'I enjoy doing both.'

William arched a sleek black brow in mock amusement when his gaze met Anna's. 'I'm impressed! You are quite an accomplished young woman.'

'Mock me if you wish, but I speak the truth.'

'I don't doubt it. And to add to all those admirable attributes the cut and thrust of your tongue is sharper and deadlier than any rapier,' he retorted.

'I'm glad you've noticed,' she replied with an impudent smile and a delicate lift to her brow.

William seemed to find her impudence utterly exhilarating. The ghost of a smile flickered across his face as his eyes locked on hers in silent, amused communication, and he seemed quite entranced about sharing her humour.

'You have spirit. I have to give you that. Do you like art, Anna?'

'Like my father before me I like looking at paintings,' she said, placing the magazine back on the table and picking up her glass, 'even though I don't always understand what I'm looking at.'

Turning to look at her as she sipped her wine, he grinned. 'Don't worry. We all have our faults.'

'I'm glad to see you include yourself among the imperfect,' Anna retorted, turning away from his condescending smile.

'I'm just as flawed and human as any man, Anna.'

'I suppose I should be flattered that you have taken the time to take an interest in me—although I sense you find me rather pathetic.'

'Not at all. I was extolling your virtues.'

'It didn't sound as though I was being complimented. Despite what my brother told you about me, after just a short acquaintance, is your vanity so colossal as to lead you to think you can understand me?'

If William felt the barb of her riposte, he didn't show it. Sitting down and stretching his long legs out in front of him, he watched as she slowly paced the floor, smiling now and then at Mrs Preston as the lady sipped her wine and was engrossed in a conversation with Mac about India.

'I know that you are caring and thoughtful, honest and sincere. I don't think it's amiss to pay a compliment and say you are a very pretty young woman—also a spirited and very determined one,' he added. 'That is clearly your style and I admire such spirit in a woman.'

Surprised by his compliment, she stared at him and smiled broadly. 'Thank you. That means a lot—coming from you.'

'I have a notion you will succeed at anything you choose to do.'

Anna's cheeks pinked. She wasn't completely lacking in human feeling. 'Thank you,' she replied. 'I intend to try—although I shudder to think what Uncle Robert might have in store for me. He won't want me living with him indefinitely, that I do know—or Aunt Constance. I suppose he's done well for himself despite inheriting neither title nor wealth. Qualifying as a lawyer of distinction, and by unstinting work, he's managed to amass a considerable fortune.

'He'll not want me cluttering up his fine house for too long so I suspect he'll probably have someone lined up for me to wed—a man I won't care a fig for. If so, he is going to be vastly disappointed for I have no intention of allowing myself to be forced into a marriage with anyone. I'm looking forward to the day when I have complete independence, to do what I want with my life and not be answerable to anyone.'

'And have you thought what you will do as an independent person?'

'I'm mulling it over. I like being with children, helping with their learning, which is what I was doing in Bombay. I might decide to open a school—or an orphanage. There are so many destitute children who would benefit from that.'

'That would be an admirable thing to do, Anna. Your uncle might not be as difficult as you expect. He might surprise you and be willing to advise you in any venture you decide on.'

'I sincerely hope so, although I suspect he'll want to marry me off to the first bidder.'

'I'm sure he's not as bad as you make him out to be.'

'You would say that. All men stick together,' she said crossly.

William turned and looked at her and said quietly, 'I want to talk, not argue. I have no desire to quarrel with you.'

'Then do not try to provoke me by implying Uncle Robert is some kind of saint.'

'I wasn't.'

'It's extremely ill-mannered of you to badger me. Why do you do it?' she asked sternly, undaunted by him.

Her words were accompanied by such a well-bred, reproving look that William laughed in spite of himself. Still smiling, his mouth wide over his excellent teeth, he looked at the outrageous young woman who dared to lecture him on his shortcomings. 'It's as well to test the mettle of one's allies, as well as one's enemies.'

Anna found herself quite intrigued by this confounding man. Her heart gave a disturbing leap as he turned

his head in her direction. It did not seem at all fair that
a man with wealth and power and a title should possess
the face and form of an Adonis. She saw there were tiny
lines around his eyes from squinting against the sun,
which gave strength and depth to his handsome face.
It was impossible not to respond to him as his masculine magnetism was dominant wherever he happened
to be. She imagined many women had been enamoured
of him, that many had fallen in love with him.

Meeting his direct gaze, she saw there was something agreeable in their depths that made her whole
body feel as if it were unwinding, growing weak with
the pleasure of it. Vividly conscious of her close proxim-
ity to him, she abruptly turned her thoughts away from
this new and dangerous direction. Her mouth quivered
in the start of a smile to match his own.

'And in which category do you place me?' she asked,
her antipathy of a moment earlier having melted away
in the most curious way.

William looked at Anna hard. His instinct detected
untapped depths of passion in the alluring young woman
that sent silent signals instantly recognisable to a lusty,
hot-blooded male like himself. The impact of those signals brought a smouldering glow to his eyes.

Recollecting himself, on a more serious thought he
admitted that Anna was appealing, but he was a man
on a mission to be reunited with his family. He had
everything mapped out and did not want complica-
tions, especially not of the kind Anna posed. He was
not about to let this young woman disrupt his life. An
act of gallantry was one thing, undue sacrifice was an-

other. Besides, she had her own agenda and he would not interfere with that.

'I will just say you stand in the middle just now. Where you end up depends on how we get on for the rest of the voyage. Now finish your wine. I think it's time I escorted you and Mrs Preston to your cabins.'

Chapter Four

The sea was as smooth as shimmering satin. The lines of the African coast could be seen in the far-off distance, a chain of islands coloured blue and green in the light of the setting sun. Anna laughed as she watched a pod of frolicking dolphins swimming alongside the ship, their shrill cries drifting up with spray to blend with the creaking of the rigging.

Seeing Anna standing alone, James Ryder left the group he was with and sauntered towards her.

'I'm delighted to see you again, Miss Harris—and without your guard dog.'

Anna turned to find James looking at her with twinkling eyes. She laughed. James was charming and entertaining and she basked in the glow of his attention. If, in her calmer moments, she doubted that what she was doing was the right thing in encouraging him, she quickly shook it off.

'I think you mean Lord Lancaster. He is only looking out for me—which is what guardians do.'

'Did I tell you—before we were interrupted by your

thunder-faced guardian—that you dance divinely, by the way?'

His grin was impudent as he subjected her to a long, lingering gaze. 'No, I don't recall you doing so—although I would hardly call it dancing. Because the ship was heaving so precariously, we almost ended up in a heap as I recall.'

'So we did. Would you care to take a turn about the deck with me before we have to retire below?'

Despite William's hostility towards James, there seemed to be nothing malevolent about him just now—and she found his relaxed detachment an antidote for William's highhandedness. What she minded, and what brought a militant sparkle to her eyes, was William's persistent and decidedly unwelcome and authoritarian attitude to direct her. The deep hostility that existed was between William and James Ryder and had nothing to do with her. She would make up her own mind where James was concerned.

Knocking the little demons that rose up to do battle away, she didn't object when he took her arm and drew her into the shadows.

When William arrived on deck, having been wined and dined by Captain Leighton, he paused and glanced around. Already the sun had dropped low on the horizon in a blood-red sunset. Sailors were going about their business and several passengers were taking a last stroll about the deck before going below for the night. That was when his gaze picked out Anna standing with James Ryder, who was looking down at her upturned face like a hungry fox looking into a hen coop.

When he saw him take Anna's arm and draw her to a quieter part of the deck, fury gripped him. James Ryder was an unscrupulous individual—in India an entire loving family had been destroyed because of him—and now William felt all the remembered fury and horror of that time surge through him.

He moved across the deck with long irate strides. 'What the hell do you think you are doing?' William exploded, looking at James, his voice vibrating with fury and contempt.

Anna turned to face him, annoyed by William's interference. 'If you don't mind—'

His face darkening into a mask of freezing anger, William turned on her. 'I do mind.' Anna was surprised how much she minded his look of contempt. 'That was a stupid thing to do. Have you any idea what was in his mind when he tried to get you alone?' He turned to James, who remained unmoved by William's anger—as did his smile.

'I meant Miss Harris no harm. We were merely taking a stroll before dark.'

Willian glowered at him. 'You can leave, but just a word before you go.'

'A word, is it? And what have you to say to me that you haven't said already?' James smirked in the face of William's anger. 'Regarding a certain person known to both of us.' It was gratuitous malice, and it hit its mark.

The words hung in the air in an oasis of stillness. The wariness in William's eyes froze into a pale sliver as cold as glacier ice. From where she stood, Anna could see his right fist clench—the only outward sign of his feelings. What she had witnessed told her that William was a dangerously unpredictable foe. There was no hiding the highly charged antagonism between the two men.

She watched them speak quietly, too far away to hear what was said, but she saw shock flash over James's face like summer lightning and his shoulders slump. He was about to say something more, but his mouth snapped shut abruptly, as though he were afraid to say more. And then, without a glance in her direction, he walked away.

When William turned back to her his face was expressionless, but his lips were white. 'Are you out of your mind? Weren't you even listening to what I said about him?'

'What did you say to him?' Anna demanded.

'It was between Ryder and me. Let it rest, Anna.'

Anna gasped, glaring up at him. 'William, how could you be so rude?'

He cocked a brow and regarded her coldly. 'Was I?'

'Inexcusably so and you know it.'

'You little fool. I thought after what I said to you the last time about Ryder and his ways, you would have the good sense to avoid him.'

'He has done nothing and did not deserve such a cruel set-down. And since when did you care a fig for my reputation?'

'When your brother put you in my charge. To encourage James Ryder can do you no good in the end. I realise that you may have been allowed to go your own way in Bombay and that you find being on board this ship confining and a different concept for you to grasp, but try to make an effort. You are too naive, too inexperienced, to take on a man like Ryder.'

His words sounded so insulting, that Anna felt as though she had been slapped. An icy numbness crept over her body, shattering any feelings she had for him. She expelled her breath in a rush of tempestuous fury as any unity they had shared was shattered.

'Contrary to what you say, Mr Ryder has shown me nothing but courtesy.'

'Nevertheless, his intentions may not be as honourable as you think and, deprived of female company for so long, he may be inclined to toss you to the deck without thought of the consequences of doing so.'

Anna was shocked by his insinuation and she glowered at him. 'Not all men are barbarians.'

'Don't you believe it,' he replied with a sarcastic twist to his lips. 'There's no accounting for some people's tastes, particularly when their need is great enough.'

Anna gaped at him. 'Such a thought never entered my head. You really are quite hateful.'

'True, but I trust I've made my point.'

'How dare you mock my feelings. What a callous, self-opinionated beast you are, William Lancaster. How excruciatingly naive you must find me. Just to set the record straight, where my reputation is concerned, I am quite capable of taking care of that matter myself. I do not need any help or interference from you.'

William stared at the proud, tempestuous young woman in silent, icy composure. Her words reverberated in his head, hitting him with all the brutal impact of a battering ram, but it failed to pierce the armour of his wrath and not a flicker of emotion registered on his impassive features.

'That, Miss Harris, was quite an outburst. Have you finished?'

Pausing to take an infuriated breath, Anna finally said, 'Far from it. There is much more I would like to say, but I won't. You are being vindictive without just cause, but if you want to carry on hating me then please do so. It does not matter one jot to me.'

Their minds and their eyes clashed in a battle of wills.

'I do not hate you.'

'No? Well, I hate you,' she told him wrathfully.

'I know you do,' he replied quietly. Not only had he heard, but also he sensed it. Cool and remote, he studied her for a moment, as though trying to discern something. She was glaring at him like an enraged angel of retribution and he realised she was on the brink of tears. He felt a twinge of conscience, which he quickly thrust aside.

'Go below to your cabin, Anna. Get some sleep.' Without another word he turned and walked away.

Anna spun round and fixed her gaze on the never-ending ocean, looking blindly at it for a long time with raging fury. A whole array of confusing emotions washed over her—anger, humiliation and a piercing, agonising loneliness she had not felt since she was fifteen years old, when she had left England.

William was thoughtful when he went to his cabin and poured himself a large much-needed brandy. With his legs stretched out in front of him he sat and slowly sipped the fiery liquid, a reluctant smile touching his lips when he remembered Anna standing valiantly against him. She had looked so heartbreakingly young, with those mutinous dark eyes flashing fire, unable to see that she had done anything wrong. And to be fair to her, apart from defying him, she hadn't, she couldn't be blamed.

But from his past dealings with James Ryder and the secret, shameful guilt he would feel to his dying day because he had not been there to save Johnathan's life on the night he had been attacked, he couldn't bring himself to tell her the truth. He was afraid, afraid she would think and feel differently about him—that she would despise him.

When he had reproached her he had seen the hurt in her eyes and it had wrung his heart.

Alone in her cabin, Anna climbed into her bunk. The memory of what had passed between them was intolerable. How dare William tell her who she could associate with, who she could speak to and who she could not? He had no right. However, when she thought of the words she had flung at him she suddenly felt ashamed. She had told him that she hated him and likened him to a barbarian. It had been an awful thing to say and, as she lay in bed that night, she was overwhelmed with shame.

She had been angered by his authoritative manner and was uncaring if her words hurt—not that she believed anything could penetrate that thick skin. Turning restlessly between the sheets, she cursed her wayward tongue a hundred times and sought forgetfulness in sleep. Sleep eluded her, however, and the image of William Lancaster and those dreadful words kept repeating themselves in her brain. She had never spoken so rudely to anyone in that hateful manner.

She had always thought herself polite and considerate to other people, yet there was something about her guardian—the lift of his brows, the quirk of his mouth—that infuriated her and yet at the same time it warmed and excited her to her very soul.

No matter how she tried to dispel the vision of him from her mind, those enigmatic eyes continued to stare into her soul—they mocked her, tantalised her and seduced her, until she felt as if he inhabited her body. When she was with him strange feelings and emotions she had never felt before tormented her.

She felt at times as if William had cast some kind of spell over her, so that she was no longer the same person. Never had she foreseen such a tempestuous awakening of her womanly desires, which had left her shaken. She hadn't wanted it to happen this way and certainly not with a man such as William Lancaster.

She had met many handsome men in Bombay and yet not one of them had impressed her. There had been no meeting of eyes to cause her heartbeat to quicken like it did when she captured William's stare. There must be something else, something indefinable about him that had the power to hold her so entranced. All her life, feeling rejected and of no consequence to her family, she had protected herself. It was a strange sensation for her to be on the receiving end.

This feeling couldn't last, she told herself. She wouldn't allow it. There were too many things she wanted to do to let any romantic feeling from any man get in the way. Her jaw tightened, her resilient spirits stretching themselves as they had done once before when her mother had sent her to live with Uncle Robert.

Once they were in England and William had deposited her with Robert, it would end and it was unlikely she would see him again.

Appearing on deck the following day, Anna let her gaze travel to where William stood talking to a group of young officers lounging against the rail across the deck. On seeing Anna, he excused himself to his friends and started to walk towards her. Having no wish to continue their argument, Anna turned to return below, but he was soon beside her, halting her.

'A moment, Anna.'

She looked at him, her face expressionless, her eyes searching his for the anger of yesterday, relieved to see it had gone. 'What is it, William? Do you have something to say to me?'

'The air is cool just now. Will you not stay a while— or is my company so distasteful to you that you are in a hurry to rid yourself of it?'

'Not at all,' she replied calmly, 'but I think it is the other way round and I'll warrant you'll find the air more conducive without my company.'

'You are mistaken.' He drew a little closer to her. 'The estrangement that has arisen between us was none of my making, Anna.'

A look of relentless obstinacy crept into her eyes. 'You must forgive me. I have a short memory.'

He looked her straight in the eyes. She met that look, unbending. Womanly pride would have suggested she should walk past him without another word, but some instinct suggested that she should remain. They could not continue all the way to London at daggers drawn.

'You will stay?'

'Very well,' she said, relenting, the slightest of smiles on her lips.

'Dare I hope that smile denotes a softening in your opinion of me?'

'I have no opinion of you,' Anna said calmly.

'I disagree. You have a very strong opinion of me. I recall you telling me that I am callous, self-opinionated—and you also likened me to a barbarian.'

Uneasy beneath his relentless gaze, Anna's face fell. 'I also remember saying that I hated you, for which I apologise. I'm sorry. I was angry. I didn't mean any of those things. I would like to thank you for looking after me—even though I insist I don't need looking after.' Her words were sincere and heartfelt.

Their gazes linked and held, hers open and frank, with gratitude in its depths.

'I realise that. If you had been with anyone other than James Ryder, it would not have mattered quite as much.' Taking her arm, he walked her to the rail which offered some privacy.

'You know James quite well, don't you?'

'Well enough.'

'Will you tell me what is wrong between the two of you?' His eyes were very intent, very serious. They held hers as if she was in some way worthy of close study. She could not look away.

'James Ryder and I go way back and things have happened that are impossible to forgive or forget. What you said about his pride having taken a battering was right. A man is most sensitive about his pride when he knows he has little of which to be proud. He's the son of an earl.'

'That first time you saw us together, what did you mean when you accused him of being under the influence of drink—or another substance? To what were you referring?'

He looked at her, his eyes piercing hers. 'Opium. You lived in Bombay in the cantonment—it cannot have escaped your notice that there are those who seek respite from the boredom of such long hot idle Indian days and nights by exciting themselves with an occasional smoke of opium. Ryder was no exception and I imagine he has a horde stashed away somewhere on board. It's expensive, but many in the Company can afford it.'

'I didn't know. I never gave such things a thought—and I would not have thought it of James.'

'Well, now you do. Ryder is a sybaritic layabout, living each moment like a well-fed cat in the sun. Women are drawn to his easy, engaging personality—and I don't suppose anyone can blame him for playing to his strengths. There might well be an heiress who will find him irresistible, but to embark on any kind of relationship with that man I can only regard as disastrous. It was Ryder's hedonistic lifestyle that got him thrown out of the Company. He thinks being the son of an earl enables him to do as he pleases with relative impunity.'

'Why—he is what—twenty—twenty-one? At that age he can hardly have had time to sink into such depravity.'

'Twenty-two, if you must know. My young brother Charles is the same age. They were at Oxford together and Ryder is every bit as bad now as he was then. Most students go to university to grow up. James Ryder went solely to have a good time—fast living and academic indifference—with absolutely no intention of learning anything. Unfortunately, he almost took my brother with him when he was sent down. Thankfully I was home from India at the time and I was able to separate him from Ryder before too much harm had been done.'

'And his family?'

'He's the youngest of four sons of the Earl of Brinkley. For the first time in his life the Earl was rudely awakened to his son's shortcomings. Thinking to teach him a lesson, he obtained him a position with the Company and had him shipped off to India.'

'Did you have contact with him in India?'

His eyes darkened and his expression became grave. 'Unfortunately our paths crossed on more occasions than I would have liked, even though I did my utmost to avoid his company. I hope you will realise now why it would be sensible for you to avoid him.'

Anna nodded, having a strange feeling that he hadn't told her everything. Was William making too much of it? she wondered. Maybe James was a reformed character—although she must not forget that he had not been dismissed from the Company without good reason.

When they finally put in at the Cape to take on board fresh water and provisions before continuing on their journey London bound, for the first time in two months they stepped on to dry land. Two vessels of the convoy were already at anchor. The glittering waters were dotted with all manner of craft, from fishing ketches and lighters to huge merchantmen. The town had a considerable English population to look after the East India Company.

The noise and the colour assailed Anna's senses and the hot African sun gilded the town and warehouses that lined the water front in a silver glow. Everywhere disorder reigned. A never-ceasing army of bare-chested workers worked laboriously, driving wagons and manning the oars of the lighters—sturdy vessels utilised to transport cargo to and from the ships anchored in the bay.

William hired a carriage on the water front and beneath the shadow of the flat-topped mountain and a perfect blue sky, they left the harbour behind. William wanted to show Anna the surrounding countryside. Her head was full of the delightful excursion as they journeyed out to the foothills. She took in with awe the land that was covered with colourful shrubs and exotic flowers and the beauty of the mountains that stretched into the interior.

Returning to the town and reluctant to board the ship just then, they dined at a small restaurant, seated on a veranda, and watched the world pass by. They ate lobster as red as any they had seen in Britain and juicy orange mangoes, and drank wine, pale and yellow and as rich as the fruits they ate.

After what Anna proclaimed had been a perfect day, toying with his wine glass, William watched her closely, delighting in her. His gaze lingered on the tiny freckles across the bridge of her nose and the smooth expanse of her cheek, which had acquired a golden glow. Her hair, which she had twisted into a thick plait, snaked down her spine, curling tendrils frothing about her face.

There were depths to Anna that every other woman he knew lacked and she never ceased to amaze him.

She was lovely, breathtakingly so, and within his grasp, but he had to deny himself the satisfaction of possessing her.

Replete and relaxing in the shade of the veranda, Anna sipped her wine and said, 'I asked Mrs Preston about you, William. I hope you don't mind.'

'No, why should I? What did she tell you?'

'Very little that I didn't already know—that your grandfather is the Marquess of Elvington and that you are his sole heir. She also told me that you had a disagreement and fell out.'

'Well, she got that right.'

'Is that why you are going to England, to make up with your grandfather?'

'I will see him. Whether or not we can forgive each other is another matter entirely. He is cantankerous and autocratic, unable to see anyone else's point of view but his own.'

'Then perhaps you should resolve your differences. If you don't and something happens to him—if he dies, then it will be too late.'

William sighed, becoming thoughtful. 'You may be right. During my time in India I've had a lot of time to think about what it is I should do. I became consumed with a desire to possess something money can't buy. That's when I realised I already had it. Cranford.'

'So you decided to go home.'

'Yes. I have to find some way back and make my peace with my grandfather. It has bothered me that we parted on bad terms—yet, when I think of his harsh treatment of my mother, I am reluctant.'

'But—if you don't make your peace with him, then you may regret it.'

'I might not.'

'Yes, you will. If you don't, you aren't the man I thought you were.'

'And what kind of man do you think I am, Anna?'

'Kind, honourable, loyal…'

His lips curled with cynicism. 'I'm flattered. I had no idea I was held in such high regard.'

'What did your grandfather do that was so terrible you fell out with him?'

'I've told you. He was not very kind to my mother.'

Anna stared at him. 'Yes, I'm sorry. I remember you telling me he wasn't happy when she remarried and left Cranford.'

'No, he wasn't. My concern now is for Charles and Tilly. It's time for me to go back—to get to know them. I've been away too long. Now our mother has died—and their father died before that—Tilly needs direction. Bearing in mind that Charles had decided on a career with the Company and that I was to return to Cranford, my mother made me the sole arbitrator of Tilly's future. She also realised the advantages to be gained for Tilly's future by making her my ward.

'I made a promise to my mother a long time ago, that should anything happen to her I would watch out for Tilly and Charles. I shall keep that promise in the only way I know how. Where my grandfather is concerned, I will tread carefully. He's a ruthless, bitter old man. The people who work for him live in fear of him. Even my father obeyed him without question, never offending the old tyrant.'

'And you are not like your father?'

'No.'

'Tell me about your mother. What was she like?'

'Gentle, loyal. She loved my father with her whole heart. When he died, she couldn't go on living at Cranford with Grandfather. She both feared and hated him. She thought she could escape by marrying again, but Grandfather refused to allow me to go with her, so I was left alone at Cranford—although he allowed me to see her on occasion. He drove my mother away. I could not forgive him for that.'

'But she was still a young woman. He could not have expected her to remain unwed.'

'He did. While ever I remained at Cranford I would never be my own master. Titles are meaningless to me. Being Marquess of Elvington was not for me.'

'So you rebelled.'

'Something like that. The mere thought of capitulating to my grandfather was anathema to me. I told him to go to the devil and take his title with him.'

'Are you the last in the line?'

'I am.'

'And you would allow the line to be wiped out?'

He sighed. 'I did consider it. At the time I did not intend to claim my inheritance because to destroy the line seemed a fitting punishment for everything my grandfather did to my mother. In my anger, my opinions and rationality clouded by youth, perhaps I was a too hasty. My time in India taught me much—and one thing I realised was that Cranford was where I belonged—where I am meant to be. I love the old place—every stone and blade of grass that grows.'

'Yes,' Anna said softly, deeply moved by what he had told her. 'I can see you do. Surely your grandfather has some redeeming features?'

'Not that I know of.'

'I can think of one. He is your grandfather, therefore indirectly responsible for your existence. You have to agree with that.'

He nodded, catching her eyes. Then he smiled. 'Yes, there is that.'

'Was he an only child—no brothers or sisters?'

'One brother, the heir, which allowed my grandfather to choose his own career. He became a soldier—reaching the rank of Colonel. It was unfortunate that his brother died. The title and the estate passed to Grandfather. It was with great reluctance that he returned to Cranford as the Marquess of Elvington. He had to watch the woman he loved marry another.'

'But why?'

'As the daughter of a cloth merchant, she wasn't suitable to be the wife of a marquess. The Lancasters have always made marriages of convenience—it was a duty, *noblesse oblige* and all that. No longer able to forge his own future doing what he loved best, he had no choice but to return to Cranford and marry a woman to suit his title.'

'That must have been heartrending for him.'

'It happened a long time again, Anna. No good brooding on it now.'

'And soon it will be your turn to take over the estate, to find a wife suitable to reside over Cranford.'

He nodded. 'Exactly. During my time in India, I began to look at Cranford differently. I began to take a deeper pride in it and was very aware that on my grandfather's demise the responsibility for everyone within its environs rested on me. I discovered within myself a need to see those responsibilities carried out and for Cranford to prosper as it has done for centuries. Everyone who depends on the estate must know their futures are secure.'

'And they will be with you at the helm.'

'I sincerely hope so. Now, I think we should be getting back to the ship.'

Chapter Five

'This has been a wonderful day for me,' Anna said, draining her glass of wine.

They stood up, close together. William took her hands and drew her towards him. He was a foot taller than she was and she had to look up to him. She thought in that moment that he was going to kiss her and she felt alarmed, particularly because she realised it was not him she was afraid of, but herself. She tried to shake off the effect he was having on her. Why was she hoping that he would kiss her? She felt a sudden rush of embarrassment and anticipation and denial, excitement and panic. Her heart beat frantically. She lifted her hand as if to touch her mouth, then withdrew it. She watched as William's mouth curved in a ghost of a smile.

'You have been a gracious host, William.'

'I can be charming when I am doing what I like.'

'And you enjoy entertaining me?'

'Absolutely.' He looked at her seriously. 'Are you happy, Anna?'

She laughed. 'As happy as I can be—as happy as everyone else.'

'That's evasive.'

'Happiness is rarely a permanent state. It varies with one's moods. I am happy now.'

'Why? Because you are here now—that you have seen Cape Town and we have enjoyed a meal together? That is not necessarily happiness, but a pleasant experience.'

'Yes, it is that, I suppose—and I do feel happy. Thank you for showing me Cape Town. I never expected to be taken on a guided tour. This day will always stand out in my memory.'

William's eyes searched her face with something like wonder in his light blue eyes. 'You confound me—do you know that? You try my patience like no other, you play chess like a master, you ride a horse like no other, and yet what an amazingly sensitive, perceptive, wise young woman you are, Anna Harris.'

'You make me sound complicated.'

'I didn't mean to,' he said as they made their way back to the ship. 'If the winds are favourable, hopefully it will be plain sailing to London. The Bay of Biscay is often rough and passing the Straits of Gibraltar can be challenging, not only because we are at war with France, but it's the corsairs' hunting ground and perhaps the most dangerous part of any voyage, where they target vulnerable merchant vessels. As part of a convoy, with any luck we'll pass unhindered.'

They returned to the ship as far over the water, layering the sky with shades of gold, red and indigo blue, they watched the last of the sun sink over the sea. That day would always stand out in Anna's memory. From the moment she set foot on Africa's Cape it became an enchanting place. She was buoyantly happy being shown the sights in one of the most exciting cities in the world by the most attractive man in the world and, before they went back on board, he presented her with a small bunch of flowers, the kind she had seen carpeting the land.

He was standing close and they were quite alone. She smelled the sweet-scented flowers and then looked up at him. He was looking down at her in a way he never had before. She should have stepped away from him, but she couldn't. Everything about him conspired to draw her in and she could no more resist him than she could resist the land and the sea and the sun and the air that drifted around and above them like an invisible cloud.

She melted into him, into his embrace, into his kiss. His arms were around her and his lips were warm on hers, and there was nothing she could do but allow herself to be carried away by the overwhelming sensation of it all.

When at last they pulled away, they stared at each other in amazement, both startled by what had occurred. William touched her face.

'I am shocked that I did that, Anna. I should have shown more restraint. But you are quite extraordinary,' he murmured. 'I had no idea what to expect when Johnathan gave me the task of escorting you to England. I imagined you to be a shy young thing, dull, even, but you are nothing like that. You have a fire inside you, a fire deep in your soul. I can feel it.'

There was a raw undercurrent to his voice that pierced

Anna's heart. Overwhelmed by him, by the moment, realising where she was and what was happening, she stepped back. What was she doing? It was as if she were someone else and not herself at all. This man was, for the time being, her guardian and more experienced than she was, and she should not be doing this—her mind told her that much, but then, why was he looking at her with such intensity?

This was something she had no experience of and she felt as if she were balancing precariously on the edge of a precipice and that one step forward would send her tumbling into the unknown. She shrank away from him and the moment was lost. She turned away and without a word returned to the sanctuary of her cabin.

For the days that followed, Anna threw all her efforts into helping more with the children and trying to forget what had happened with William. She spent time with Mrs Preston and Celia and tried hard to concentrate on their conversation, but try as she might she couldn't stop her mind from casting back to that kiss. Had it affected William as much as it had her, she wondered, and had he acted on impulse? Was he feeling as lost as she was?

And so she struggled through it, unable to say who was to blame, and gave up in the end. They had both been complicit in allowing the kiss to happen—and a little voice in her head told her she had enjoyed it—her first kiss.

Two weeks out of Cape Town the winds rose and began blowing with a force that Anna found terrifying. The expanse of hostile sea was all around them, the waves capped with curls of foam. The tackle creaked and the sails cracked overhead as the wind caught them. Suddenly all about her became a grey, watery world, with heavy clouds racing across the sky as far as the eye could see, salt spray and massive waves rising and falling in a froth of boiling foam.

'We're sailing right into a storm,' Mrs Preston said as she came down from the deck. 'With any luck it will blow itself out, but stay in your cabin, Anna. It will become dangerous on deck—you're most likely to be blown overboard.'

Left to herself, Anna retreated to her cabin. The vessel was pitching badly in the turbulent sea. The grey waves fell into deep hollows as though the sea would swallow them up. As the day wore on it began to rain, the conditions becoming worse. Flashes of lightning illuminated the cabin and the rolling sea beyond the porthole seemed even blacker as darkness began to shroud the ship.

Anna shivered as she crouched on her bunk. She couldn't imagine what the seamen were going through on the deck of the pitching ship. The rain had become a downpour and on several occasions she was almost thrown from her bunk to the floor. Suddenly there was the piercing scream of a woman outside her cabin. Immediately she flung open the door and, clinging to the frame, looked out. A woman with a crying babe in arms was trying to keep her balance as she went from cabin to cabin in search of her daughter who had gone missing. She was fraught with worry.'

'Go back to your cabin,' Anna called to her, knowing

the child she was looking for. 'I'll see if I can find her. When did you last see her?'

'About ten minutes ago. She—she went to the cabin next to ours to play with her friend, but she is not there. Where can she be?' she wailed, her eyes darting all over the place in her attempt to locate her.

'She can't be far away,' Anna said, having to shout above the noise of the storm to make herself heard. 'I'll see what I can do.'

As she staggered and groped her way along the narrow companionway and up the stairs, her stomach knotted with fear. Up on deck the rain was cold and slashing, and she was drenched in seconds, her dress plastered to her body and her hair loosened and clinging to her face. The clap of thunder overhead startled her.

Captain Leighton was at the helm, calling on every ounce of skill he possessed to hold a course in the rough sea. She could see the figures of men high above her head, illuminated by the flashes of lightning that streaked across the sky. It seemed that at any moment the wind would pluck them from their perches and fling them down on to the deck or into the boiling sea. Men were rushing about on deck, battling the elements, paying her no heed, being so absorbed in their work.

Frantically Anna's eyes scoured the deck for a small child. Holding on to anything that didn't move, she searched but without success. She was flung on to the boards when a wave broke over the port rail, spewing a foaming cascade down upon the ship. She found herself clutching at anything within reach. She grasped and scrambled while the wind and the rain seemed to snatch away her breath as she tried to pull herself upwards, cursing the sodden wetness of her clothes. Lightning flooded everything with a blinding glow of white fire. She knew she had to hang on to something, anything, and not lose her grip, for she was in danger of falling into the swirling torrent perilously close.

Seawater ran off the scuppers as another flash of lightning shot across the sky, followed by another gigantic wave that propelled her across the pitching deck, causing her to hit her head and knocking the breath from her lungs. Desperately she reached out for anything to hold on to and then, just when she had lost hope, almost disbelievingly strong fingers gripped her arm and she began to slide upward, unbelievably, joyously.

Her skirt caught on something and ripped, but what did it matter? She was being dragged higher and higher. She looked up, wiping her hair from her eyes to see William glaring down at her, his hair plastered to his head and water streamed down his face. And then she heard his voice. Was it possible that there was a note of anxiety, almost desperation in it?

'Good Lord, Anna, what are you doing up on deck in this storm? This is not the place for you to be. Just look at you—you're hurt. You could have been washed overboard.'

She could scarcely hear him above the noise of the storm. She stared up into William's shadowed face. Lightning flashed again, and in the unnatural brightness, William saw that her eyes were wide with terror. A shower of spray burst on to the deck as the ship pitched to starboard. She would have fallen except for his powerful arms that came round her and pulled her close. He tried to pull her back inside, but she clung to him, her head spinning from the bang it had received.

'William, listen to me,' she cried over the howling wind, clinging to his shoulders. 'There's a child missing. She isn't down below and there is a chance she may be on deck.' At that moment, with a shower of spray the ship pitched. 'Please help me find her.'

A muscle flexed in William's jaw and he looked as if he would refuse, until a crewman shouted and pointed to a small figure being carried by one of the crew. She was clinging to him for dear life, her face buried in his shoulder.

'Take her below to her mother,' William shouted down the length of the deck. 'And while you're at it, inform Mrs Preston that Miss Harris is safe—that she will return shortly.'

The seaman hurried away with the child, disappearing down the companion ladder.

William turned his attention back to Anna. 'Come with me. We have to get out of the storm.'

Taking her arm, he helped Anna down to his cabin which was much closer than her own. She collapsed into a chair and closed her eyes, coughing on the water she had swallowed. Bending over her, William inspected the wound on her head, producing a handkerchief and dabbing the blood away.

'Open your eyes, Anna.' When she did as he bade, he smiled. 'Thank goodness. You gave me a fright when I saw you on deck. The wound to your head isn't serious, but hold the handkerchief against it for a while until it stops bleeding. It was a foolish thing to do to go on deck in a storm.'

'I had to find the child. I knew how frightened she would be."

'It was commendable of you. The little girl is safe now—with her mother.'

'It's a relief to know that,' she said quietly. 'The man who found her probably saved her life.'

'Maybe. I'll slip next door and get Mac.'

He returned a moment later, looking none too pleased. 'Mac is horizontal, I'm afraid. He doesn't care for ships—and certainly not in a storm. He won't show his face until the storm abates and we sail in calmer waters.' He looked at Anna, who was sitting with her elbows on her knees, her head resting on her hands, her body trembling. Hunkering down in front of her, he touched her hands. 'Anna, are you all right?' Placing a gentle finger under her chin, he compelled her to meet his gaze.

Raising her head, she nodded. 'Yes,' she answered quietly.

She was still in her wet clothes, chilled to the bone. But it was not the cold that was making her tremble, but the realisation of what might have happened had William not found her in time. Wordlessly he rose from his knees and raised her up from the chair, his arms close around her.

'There's nothing to fear now, Anna. You are quite safe.' Holding her from him, he stroked the wet hair from her face. 'Until it's safe for you to return to your cabin, you had best stay here. You will have to get out of your wet clothes otherwise you'll get more than a chill.'

'Will you hold me a moment longer?' she whispered.

Distressed by the sight of her, drawing her to his

chest he wrapped his arms round her once more, resting his cheek against her hair. 'Don't ever,' he said, remembering that devastating moment when he had seen her being swept along the deck when a wave hit her, 'do anything like that again.'

'I won't,' she mumbled against his chest. 'I promise.'

William suppressed a smile, but then on a decisive note he held her from him and said, 'I'll find something for you to wear until you can return to your cabin.' Finding a towel, he rubbed as much water from her hair as was possible. Then, producing a warm robe, he sat her back down on the chair.

'You are shivering, Anna, and so cold. Are you able to remove your wet clothes—it isn't appropriate for me to do it and it would create one hell of a scandal should anyone walk in.'

'I—I can't,' she uttered, her chin trembling with the cold. 'You will have to help me.'

With a feeling of urgency, William knelt down and proceeded to remove her shoes and peel the stockings from her legs, rubbing her shapely calves to warm them before standing up once more.

Anna was aware of the impropriety of what he was doing and knew should anyone walk in her reputation would be in tatters, but with the storm still raging and everyone concerned for their own safety, it was doubtful anyone would come. Besides, she was too shaken by what had happened to her to think about proprieties and her body was trembling so much she had little control over her limbs.

'Would you like me to help you off with your dress or do you think you can you manage? You can wear my robe for the present.' His eyes were drawn to her face and her trembling lips and he felt his heart flood with tenderness. 'Here, let me help you.'

She put up no resistance when he turned her round and unfastened the buttons down the back of her dress, slipping it off her shoulders and down to her feet, both of them doing their upmost to remain upright as the ship dipped and swayed. Draping the robe about her shoulders to save her modesty, he told her to remove her undergarments.

She stood rooted to the floor. 'I think I would like to keep them on,' she said, feeling dwarfed by his towering height.

'I think you should take them off,' he insisted quietly. 'They're wet and you're shivering.'

Anna nodded. 'Yes, I know. I think I can manage to remove them.'

'I'll leave you to it and return in a moment.'

She proceeded to remove her wet undergarments and, throwing them on to the floor, drew the robe about her, glad of its warmth. Reaching for the towel, she managed to get to the bunk as William returned. Sitting down, she began rubbing her hair, unconscious of the seductiveness of her gesture as she put the towel down and combed her fingers through it, twisting it into a thick cable which she shoved over her shoulder.

Glancing at William, she saw him standing perfectly still beside the chair she had vacated, watching her. Something in his expression made her hastily drop her hands, but the effect of that warmly intimate look in his eyes was vibrantly, alarmingly alive, and the danger of being here alone with him made her quake inside.

Seeing that she was still trembling and unable to resist the appeal in her eyes, William went and sat beside her. Before he knew what he was doing, he had taken her in his arms and gathered her to him.

She huddled against his chest like a small animal seeking the sanctuary and comfort of another. Her hair, which she had so painstakingly put into some semblance of order, was released once more and it sprang about her head in a tumbled mass of damp curls. He brushed the tendrils from her cheeks. She wasn't trembling so much now, but she still clung to him as the storm continued to rage and the ship to tilt this way and that precariously.

'Are you feeling better?' he asked.

'Yes, much better,' she whispered, her sweet breath fanning his lips. Her eyes, as she looked at him sitting beside her, had darkened so that they were almost black and her parted lips were moist and pink.

There was no intention on William's part to offer more than comfort and on hers to receive it, but in the close, intimate confines of the cabin, taking the initiative away from William, Anna put her arms about his neck, drawing him to her, and his own tightened, crushing her.

His hand cupped her face, then moved down to caress her throat before sliding inside the robe and caressing her small, round, rosy-tipped breast. The robe fell apart, sliding away from her thighs, and his hand moved to touch more exposed flesh, white and smooth as silk beneath his brown hand.

His hand was warm and his very male scent seemed to surround Anna. Her breath caught in her throat as she placed her sweet lips on his in a tender kiss, her eyes watching his face. His warm breath stirred her hair as he slid his lips to her ear. Imprisoned by his protective embrace and seduced by his mouth and caressing hands, Anna clung to him and, as his mouth began to move from her ear, she turned her head to fully receive his lips while her hands travelled over his chest.

What little remained of her good sense was warning her that this was wrong, a mistake, but she ignored it, because at that moment it didn't feel like a mistake. An impulse of the moment was beginning to consume her and she couldn't help it. Dragging her mouth from his, she looked at him.

'Your clothes are still wet,' she whispered. 'You'll catch your death if you don't take them off.'

His lips curved in teasing mockery. 'Why, Miss Harris, are you suggesting that I remove them?'

She laughed softly, her cheeks flushing a delightful pink. 'Yes—I mean, no. Oh, dear,' she whispered, her eyes on his lips hovering close to hers. Too naive to know how to hide her feelings, Anna raised her eyes to his and her longing for him to kiss her again was in their soft depths. 'I don't know what I mean. Please kiss me again, will you?'

William hesitated, but he did not disrobe. Anna was vulnerable, traumatised. He could not take advantage of such an innocent. He knew that what she needed right now was someone she could trust, not some ardent guardian set on seduction. The enduring ache of suppressed passion stirred his blood. His heart seemed to soften before he felt something like a stab to the chest. For a moment his resistance wavered, making him pause. It was a small warning, but a warning just the same, but it was too late.

The sweet offering of her mouth was too tempting for him to resist and his lips seized hers in a kiss of melting hunger that increased to scorching demand.

He tasted the honeyed softness of her, finding himself at the mercy of his emotions, when reason and intelligence were powerless. Savouring each intoxicating pleasure he gloried in her innocence, her purity, painfully aware of the trembling weakness in her scantily clad body pressed against his own.

She clung to him, her body arched against his and he felt his heart slam into his ribs. He kissed her with unleashed passion, his hands continued to explore her flesh beneath the robe. Dragging his lips from hers, he lowered his head and nuzzled her breast, his lips closing tightly around the taut nipple.

William's conscience, which he had assumed was long since dead, chose that moment to resurrect itself. Expelling a ragged breath and out of sheer self-preservation, he flung himself away from her, raking fingers of angry self-disgust through his hair as he fought to reassemble his senses and bring his desire under control.

Devil take it, he cursed silently as he fought to tame his body's fierce, frustrating urges—what the hell had happened to him? He was using Anna as he would one of his sexually experienced mistresses. But she was not like them. She was uncompromised and untainted.

Drawing a long, tortured breath, he looked down at her. 'Anna, we have to stop.'

Kissed and caressed into almost unconscious sensibility, a moment passed before Anna realised something was wrong, that there was an unexpected lull in their kisses. She opened her eyes in a daze of suspended yearning, newly awakened passion glowing in their velvety depths. Reaching out, she gently touched his arm.

'We must stop, Anna, before things go too far for us to draw back.' His voice was tight. He was unable to believe this innocent temptress had surrendered in his arms, returning his passion with such intoxicating sweetness that had almost shattered his self-control. No woman had looked like this. He was in thrall to her beauty, to her sweet face and her body, so achingly lovely. In her wild entanglement she looked like something artists of old would paint, a lawless goddess come to life.

Anna gazed at him, dazed by his kisses, as her swirling senses began to return to reality. Looking down and seeing her nakedness where the robe had slipped apart, passion gave way to anguish and then shame.

'What must you think of me?' she murmured, pulling the robe over her nakedness. 'I cannot believe what I have just done—that I actually asked you to kiss me and you have seen me practically naked. I—I don't do this...'

Gently he placed his finger beneath her chin and raised her face to his. 'Stop it, Anna. You have done nothing wrong. You are a very lovely and delightful young woman.'

'I never thought a kiss could be like that.'

He brought his gaze down upon hers heavily and with a slight smile, reaching out his hand, he gently touched her cheek with the tip of his finger. 'It was a little more than a kiss, Anna.' Taking her hand, he placed a kiss on its palm and stepped back as the ship continued to dip and sway. Picking up some dry clothes, he made his way to the door where he turned. With her hair tumbled around her in a glorious silken mass, she half sat like a beautiful, pagan goddess among the ruins of the bed.

'This should not have happened, Anna. It was a mistake. When Johnathan placed you in my charge, I agreed to take care of you. I will not break that agreement by seducing you. Not only would I be failing in my duty to your brother if I did that—but I would also despise myself. Get some rest. I'll arrange for some dry clothes to be brought to you.'

Leaving her alone, William went to see out the storm with his valet in the cabin next door, and when the wind dropped and the ship was more stable, he went to find Mrs Preston to tell her Anna was safe.

When he next saw Anna he needed to make her understand that the passion that had erupted between them should not have happened. His mind kept flashing back to that galvanising moment when she had reached up and twined her arms about his neck and placed her sweet lips against his. That single gesture had undone him, for no woman had ever kissed him so tenderly and he had found himself lost in temptation. He doubted she had ever been kissed before. The innocent sensuality of her response had taken him by surprise. But he couldn't allow such a thing to happen again.

However much he was attracted to her, however much he admired her and wanted her, he could not marry her. Very soon she would be an independent young lady, free to do anything she liked. She had told him how much this meant to her, how she would spend her money wisely but usefully—on a school or an orphanage for needy children—perhaps both. Like a bird she would fly free. He could not take that away from her by stifling her in a marriage she was not ready for and he sincerely hoped her uncle would feel the same.

The following morning Anna rose early. She had awoken with the awareness that something had happened to her, something that was to change her whole life. With a slow smile of contentment, she remembered what it had felt like to have her body pressed close to William's, for him to have kissed her with such passion.

Making her way on deck, she watched the early morning light catch the water so that it shone a luminous blue towards the distant horizon. On the main deck the shouts of the crew rose, their bare feet pattering over the wooden boards. There was little sign of the storm which she was certain had almost sent the ship to the bottom of the sea.

Strolling along the deck, she turned when she felt someone touch her arm. William stood beside her, looking down at her upturned face. Anna saw a world of feelings flash across his set features when their eyes locked. Tenderness welled up in her heart as she remembered how he had come to her aid at the height of the storm and she remembered how desolate she had felt when he had left her.

A slight flush sprang to her cheeks, which was ridiculous, she thought crossly, remembering that as the storm had battled around them, she had been lying almost naked in his arms. She averted her eyes, push-

ing away the erotic images that leapt to mind, for as
her guardian and an experienced man of the world, he
should not have taken advantage of her weakness. But
she could not deny that where he was concerned, there
was something about him that seemed to bring out the
worst in her and made her act more outrageously than
was wise.

'You are recovered, I hope, after the storm?'

'Thank you, yes, I am.'

'I'm glad to have caught you alone,' he said.

'Mrs Preston is resting. She didn't get any sleep during the storm.'

'That is understandable. Anna, I want to apologise
for last night.'

'You do?'

'I had no right to take advantage of you. I beg you to
accept my apology. It won't happen again.'

Why did hearing his words cause a heaviness in Anna's chest? It was prudent that he should say this, but
that didn't stop her from wishing things were different.
His ardour had been overwhelming and now there was
no sign of that man. He was very good at masking his
feelings. Either that, or she'd imagined those feelings
when he'd held her in his arms. She nodded, wanting
to conceal how deeply she was affected by what had
happened between them.

'No, I don't suppose it will. You must forgive me if I
appear stupid—but I am confused, you see. Will you tell
me why you kissed me? A man of your experience—you
knew exactly what you were doing. I'm not used to that
sort of thing, you see. I don't go around kissing people.'

'I should hope not.' Raking his fingers through his

hair, he sighed. 'I'm sorry, Anna. I never meant for it to happen. You must forget it happened.'

But I can't, Anna almost shouted at him. That was the trouble. The memory of what had happened between them in the storm lingered far too strongly for her to discount its effect on her. In the depths of her misery, she might have yielded to her disappointment, but then all at once her father's face came into her mind, proud and loving as she had last seen him, and Johnathan, so handsome, so intelligent and all fired up with a spirit of adventure when he had come to India—and with that the vulnerable and desperately loving Anna shrank away.

'So, William,' she said, sounding intentionally flippant, 'your intentions weren't honourable when you took me to your cabin and took advantage of me in my weakened state.'

'I took you to my cabin because it was closer than your own. There would have been the danger of us both being washed overboard otherwise. You were distressed. I wanted to comfort you—and it should have stopped at that.'

'We kissed, William, and it may have gone further than either of us intended, but no harm was done. No one knows of it but us.'

'Maybe not. Despite the feelings and emotions we aroused in each other, the depths of passion we reached, I'm relieved to see you do not fool yourself into believing it had anything to do with love.'

Anna's heart plummeted. An icy numbness crept over her body, shattering all her tender feelings for him. Deeply regretting what had happened between them, that she had even kissed him, urging him on when he would have stopped, she expelled her breath in a rush of tempestuous fury as the fragile unity they had shared was splintering.

'How dare you mock my feelings—and how dare you take liberties with me and then try placating me with a lame attempt at an apology? What a callous, self-opinionated blackguard you are, William Lancaster.'

He arched his eyebrows, his tone one of irony when he spoke. 'Yes, I am all those things. What did you expect—some infallible being? It was a mistake—my mistake,' he said, his voice strained. 'However, seducing a gently reared virgin—and one who happens to be in my charge—violates even my code of honour where women are concerned, no matter how degenerate you consider me to be. I am not proud of myself.'

Anna's eyes flared with anger. 'How excruciatingly naive you must find me. Just to set the record straight, *My Lord*, I do not expect a proposal. It never entered my head, so you need not concern yourself that I will demand any kind of commitment from you. That would be too extreme.'

'Nevertheless, this changes things between us. You showed me so much vulnerability when you were in my arms, so much generous passion, I cannot deny that I wanted you, Anna—all of you. After meeting you it didn't take long for me to realise that we have something in common. Like me, you like to make your own choices. I owe no man a living and I owe no woman a duty. In short, I am my own man, free to do what I choose.'

The impact of his words was like a punch in the

stomach. Anna did not feel particularly flattered or complimented by his words. 'And I am my own woman, William,' she said with a proud lift to her chin and in a tone made carefully neutral, feeling the need to give back hurt for hurt. 'I comprehend perfectly how you feel. Yes, I gave you freedom with my body and I thank God that you did not carry it too far.'

She could see that her words had pricked his anger.

Holding her gaze, he stood before her, tall and powerful, his face austere, his eyes challenging. 'And if I were to propose marriage?'

'My answer would be no. My background hardly recommends me to be the wife of the future Marquess of Elvington. You would only be asking me because you would feel obligated. I will not marry any man because he feels obligated. I am not some foundling you are obliged to propose to when you have a touch of guilt. I will not live the rest of my life with any man in a loveless marriage made as a result of his temporary passion, to expunge his guilt. I am not angling for a husband. I still comprehend the benefits of a life not confined to the dictates of one man. I want nothing from you.'

'And if I had taken your virginity? What then? For heaven's sake, Anna, if you think I would take your innocence and not do right by you, then you do not know me, my position in life or my honour as a gentleman.'

'I do and it matters to me that you have some regard for me. For myself I want to manage my own life. I want independence and autonomy. I want to be accountable to no one.' She pressed her lips together. Resistance was in every line of her, in her pose, in the stiff rigidity of her body, in the distance between them. They stood just three feet apart, and yet the gap between them at that moment seemed wider than the Atlantic Ocean.

'Your ability to wound my vanity, Anna, is boundless, it seems.'

'I'm sorry about that, but that's how it is. You owe me nothing and I will take nothing from you.

Stepping away from him, she paused and looked at him. 'And now, what will we do in the time it takes the ship to reach London? Avoid each other? Which will be no simple matter on board a ship with few places to hide.'

'We don't have to do that. I'm only trying to protect you.'

'I know you are. I understand. Be satisfied that your responsibilities where I am concerned will soon be over.'

In the tearing, agonising hurt that enfolded her, Anna was ashamed at how easy it had been for him to expose her vulnerability. With her head held high she left him then. Tears blinded her vision as she made her way down to her cabin, silently weeping for her lack of will and with a fear of her feelings for William she seemed unable to control. Why did she keep tormenting herself with memories of what they had done while the storm raged, memories that were better forgotten?

Chapter Six

Anna's conjecture, however, was very much mistaken. Whenever William laid eyes on her, he found just the sight of her and the remembrance of the intimacy in his cabin more than capable of arousing him. The sudden tautness of his own body proclaimed lounder than words how much he was attracted to her and how difficult he was finding it to control his physical attraction to her.

Anna had suddenly turned cold and, in all fairness, after the way he had treated her he could hardly blame her. It was clear she didn't want his company. For the time they were on board after that night, he didn't try to press the issue. But he was disgusted that their passionate interlude together had left him throbbing for her like a youth hungering for his first woman. Yet there was nothing he could do to control either the lust licking at his veins or the disquietingly tender feelings that were prodding at his heart.

William had become quiet since leaving the docks. Now there was a cynical edge to his voice and a coldness in his eyes. Leaving Mac behind to organise the transportation of William's baggage to the Lancaster town house in Mayfair, a dark and ominous figure at her side, he accompanied a silent Anna back to a world she had left four years before. The happiness India had brought her had become plagued with remorse and fear.

Looking at the house in Kensington as they approached, she became quiet, so quiet and so still.

'I don't want to be here,' she said, her voice so quiet that William almost failed to hear it.

William sat watching her, filled with compassion and guilt, for she spoke in a tone of unutterable sadness. He felt a surge of reverent admiration for her, for what she had overcome, and his admiration was reinforced by the pain and loneliness she had endured throughout her short life. He silently cursed her mother for her despicable treatment of her daughter—and his own hadn't been much better. He knew how it felt to be deprived of a mother's love at a time when it was most needed.

'Are you ready to see your uncle?'

Anna looked at his face. He was looking at her hard. He smiled and his eyes were suddenly warm—warm with what? Understanding? Pity? She hoped not. Quickly she looked away.

'Not really, but I'd best get it over with.'

It seemed to Anna that she was going back in time, as if she had never left London four years ago, as they passed through the tall wrought-iron gates of Melcot Lodge and proceeded up the short, curved drive. The carriage came to a halt at the front of a low flight of stone steps on which a smartly dressed man stood to receive them.

'There's Uncle Robert,' she said, reluctant to get out of the carriage while knowing she must. A tall thin man with greying hair and piercing grey eyes, he was little changed and bore no resemblance to his sister, Anna's mother. Dignified and self-important, he had none of her mother's lightness of spirit either.

William got out of the carriage and assisted Anna before turning to Robert.

'So, the voyager returns,' Robert said, stepping forward, looking his niece up and down with narrowed eyes.

Anna bobbed a small curtsy and her uncle gave her a small peck on the cheek.

'Uncle Robert, this is William Lancaster—Lord Lancaster. Johnathan put me in his charge for the voyage to England.'

'It's a pleasure to meet you, Lord Lancaster. Thank you for taking such good care of Anna,' Robert said brusquely. 'After the long voyage from India I can only imagine what it must have been like on board. The experience must have been very trying.'

'Not at all, Uncle,' Anna remarked quietly, her eyes still shadowed with the memory of her time spent on the ship. 'I was comfortable. In fact, there were times when I found the voyage quite exhilarating.'

'Naturally we were shocked to hear about Johnathan. Wounded in a skirmish, I believe.' William nodded and did not elaborate. 'Were you with him when he died?'

'I was. Before he died, his last thoughts were for his sister. Naturally he was concerned that without him she would be alone in India. Knowing I was coming to

England he asked me to take care of her—to bring her to you.'

'Yes—well, she has no one else. Will you not come inside? Constance is not at home—some charity function or other. I'll have one of the servants bring in your bags, Anna. You'll take refreshment before you leave, Lord Lancaster?'

'I'll just come in for a moment. There is a matter I have to impart.'

William's words caught Anna unawares. Her eyes flew to his, the sharpness of her disappointment taking her by surprise. 'You—aren't leaving straight away?' she asked as her uncle disappeared inside to order refreshment for his guest.

William heard the sudden break in Anna's voice. It was so touching and tragic, suggesting something very like distress, that he was moved in spite of himself. He shook his head. 'I'm sorry, but I'm afraid I have to go. I have important matters to take care of myself.'

His tone suggested such finality that Anna turned her head away. It shouldn't hurt so much, being told that he was leaving her totally undefended. But it did.

'Then of course you must go,' she heard herself say. 'I quite understand. I have taken up far too much of your time as it is.'

Before she could move away, William had closed the distance between them and grasped her arm. When he looked at her, Anna could see the light in his eyes and the crinkle of laughter lines at the corners.

But William wasn't laughing. He searched her face for a long moment, then reached up to gently touch her chin with his forefinger. 'Anna, believe me, you'll be fine. It's time to return to reality—for both of us.'

She looked into his fathomless eyes and for the first time she realised he wasn't handling their parting as easily as she thought.

Anna and William followed Robert inside the tastefully furnished house where refreshments were served. Anna remained silent while her uncle and William engaged in stilted, formal conversation before William mentioned Johnathan's death and what it meant for Anna.

'Johnathan amassed a small fortune. I know he didn't spend much of it. He's left his entire wealth to Miss Harris.

Robert looked at Anna, but did not address his words to her. 'Then she is indeed a fortunate young woman.'

'I have correspondence from Johnathan and the paperwork. You have offices in Lincoln's Inn Fields, I believe?'

Robert nodded.

'Then I will call on you there.'

William took his leave. Anna followed him outside. He turned and looked at her. 'There. That wasn't so bad, was it?'

She shook her head. 'No. It was better than I expected—but he said not one word about my mother.'

William placed his hands on her shoulders, forcing her to look at him. 'Life is about being let down, Anna. One has to learn to deal with it. Will you see her?'

Anna was silent. Then, 'I will, at some point.'

'You must begin to realise that what you have learned since leaving England for India has released you from the bonds of loyalty and devotion that binds you to her. From now on your life can be what you want it to be. Take stock of what you've got, lose what makes you miserable and hold on to what makes you happy. You are nineteen years old, with an aunt and uncle who are willing to let you live with them. You are on the brink of a new life.'

She managed a wobbly smile. 'Not until I have sway over my inheritance. I wish I was as wise as you.'

Mild cynicism marred the handsomeness of William's lean features. 'My dear girl, I do assure you that no life has been lived less wisely than mine.'

'Until I went to India, I didn't know what it was like to feel so happy.' She gave him a slanting look. 'And then I met you.' She swallowed. 'I—I wish—'

'I know,' William said quickly, gently. 'Believe me, Anna, I do know.' With a sigh he placed his hands on her shoulders once more. 'I think there is something I should say to you before I leave and I want you to listen to me very carefully.'

Anna looked at him, holding her breath for what was to come. His face was as still as his body, expressionless, except for his eyes searching hers. She felt those eyes, felt them as a physical force, as a powerful, physical force, probing deep within her.

'I want you to know how much I both like and admire you. I think you are an extremely lovely young woman, mature and brave. You've had more to contend with in life than most girls and you have coped magnificently. I will miss you in the days ahead, but we both have much to think about as we go forward.'

Anna flinched at his words, feeling suddenly bereft even though he was still with her. What was happen-

ing to her? How was it that this man she had never set
eyes on until she had embarked on the journey back to
England could have made such a difference to her life?
How was it that his mere presence made her happy?
And how was it that his absence would leave her feeling so very sad? And how was it that when they had
argued and she had told him she hated him, the very
idea of him disappearing from her life altogether filled
her with sadness?

Quickly she recovered. She wouldn't show him her
hurt feelings. 'Yes, of course we do,' she said, trying
to keep her voice steady and light.

Dropping his arms, William looked at her hard, tracing every line of her face, every warm, beating part of
her. He breathed in the essence of what lay between
them, as if to imprison her image into his memory. His
manner suddenly changed, becoming brusque. 'I will
be in town for a week or two, probably longer, then I
must leave for Berkshire. When I return and you are
out with your aunt in society, we might very well encounter each other.'

Anna searched his face for some indication that he
was sorry they were parting, but his expression was
completely unemotional, his tone suggesting such finality that she turned her head away. She so wanted him
to put his arms around her, to hold her tight and offer
her the comfort she yearned for, but he was unlikely to
do that. Even his companionship was to be denied her
in the days ahead. He had fulfilled his obligation and
now he was doing his utmost to distance himself from
her. It shouldn't hurt so much, but it did.

She was wise enough to accept with piercing clarity
that the huge differences in their backgrounds stood be-

tween them like an impenetrable wall. Yes, she was a wealthy young woman now and Johnathan had been his closest friend, but it made little difference where William was concerned. He was Lord Lancaster, the future Marquess of Elvington, while she was the daughter of a man who had died in the Fleet prison and a woman who was free with her favours. That was the moment when she realised that she was finally saying goodbye to William once and for all.

She would have to move on, as William would surely do, and face an unknown future as she resolved to let go of the sad, destructive feelings she carried in her heart for him. That was the moment when she realised the old Anna had been cast off and, newly awake, she had stepped out of childhood. Her world had suddenly become a very empty and lonely place.

It remained only for her to extricate herself from this awkward situation as gracefully as possible. Trying to maintain her control, she stepped away from him, knowing that in his mind he had already left her. Forcing a smile to her lips, she managed to answer, 'I'm sure we will. Thank you for looking after me. You've been very kind and I'm extremely grateful. Goodbye, William.'

Without another word she turned from him and went back into the house, her throat and eyes hurting from the tears she adamantly refused to shed, dazed from her futile effort to shut out the painful knowledge that William had left her.

William steeled himself to let her go. He was torn between an impulse not to go after her and prolong their goodbye, and another to offer her some sort of support and comfort. The latter impulse was the stronger, but it was the first that won out.

When he'd left Oxford and then Cranford behind and gone to India, apart from his mother and Charles and Tilly, he had not believed in the inherent goodness of anyone, until he'd met Johnathan—and then Anna. He could still hear her musical laughter. With her he had relaxed his guard and allowed her to come closer than he'd intended.

He would take the golden memories of Anna with him, the sound of her voice, the taste of her lips and the way she had looked when she stood on the deck of the *Bengal*, looking out to sea with a faraway look in her eyes and her hair flowing behind her like a pennant. He would keep her image in the deepest recesses of his memory—like a box that would remain closed for ever.

And so with the skill he'd perfected when he had left England and his birthright behind, already restrained, guarded and world-weary, he calmly dismissed Anna from his mind—at least this was what he tried to do, but it was no simple matter. Why, he asked himself, did she occupy his thoughts? Why could he not break the hold she had over him?

Constance arrived home accompanied by her two daughters. Attired in a warm claret dress and furs around her shoulders, she swept into the house appearing very grand. Of medium height with brown hair and eyes and on the plump side, Constance spared no expense on her clothes, or her daughters', and always wore the latest fashions.

She greeted Anna with a haughty look full of disdain, without kissing her or offering her condolences for Johnathan. Her daughters, Mary and Dorothy, twelve and ten respectively, were equally as cold. After greeting Anna as if she were one of the servants, they disappeared to their rooms.

'I'm sorry, Aunt Constance, for any inconvenience my being here has caused you,' Anna said.

'Sorry!' Constance sniffed, speaking through stiff lips. 'Well, you're here now so we'll have to make the best of it. You can help with the girls—Dorothy, in particular. She is struggling with some of her lessons—mathematics in particular, which, as I recall, you were very good at.'

'I'll be happy to help in any way I can.'

'Robert tells me Johnathan placed you in the care of Lord Lancaster for the journey, Anna. Was it wise of your brother to place you in the charge of a single gentleman—for you to spend the entire voyage in his company?'

'Johnathan was dying, Aunt Constance, and he knew I would have to return to England. Lord Lancaster placed me in the care of a Mrs Preston for the journey.'

'Well, that's something, I suppose, otherwise your honour would have been compromised beyond what is proper.'

'He did not do that.' Anna didn't know why she was defending William except that Aunt Constance was attacking his integrity.

'And your face, Anna,' Constance said after close scrutiny, unable to hide her shock and distaste at what she considered to be Anna's unhealthy complexion. 'Why, it's so brown. You really should have taken more

care of yourself and carried a parasol when abroad.
Hopefully it will have diminished somewhat before you
meet people. What will they think if you present yourself as you are?'

'Then to save any embarrassment, Aunt Constance,
I will keep to the house until I'm as pale as can be.'
She almost said *as pale as you are, Aunt Constance*,
but resisted the jibe.

Constance did not comment on Anna's flippant reply,
instead she said, 'I trust Mrs Wilson has shown you
to your room—the small guest room at the end of the
landing. It's in a quiet part of the house overlooking the
stables. I'm sure you'll be comfortable in there. Mary
has taken the room you occupied when you were here
before.'

'The room is very nice. It will do me perfectly.'

'Well, that's something, I suppose,' Constance remarked, sweeping out of the room to consult the cook
about supper.

Anna watched her go. Her aunt's attitude told her
that she must not forget that she was a tolerated guest
in this house.

Not until she was alone in her room and ready for
bed did Anna's defences crumble. Already she missed
William in a way that shocked her with its intensity. The
feelings she had for him were so confused she found
it impossible to analyse them, but what she did know
was that she had never felt these devastating emotions
for anyone else in her life.

Tears streamed down her face. She was suddenly
afraid. She, who had always faced what the world threw
at her bravely, who had journeyed to a country far away

and tried to make it her own, was afraid, because she knew now what the worst thing was that could ever happen to her: losing those she loved most in the world.

And so began the most miserable existence of Anna's life. In the days following her parting from William, she missed him dreadfully and could not stop thinking about hm. She was tormented by memories of how it had been between them on the *Bengal* and the passion they had shared on the night of the storm. Now she mourned and for what? she asked herself time and time again—a dream lost? A future in which he played a part? She didn't know. She only knew that with their parting, something vital had gone out of her life, as if something inside her had withered and died.

She existed in her uncle's house without complaint. In fact, she was the perfect guest. With gritted teeth she gave Aunt Constance no cause for reproach. Robert had a library with a collection of fine books. It helped to make her life bearable as a place of refuge, if only for a few hours. The days were tedious, the meals tense. When at home Uncle Robert spent most of his time in his study. Constance was out doing her charitable works and despite her sunburned face, which did not fade as quickly as Constance would have liked, she began taking her along to help, which Anna looked forward to, finding it rewarding and worthwhile.

It gave her an insight into another world, a world inhabited by people who had very little of their own, some even without hope. It was clear there was a need to provide aid and provision for destitute children. The day when she would have access to her inheritance couldn't come quickly enough, so that she could try to make their young lives more bearable.

Anna travelled to Curzon Street to visit her mother with a cacophony of bells ringing out since first light. She would never get used to it. Noise was everywhere. Mud caked the thoroughfares, clinging to shoes and soaking the hems of women's skirts. The air of the city was clogged with soot and fog. It was cold and dank from the river that snaked its way through. Carriages carried their fashionable occupants here and there and the coffee shops were doing a good trade. But Anna couldn't help thinking that it was all so different from the colour and the sunshine of India.

The carriage pulled up in front of the house and Anna was relieved to see it was an elegant building and in good repair. She rapped the brass knocker and stood back when the door was opened almost immediately by a servant, an attractive young woman of perhaps twenty or twenty-one. Unruly chestnut curls sprang from beneath her mob cap and a pair of bright blue eyes assessed Anna.

'I have come to see Mrs Harris. Is she at home?'

'Mrs Harris isn't seeing anyone at present. She—she's indisposed.'

'Indisposed?' Anna repeated. 'Do you mean she is ill or just doesn't wish to receive visitors.'

'Both. The mistress isn't well. She won't want to see you.'

'You may well be right, but I must insist. She is my mother,' Anna provided when the serving girl didn't appear to want to step aside.

The girl's eyes opened wide and her mouth opened in a silent *Oh*. 'Well, in that case you had best come in— although her temper is not at its best today.'

Anna sighed, stepping into the hall and removing her bonnet and gloves. 'I'll take my chances. I've been out of the country for the past four years and now I'm back I thought I'd surprise her. How ill is she?'

'She's been poorly for twelve months past or more. It started with a cough, which became more persistent. When she finally let the doctor take a look at her he confirmed that she has consumption of the lungs. She took to her bed three months back and has not been out since.'

'I see.' Anna was silent as she absorbed what she was told, unable to believe her mother, that once vibrant woman, had succumbed to such a devastating illness. 'And who is taking care of her?'

'Why—just me and Cook. We do our best.'

'I'm sure you do…?'

'Alice. My name is Alice Simpson.'

'And how long have you been employed by my mother, Alice?

'Two years, miss. Shall I announce you?'

Anna smiled. 'No, Alice, there's no need. I'll announce myself. Show me to her room, will you?'

Anna followed Alice up the stairs. The house was quite spacious and, from what she had seen so far, tastefully furnished, soft and feminine and very much in keeping with her mother. Anna was under no illusions as to where the money had come from and she did wonder how the gentleman responsible had responded to her mother's illness.

On reaching a landing with several doors leading off,

Alice gently knocked on one and went inside. Anna, suddenly reluctant to enter, hesitated in the doorway before taking a deep breath to summon her confidence and stepping inside on to the flowered carpet. It was a lovely room, decorated in pastel blue and a restful shade of peach. It was warm and intimate and her mother's perfume hung in the air, a scent of jasmine and honeysuckle which Anna would always associate with her mother. A fire burned brightly, giving the furniture an extra glow. It was on the occupant in the bed that Anna's gaze settled.

'Hello, Mother,' she said softly. 'I'm so sorry you're not well.'

The woman, Beatrice Harris, wrapped in an expensive rose-pink silk robe, was propped up against a mountain of pillows clutching a handkerchief. On seeing her visitor, she struggled to sit upright. Alice helped her, smoothing the quilt in front of her. When she was done Anna's mother swatted her away. She looked Anna up and down. Anna felt shy, as though she were an awkward child again.

'Heaven help us! Anna!' she exclaimed, her voice raspy from her illness. 'Leave us,' she said to Alice, 'and bring some tea.' She waited until Alice had departed and then looked at her daughter. 'Well, now, just look at you. All grown up. I see you take after your father—you have his eyes and hair. You always were his little darling. How old you make me feel all of a sudden—old and worn out and quite useless.'

'I'm sorry you are ill, Mother. I didn't know.'

'It would have made no difference if you had. You were in India—no use to me there,' she uttered grudgingly.

'You were the one who wanted me to go to India when Johnathan went.'

'I thought you'd be better off with Johnathan—and that it would be good for you to see something of the world.'

'Yes,' Anna said softly. 'It was. As it turned out I spent all my time in Bombay, where I lived with Mr and Mrs Andrews. Johnathan was always too busy to take care of his sister. I rarely saw him. I did write telling you of this.'

Her mother nodded, a faraway look in her eyes, not really interested, Anna thought bitterly. Approaching the bed, she was shocked by the change in her mother, who was just a shadow of her former self. Seen through a daughter's eyes she had always been beautiful. But now, with the illness upon her, her skin so pale it was almost transparent, there was an ethereal quality about her. There was also a refined sensuality about her that Anna had never been aware of before and it was easier now to see her as the opposite sex did. Her light brown hair streaked with silver was neatly braided and draped over her shoulder.

Her mother had never tried her best where she and Johnathan were concerned. She had never loved them as deeply as their father had. Her mother had rarely held her and Anna could not remember her coming to her room to kiss her goodnight. Often when she had tried to hug her mother, she had been gently put away from her, whereas her father had been more affectionate, sitting her on his knee while he read her stories and giving her bear hugs when she hurt herself.

Anna had always assumed she was too much trouble for her mother, that later, when her father had died, she had been happy for her to go away to school and later to India.

Without her father to turn to, Anna had taken the pain and turned it inwards and for a while she had been adrift—until she had gone to India. But now, seeing how ill her mother was, she would try to ignore the insecurity, instability and anxiety that had beset her all her young life.

'I had to leave India when Johnathan died,' she said, surprised by the calmness of her voice. 'You do know about Johnathan, Mother.'

'Of course I do. Robert had the presence of mind to inform me—in a letter, mind you. He did not come in person, which is to be understood,' she said, unable to conceal the bitterness that still existed between her and her brother, which had been there since her husband had been imprisoned for debt. 'It would be beneath him to cross the threshold of a kept woman.'

'His death must have come as a terrible shock to you—as it did to me,' Anna said, having no wish to make comment on her mother's lifestyle.

'Yes—of course it did. I was his mother, don't forget.' Anna noted her voice and expression were devoid of sadness or grief. 'And so you're back in England for good now, I expect.'

'At present I'm residing with Uncle Robert.'

'Good luck. You'll need it.' She looked at her daughter. 'So, Johnathan left you his money, did he? All of it?'

'I believe so. Uncle Robert is dealing with it.'

'Who else?' she retorted with a scornful twist to her lips. 'Make sure he doesn't cheat you.'

'He wouldn't do that. He has given me an allowance to be going on with—I shall need some clothes. What I have is unsuitable for the English climate.'

'Johnathan did well for himself with the Company— and that friend of his, Lord Lancaster. It is only right that Johnathan left his money to you. Besides, who else is there? I certainly have no need of it. And what of that high-and-mighty Lord Lancaster who escorted you back to England?' she said, with a belligerent tilt to her chin. 'Do you still see him?'

Anna frowned. 'I had no idea you were acquainted with Lord Lancaster.'

'I'm not, but I know of him. Well-heeled and titled he may be, but from what Martin has told me he has nothing whatsoever to recommend him.'

Her mother's tone caused Anna's hackles to rise and she was quick to come to William's defence. 'Lord Lancaster was very kind and considerate to me, Mother. And who, may I ask, is Martin?'

'The man who pays for all this,' she said, throwing one of her arms wide. 'The Earl of Brinkley, of course—Martin Ryder. He's been good to me. Despite my illness he refused to turn me out. Generous, he is. I couldn't ask for more.'

Anna's eyes opened wide. The Earl of Brinkley. James Ryder's father. He had to be one and the same. She stared at her mother as if awaking from some bizarre dream. Had Anna had her wits about her, she would have realised that her mother had had the opportunity to see her surprise.

'Anna? Are you quite all right?'

'Yes—yes, of course,' she replied, for some obscure

reason reluctant to reveal that she had sailed from India on the same vessel as Lord Brinkley's son. 'And is Lord Brinkley acquainted with Lord Lancaster? Has he met him?'

'On occasion, I believe—the last time was when Lord Lancaster was in London,' she informed Anna knowingly. 'Martin's had some unpleasant dealings with him in the past—interfering in things that were none of his concern—some business involving Martin's son when he was at Oxford and getting him sent down. And then there was that scandal when he went to India—turning his back on his grandfather and telling him to go to the devil.' Beatrice glanced at her sharply. 'I don't like the sound of him, not one bit.'

'Don't listen to gossip, Mother. Lord Lancaster is the grandson of the Marquess of Elvington, with a sterling reputation in the Company before he left to go his own way.'

Beatrice fixed Anna with a hard look. 'You haven't done anything ridiculous, have you, Anna? You haven't fallen for him.'

Anna stiffened. 'Absolutely not. And please do not speak ill of Lord Lancaster in my presence. He's shown me nothing but consideration and kindness.'

'Well, now you're here, delivered safe and sound, you can put Lord Lancaster out of your mind. Although now you are here, we must consider what is to be done with you.'

'Does anything have to be done with me?'

'Oh, yes. You are nineteen, Anna. High time you were wed to a suitable gentleman. I shall consult Martin—as I always do on matters of importance. He will advise us.'

'I'd rather you didn't. I don't want a husband.'

'We shall see. What will you do with the money Johnathan left you?'

'I'm still thinking about it. I'm helping Aunt Constance with her charity work at present. I would like to put some of the money to good use—perhaps open an orphanage or a school. There are so many needy people who need help.'

'I'm surprised—I never took you for a charity worker, Anna, but once it gets out that you have money you'll have every male—attached and unattached, with no wealth of their own, lining up for your favours.'

'I won't be any man's mistress.'

'Like me, you mean.'

'Yes.'

Her mother sighed and closed her eyes. 'I can't say that I blame you. I loved your father—the only man I have ever loved, but I could not forgive him for leaving us destitute. All I had was my looks and I made use of them. I was fortunate when I met Martin. I don't love him, but I am fond of him—and he's been generous to me.' Opening her eyes, she looked at Anna. 'It's easy to put up with certain things when the heart is not involved. You are my daughter. You will manage to survive just as I have.'

'Mother, I shall do my best by you,' Anna told her, with special emphasis on the relationship, which she sincerely hoped would become less strained, 'and for that reason alone I shall see you are taken care of and help in any way I can.'

'Help? I don't need help,' Beatrice said ungraciously. 'Martin sees to all that—and Alice does what she can.'

'I'm sure she does. Alice appears to be a capable woman, but I will visit you often and do what I can.'

Her mother looked at her sharply. 'Why, what is this, Anna?' She chuckled softly. 'Tired of Uncle Robert already, are you? Now why am I not surprised. He always was an uninteresting brother as we were growing up.'

She sighed, closing her eyes. 'You see me now in all my human frailty. While you are a young woman with your whole life before you, I will not have you coming here day after day to watch me become weaker, wasting away before your eyes. Visit me on occasion if you wish, you will be welcome, but for you to be seen coming to the house of a fallen woman, even if that woman is your mother, would damage your reputation irreparably.'

Anna carried the memory of her mother's bitter words as she made her way back to Kensington. She had hoped that things might be different between them, that their relationship might become closer after so long an absence, but it was not to be. She had only just come back and already her mother was wanting rid of her. How had her mother come to this? Anna felt the tears filling her eyes and she took a deep steadying breath, willing herself not to cry as she remembered her father and how saddened he would have been.

Anna became a frequent visitor to her mother's house. She would sit in the luxury of her bedroom, drinking tea from fine bone-china cups. During these times she began to see a side to her mother she could never have imagined. She insisted on wearing silk and the flimsiest of nightclothes in bed—which was where she spent most of her time when she was not sitting in a chair by the window.

Alice would thread ribbons through her hair and she wore a ring on every finger. In fact, she was quite outrageous, like an exotic butterfly. There were refinements in her sensuality and Anna could well imagine that before she had met the Earl of Brinkley, she had charmed and held many men under her spell.

When the Earl came to call and her mother summoned her to her bedroom to be introduced, Anna didn't much care for him, but she considered it prudent to be polite. He was a man of medium height and still handsome, but his eyes were cool and assessing as they looked at her with a thoroughness that made her want to turn and run.

'So you are Beatrice's daughter—recently arrived in London from India, your mother tells me.'

'Yes, Lord Brinkley.' As she curtsied, she heard that he spoke with polite gravity, as if she were entitled to his consideration.

'You do not resemble her—perhaps a little about the eyes.'

'I take after my father.'

He nodded. 'And you travelled to England on the *Bengal*?'

'Yes.'

'You were with Lord Lancaster, I believe.'

'You are well informed, My Lord,' she replied, resenting his question for some reason since it was none of his concern who she had travelled with, but answered anyway, wanting no unpleasantness.

'I make it my business to be. My son James was on the *Bengal*. The two of you must have come into contact.'

'Yes—we did. Being on a vessel at sea for several months, it would be hard not to.'

'Strange he didn't mention it.'

'Perhaps he did not deem it important.'

'I'll make a point of asking him when I next see him—which could be any time. James comes and goes as he pleases—he's staying with friends in town at present.' He turned away and made himself comfortable in a winged chair beside the bed, taking her mother's hand in his own.

After that introduction, whenever Lord Brinkley was expected, Anna made a point of staying away, but he often called unexpectedly. Seeing them together, her mother became a different person. There was a sense of intimacy and ease between the two of them and it was plain to anyone observing them together that they were fond of each other. Her mother's tinkling laughter would fill the house and champagne was her favourite tipple.

Whatever his son was guilty of, Anna was grateful to Lord Brinkley for bringing some happiness to these final days of her mother's life.

Chapter Seven

It was on a cold day in November when Anna decided to pay a visit to the Royal Exchange to do some shopping. Aunt Constance insisted on accompanying her. Anna was feeling the coldness of winter and had few clothes suitable for the English climate. There were also several social functions Aunt Constance thought she should attend, but before she could do so she must have some fashionable dresses.

Before going on to the Royal Exchange they visited the shops along Bond Street, mingling with well-dressed ladies and fine gentleman who crowded the shops. Anna felt her spirits rise as she chatted with shopkeepers and was measured up for a couple of new gowns for day wear, choosing warm material suitable for the cold climate, and two gowns for evening wear, along with accessories. Afterwards they proceed to the Exchange. Anna stared with excitement at the immense stone front of the façade of the Exchange with its high arcades and column and the clock tower reaching skywards.

'What a wonderful place this is,' Anna murmured,

breathing in the different smells that reached her, from roasting chestnuts to hot pies and horse dung. She was captivated by the sight and would have stopped, but Aunt Constance was moving on through the yard.

They spent a pleasant half-hour browsing among the stalls with Aunt Constance dipping into her purse for coins to buy fripperies for her daughters. Mounting the staircase, they strolled along the upper gallery. It was thronged with shoppers, some buying gifts to give their loved ones at Christmas. Open doors allowed shoppers a glance of a busy shoemaker and a tailor, and another showed a dressmaker, with bolts of gorgeous materials in the bay window.

Anna found it difficult to keep her aunt within her sights at times. When she disappeared inside a shop to take a look, telling Anna she wouldn't be long, Anna slipped in after her. She was having fun in just looking and she was distracted when a blue bonnet caught her eye.

She had not been in the shop very long and was trying on the bonnet when she had an odd feeling that she was being watched. As she began to turn round, she was half expecting to see her aunt behind her. Still holding the bonnet, she flicked her eyes round the shop, passing the stranger with hardly more than a glance, not even pausing for the sake of politeness as the man swept his hat from his dark head.

Instead, she put the bonnet down and lifted her skirts to descend a step, but something made her eyes look back and she gasped and gaped at him, her eyes arrested by the impeccably groomed gentleman, faultlessly arrayed in dark green coat and dove-grey trousers.

He was standing a short distance away, watching her. She stopped as abruptly as if she had walked into a sheet of glass and stared at him—the silence held for what seemed like an eternity as all the memories she had tried so sensibly to forget overwhelmed her. Her heart turned over on finding herself face to face with the man who had occupied all her thoughts since the day they had parted—tall, lean and strikingly handsome, recklessly so.

Deprived of him for so long, all Anna could do was gaze at him. Her feelings where William Lancaster was concerned were the same—although perhaps that was not quite true. Now they were deeper, more profound. She met his eyes, his warm, smiling deep blue eyes. Her enchanting face was aglow with the heady surge of pleasure she experienced on seeing him again.

He was leaning back against the fixtures. He smiled his appreciation as his eyes caressed her. Staring at him in disbelief, all Anna could think about for the moment was being with him again and how happy that made her. Just when she had thought she might get over him, that he no longer affected her, he'd appeared, and all her carefully tended illusions were cruelly shattered. The violence of her feelings for him continued to shake and shock her.

'William,' she gasped, giving him one of her unforgettable smiles.

'The same. I'm pleased to see you haven't forgotten me.' Now having her full attention, he held his hat before his chest in a bow of exaggerated politeness, before taking her arm and drawing her to a quiet corner.

'I could never forget you, William.'

He took her hand and, raising it to his mouth, brushed it with his lips. His smile sent a flood of warmth through her body to settle in a hot flush upon her cheeks and other, less exposed places.

'We were together for too long for me to do that.' She found herself standing so close to him that she could almost hear the beating of his heart. Seeing him again made her mind shy away from delving too deeply into the exact nature of her feelings for him.

She had little faith in trying to judge her own emotions, but she did care for him, there was no use denying it, and she had missed him dreadfully. He looked down at her so intently that he might have been trying to commit every detail of her features to memory.

'You look exquisite,' he said.

She gazed at him with a tentative half-smile. 'I'm glad you think so.'

'When you emerge on the London social scene, you will have every young man at your feet.'

She laughed, her laughter a pure cascade of sound. 'I sincerely hope not. I have no desire to emerge on any social scene.'

'This is a trace of luck, our meeting like this. Are you alone?'

She shook her head. 'No. I am with Aunt Constance. She's wandered off somewhere. The clothes I brought with me from India are most unsuitable for the English climate and she insisted I must have some more before she introduces me to her friends and acquaintances. I suppose I must go and find her before I lose her altogether.'

'And how are you finding London?'

'Very much the same as when I left it. Although I have to confess that it is so very different from what I have since become used to. I am surprised to see you still in London. I thought you would be settling into country life at Cranford.'

'I have things to do in town before going to Berkshire.'

'Do I detect a reluctance in your tone, William? Are you not impatient to see Cranford?'

'And my grandfather, don't forget. I intend to be there for Christmas.'

She smiled. 'But that's still weeks away. I hope you find enough excitement on being home to satisfy your adventurous heart.'

'I imagine you are missing India.'

'Yes—very much.'

'And your Uncle Robert and his family? Have you settled into living with them?'

She sighed, shaking her head. 'As best I can.'

'And your mother? You have seen her?'

Anna nodded. 'Yes. She is very ill—consumption, the doctor says. I see her when I can. As her daughter I have a duty of care towards her.'

'I can understand that. And as a mother she had a duty of care to her daughter when she was a child.' William found it hard to conceal the reproach and his bitterness he felt for her mother.

'Please, William, don't do this.'

'I'm so sorry, Anna. I am truly sorry she is so ill. Consumption is a terrible condition. Perhaps, at this time, she will be glad to have you with her and the two of you can form some kind of closeness. But—you aren't thinking of living with her?' She shook her head.

'Well, that's something. It would be a huge mistake for you to do that. Being the daughter of a courtesan is bad enough, but to take up residence in her house would ruin your reputation. Who pays the bills for your mother's house on Curzon Street? Not that it is any of my business.'

'No, it isn't,' Anna was quick to reply, as irritated by his authoritarian manner as she had been on the *Bengal*. 'And, in any case, I'm not at liberty to say.' Knowing how furious he would be, she was reluctant to divulge the identity of her mother's lover.

William looked at her hard through narrowed eyes. 'I see. Then I won't ask again.'

'I would appreciate that,' she replied tightly. 'How my mother conducts her life and who she associates with is her affair. I know better than to question or reproach her.'

They were unable to converse further when a very pretty, fashionable young woman dressed in a maroon coat with warm fur at the throat and a matching hat perched atop a riot of gleaming black curls appeared at William's side.

'William, so this is where you are. Little wonder I couldn't find you when you were lurking at the back of the shop.' Her gaze shifted to Anna and she looked her up and down in an appraising way. A little smile formed on her lips. 'And I can see why. Will you do me the honour of introducing me to your companion, William?'

'Of course. Allow me to present to you Miss Anna Harris. Anna, my sister, Matilda Anderson—she likes to be called Tilly. Anna is the young lady I escorted from India, Tilly.'

The two young ladies bobbed respectful curtsies, looking from one to the other.

'I am so happy to meet you, Anna. William has told me all about your journey from India and how your brother placed you in his charge. I was so very sorry to hear about his demise. That must have been very distressing for you.'

'Yes, it was. We were close. His death meant I couldn't remain in India.'

'And you would have liked to?'

'Yes, yes, I would.'

'It will be Christmas very soon. I can't imagine what it would be like to spend the festive season in a hot country like India.'

'You have left the academy? Your brother told me about you,' Anna explained when Tilly's brow rose in mild enquiry. 'It was a long voyage and your name cropped up several times. He was so looking forward to seeing you.'

'I know—and I him,' she replied, looking at her brother adoringly. 'With Charles being so busy all the time, William has been so attentive—although like all big brothers he expects to be obeyed all the time. I am already bored.'

William gave her a mock frown. 'How old fashioned you make me feel, Tilly—and as old as Methuselah. I'm responsible for you, remember, so I'm counting on you to behave yourself.'

Seeing a cross frown wrinkle Tilly's forehead, Anna

laughed. 'Believe me, Tilly, I was under his charge for months on board ship and he means every word.'

'You poor thing,' Tilly sympathised. 'How dreadful that must have been—with nowhere to escape to—only to throw yourself overboard. Are you in London for Christmas?'

'Yes—I am staying with my uncle and his family at present.'

'William is disappointed that I shall be away until then. I have a friend in Kent who has very kindly asked me to stay with her and her family. We were together at the academy. I have assured William that I will be back in good time to spend Christmas with him and Charles at Cranford.'

'We have just become reunited and she is off already,' William said in mock offence while smiling fondly at his sister. 'Still, I can't complain. Tilly and Charles are to make their home at Cranford. It will give me time to warn my grandfather he is about to be invaded by another branch of my family.'

Anna looked at Tilly and the smile she was giving her adored brother told her this young lady would have the old man wrapped round her finger in no time at all. Although she was just seventeen, with her high cheekbones and almond-shaped eyes of a startling violet hue, Tilly was already developing into a beautiful young woman. She had a wealth of shining black curls peeking out from beneath her bonnet, as well as a softened version of William's chin. There was something almost exotic about her and, having spent much of her childhood in an academy like Anna herself, she had acquired the confident air of a girl who slotted into her rightful place in life.

Her cheeks flushed like a wild rose when a young soldier smiled at her as he left the shop. There was a playfulness about her, a harmless mischief in her eyes. This young woman didn't only want to live life to the full, she wanted to love it to the full. Anna knew that she was going to be a handful for William.

Glancing towards the window and seeing her aunt looking rather fraught as she walked past—no doubt she was put out by Anna's prolonged disappearance—she moved aside as she was jostled by a shopper.

'Forgive me, but I must go. I think Aunt Constance will be looking for me.'

'But of course,' Tilly said. 'It's been lovely to meet you, Anna—has it not, William?'

William met Anna's gaze. 'It's always a pleasure to see you, Anna. Take care.'

Without another word Anna left them, feeling as bereft as she had the last time she had parted from William.

William left the Exchange with Tilly, deeply affected by his meeting with Anna, who was looking heartbreakingly young and lovely. When he had left her outside her uncle's house, he had thought she would soon forget him and get on with her life. That was what he had told her, what he had wanted her to do. It had been a lie. He'd been unprepared for his own sense of loss. Being without her had been like a bereavement. He'd had to stop himself communicating with her, telling himself he was a fool, when all the time he wanted to look upon her face, to hold her in his arms.

In the carriage Tilly talked non-stop about her shopping spree, but he wasn't listening. It was Anna he was thinking of and Anna he saw in his mind—Anna as she had looked when she had ridden hell for leather over the dusty Indian landscape when he had first seen her. Anna as she had looked on board the *Bengal*. Anna as she had looked on the night of the storm, when he had taken her to his cabin. Her lips, when he had kissed her, had been soft and eager, her flesh like silk.

Before she had turned to face him in the shop, he had stared at her profile, tracing with his gaze the classically beautiful lines of her face, the unexpected brush of lustrous dark eyelashes. He had never seen the like of her. She was quite extraordinarily lovely. She had an untamed quality running in dangerous undercurrents just below the surface, a wild freedom of spirit that found its counterpart in his own hot-blooded nature.

Seeing her again had had a profound effect on him. He admitted he could not continue with this battle between his pride and the feelings he had for Anna. He must decide between the two or the conflict would tear him asunder and ruin any chance he might have of happiness. He never had understood why she always had such a volatile effect on him, but since their parting and missing her like hell, he understood that he wanted her back in his life.

The time had come, he realised, for him to make a choice. He could not continue as he was, constantly buffeted by conflicting emotions, torn between the demands of his wayward heart and the need not to betray his family name and honour. Thoughts of his grandfather came to mind, of how he had given up the woman he had loved for family honour, and how miserable his life had been. Was he, William, about to make the same mistake?

Marriage to some unknown heiress did not appeal. Not just any woman would do. If he was to live with a woman for the rest of his life, it had to be someone he could love, someone he liked to be with, and there was only one such woman he could think of: Anna.

That was when he realised there was no choice to make. Foolish or not, disloyal or not, he wanted Anna in his life, as his wife, and he realised that clinging to family honour would be folly. And yet choosing Anna did not make things simple. If he were willing to ignore her background, to put aside his misgivings about her parents, it did not mean that she would do so. She had stressed she wanted her independence, to make her newly acquired wealth work for the common good.

In short, *she* might not want *him*. However, if she did agree to become his wife, he would not expect her to abandon her ambitions. There was no reason why she could not be Lady Lancaster and successful in her charity work.

Aunt Constance, whose life revolved around her charitable deeds along with many other benevolent ladies, became busy with her charities as Christmas approached. To raise money for the poor and needy, tickets were offered to entertainments: musical concerts, bazaars, art exhibitions and balls. Anna was glad to help where she could since it alleviated the tedium of the days.

One such event was a ball at Lord and Lady Hartley's house in Piccadilly. She didn't mind the bazaars and gallery exhibitions, but she was apprehensive about attending a ball. Her experience of dancing was in the cantonment in Bombay, where protocol wasn't quite as strict as it was in London's society.

If there had been a way out of this dilemma Anna would have taken it, but Aunt Constance, eager to find her a husband as soon as might be—which should not be too difficult now she was a wealthy young woman and hopefully her background overlooked—had been adamant that she would attend. Thinking that Anna had not been properly tutored in what to expect at an English ball, Constance was relieved to find she had been well instructed.

She also made sure she knew how to curtsy without wobbling and how to utilise her femininity in the art of the correct use of the fan—how to hold it, how to close it—which almost drove Anna to distraction. She also directed many dos and don'ts at her bewildered niece, giving her no time to protest—that she must be discreet and blush at the right moment, to open her eyes wide and hang on to every word her partner directed at her.

On the day itself, with her thoughts on what lay ahead and the many difficulties she might encounter during the evening, Anna was fastened into a fashionable, high-waisted gown of rose-pink satin, with an overskirt of matching tulle, intricately embroidered and decorated with seed pearls. The sleeves were elbow length, with a flow of delicate Brussels lace caressing her forearms.

With her hair arranged in curls about her head, gazing at herself in the cheval mirror, Anna could not believe it was herself looking back. Even Uncle Robert
appeared stunned when she descended the stairs, even
going as far as to compliment her on her appearance.
Mary and Dorothy, as yet too young to attend balls,
looked on with awe and envy, eager for the day when
they, too, could attend such exciting and glamorous
events.

The streets around Lord and Lady Hartley's house
were congested with carriages depositing the cream of
London society outside the open doors. Inside, footmen
in powdered wigs and scarlet and gold livery lined the
stairs up to the ballroom. There was much fluttering of
fans, curtsying and bowing of elegant heads.

In the carriage taking them to Piccadilly, although
Anna was wrapped in a warm cloak lined with fur, her
body was cold. She dreaded the thought of appearing in
public, knowing people would be speculating about her.

It was a glittering affair and it seemed the whole
of London society had made the effort to attend, even
though many families had retired to their country es-
tates for Christmas. The ballroom, with its highly polished parquet floor, glowed with light from the crystal
chandeliers and reverberated with gaiety. Between the
long French windows opening on to a balcony were
huge urns on pedestals, bursting with a profusion of
flowers, and elegant gilt chairs were placed at intervals
along the walls. The ball, held at the same time every
year, was a popular event and the dance floor was already a splendid crush. Anna stood with Uncle Rob-

ert while Aunt Constance, a popular figure, chatted to friends and acquaintances.

The musicians played a variety of dances and couples took to the floor. Under Aunt Constance's watchful gaze, Anna had no shortage of partners. Uncle Robert had been concerned that her appearance on the social scene was not going to be met with resounding acclamation, so he was relieved that when her identity became known, although she was gossiped about, the fact that she was rich overrode her background. Besides, her father had been of the gentry and he was not the first and nor would he be the last of that ilk to end up in a debtors' prison.

Anna danced and smiled and managed to respond intelligently to the conversation that was directed at her. She accepted compliments graciously and some of her partners made an effort at flirtation, but with a fixed smile on her face she brushed them off easily, having no desire to form any kind of relationship with any of them. Her feet already beginning to ache, she was relieved to stand one of the dances out, but Aunt Constance had other ideas.

'Don't look now,' she said, 'but there's a young man who hasn't taken his eyes off you all evening—he's rather dashing, in fact. Perhaps you know who he is.'

Unable to resist, when her aunt turned to acknowledge an acquaintance, Anna lifted her head and looked straight at him. It was James Ryder and he was indeed looking at her, with one eyebrow raised and a smile curling to one corner of his mouth. He sauntered towards her.

'I'm delighted to see you again, Anna,' he said with a grin as he swept her a deep bow. 'You haven't forgotten me? I hope you've saved a dance for me.'

'No.' She laughed, warming to his natural charm and easy manner. 'Of course I remember you—and, yes, I shall be delighted to dance with you.'

His grin was impudent as he subjected her to a long, lingering gaze. 'More than one dance? And then perhaps you will permit me to take you into supper.'

'More than two dances would be quite improper and commented upon,' she chided teasingly, amused by his persistent manner. 'And I have arranged to have supper with my aunt and uncle. I have my reputation to uphold and—since my aunt insists—I must do everything in a proper manner.'

'Perish the thought that I would do anything to tarnish your reputation—so I will be content with just the one dance and hope for better things in the future.'

'I'm surprised to see you. What are you doing here?'

'I'm with my older brother, who's escaped to the card room. I was most surprised when Father told me you were Mrs Harris's daughter. I had no idea. I would have called on you there but—well, visiting the house of my father's... You know what I mean.'

'Yes, I do and I understand perfectly,' Anna replied stiffly. It pained her to hear her mother spoken of with such disparagement, but she could not deny her mother's chosen profession or the fact that she was Lord Brinkley's mistress. 'I met your father on one of my visits to my mother.'

'He told me. I'm glad you're here tonight. I was hoping you would be. Do you see Lord Lancaster?'

'Just the once since arriving in London—and quite by chance. Why do you ask? I believe you knew him before you went to India.'

The sound he made was like a curse. 'Knew him? I wish to God I did not.'

Anna asked no further questions about his encounters with William.

'I can't imagine it's much fun for you in London at this time. I remember you told me you like to ride. You won't get much chance to do that here. I ride in Hyde Park most mornings. Several of my friends are meeting in the park tomorrow to let off a bit of steam. You're welcome to come along if you like. We can ride in the park. It should be fun.'

Fun! Anna couldn't remember the last time she'd had fun. Her ears pricked up at the idea of riding. 'I'd love that—but I don't have a horse.'

'My father has plenty. If you visit your mother tomorrow, I'll bring the horses, so you don't have to worry about that.'

Anna stared at him, impressed. 'You would do that for me?'

'Absolutely. If visiting the house of my father's paramour is the only way I can get you to myself, then so be it.'

Recalling the times they had been together on the *Bengal*—as well as William's reaction to them—Anna hesitated. Because of William's dislike of James she was reluctant to accept his invitation, but she was unable to come up with an excuse. And why should she? she asked herself rebelliously. Now that she was no longer under William's guardianship, she could see whom she liked. Wanting so much to take the reins of a horse again, she said, 'Yes, I would love to. I've missed riding out.'

'Splendid. I'll meet you at one o'clock.' He paused

and looked towards the musicians as they began to play the next dance. 'Come, let's dance.'

He proved to be a superb dancer and Anna happily abandoned herself to his encircling arm as he twirled her about the floor. Unashamedly he flirted and flattered her and made her laugh, but their entertaining conversation came to an end when someone caught his attention.

'Damn it! I had no idea he would attend the ball. Did you know he was still in London?'

'Who?'

'William Lancaster.'

Anna felt her heart beat quicken and her thoughts scattered. She could feel William's presence with every fibre of her being, and, despite the shock of seeing him again, a comforting warmth suffused her. A strange sensation of security, of knowing he was close at hand, thrilled her. But she was assailed by the memory of the times on board the *Bengal* when he had seen her with James and how angry he had been.

Through the bodies of the couples on the dance floor she saw him standing on the side lines, powerfully masculine and attractive. Her heartbeat quickened. Charming and perhaps the most wickedly attractive man she had ever seen, he was the embodiment of a young maiden's dream. He was conversing with a gentleman, who held his attention. James immediately danced her to the opposite side of the dance floor, where their presence was concealed by other dancers. Taking her hand, he drew her aside.

'I must apologise for ending the dance so abruptly, Anna, but I would prefer not to encounter Lord Lancaster, if you don't mind. We—don't get on, as you already know. I'll slip quietly away. You will be at Curzon Street tomorrow?'

'Yes. I'll look forward to it.'

With that James slipped away. Anna couldn't blame him and she had no wish to get into further argument with William about James Ryder. She returned to Aunt Constance, who was wearing an anxious look.

'There you are, Anna,' she said crossly. 'Where have you been?'

'Dancing, Aunt Constance. I think I might sit the next one out. My feet are beginning to ache and I would like to visit the ladies' rest room.'

'Very well. Don't be long. We'll be going in to supper shortly.'

William was attending the ball on the invitation of an old acquaintance. On entering the ballroom he let his eyes wander over the crush of guests. It didn't take him long to single out James Ryder among a rowdy group heading for the card room. He cursed to himself. He seemed to be bedevilled by Ryder's presence wherever he went.

Then his gaze was arrested on seeing a lovely young woman in a rose-coloured gown heading for the ladies' rest room. Propping his shoulder against a pillar, he waited for Anna to emerge, keeping an eye out for Ryder. If he made any attempt to approach her, he would step in—unbeknown to him, had he known the two had already danced together and arranged an assignation for the following day, he would have been incensed.

When Anna finally emerged from the rest room,

William watched her literally float in his direction and his heart soared at the sight of her. All the beauty in the world was embodied in that single female form. Her golden hair had been arranged in intricate curls about her head and her face was like a jewel above the gown she wore.

Mesmerised, he stood there, watching her incredible smile, and the shattering tenderness he felt made him ache. She looked stunning, adorable. Her skin was iridescent perfection, the colour of mother-of-pearl. Dear Lord, how he had missed her and he swallowed over the knot of guilt in his throat when he remembered how hard he had tried to dismiss her from his life without success.

Returning to her aunt, Anna could not help but smile on seeing William heading towards her. As he made his way through the pressing throng, he sent her a seductive look with a mischievous little flare of his eyebrows. She felt a tingling of pleasure when he finally reached her. Taking her hand, he raised it to his lips, his eyes capturing hers.

'This is a pleasant surprise, Anna. I did not expect you to be here. I ran into Robert and he told me he had brought you along.'

'Yes—my first ball in London. It's all rather exciting.' Aware of her aunt watching them with interest, she turned to her, but before she could introduce William, her aunt took it into her own hands.

'You must be Lord Lancaster,' she said with ingratiating sweetness.

William made a polite bow. 'It's a pleasure to meet you, Mrs Payne. I understand the proceeds for this splendid event are to go to many good causes. The turn-out is impressive and a wonderful success.'

'Yes—well, we do our best for the needy—particularly with Christmas almost upon us.'

Anna stared at her aunt. Her cheeks were flushed and her eyes held a brilliance they usually lacked. Was it possible that her aunt, usually so reserved, so stoic, had fallen prey to those deep blue eyes that seemed to see through her defences?

'Do I have your permission to dance with your niece, Mrs Payne?' William asked.

Constance looked unusually flustered. 'But of course. Away you go,' she said, as the musicians struck up the next dance, snapping her fan open and proceeding to waft her hot cheeks.

'Oh, dear,' Anna whispered, grinning from ear to ear as William led her on to the dance floor. 'I believe you have a conquest, William. Aunt Constance never allows anything to affect her—and certainly not a handsome gentleman. What on earth have you done to her?'

He chuckled softly. 'Ah, well, that's my charm. It seems to be the effect I have on most ladies. But I am only interested in charming one particular lady,' he said, looking at her tenderly. 'How are you enjoying the ball?'

'Very much. Aunt Constance insisted I should attend. I think she'd like to have me off her hands and that a husband will do the trick. She can't wait to marry me off.'

He laughed. 'And she believes you will find one here?'

'I'm afraid so.'

'And have you—found anyone who would make a suitable husband?'

Anna smiled playfully, a dimple appearing in her cheek. 'Not yet, but the ball is not yet over. Aunt Constance will be delighted to see me dancing with you.' Her voice was light, but beneath the lightness was a faint teasing undertone. Before he could reply, she said, 'Are you here with your sister?'

He shook his head. 'Tilly has left to spend the weeks leading up to Christmas with her friend in Rochester. Besides, at seventeen she is not yet old enough to attend balls.'

'Of course not. So, when do you leave for Berkshire?'

'In a few days. I won't be there long before I return to London.'

'Your grandfather will be relieved to have you home, I think. Does he not get to London?'

'Not any more. When he was well, he divided his time between Cranford and the London town house. He had the stamina of two men—always up before the dawn and the last to bed. When he became ill and no longer able to travel, he kept the London house on, hoping I would come back and would want to retain it. Which I shall do. I have no intention of selling it. You look exquisite, by the way,' he said softly, his expression boldly admiring as he gazed down at her.

As he bent towards her, the soft scent of his cologne touched her senses with an acute awareness that made her almost giddy. Unprepared for this attack on her senses, she felt her cheeks burn. A half-smile twisted a corner of his mouth as his eyes warmly caressed her. There was a vibrant life and intensity in those incredible eyes that no one could deny.

William met Anna's gaze, tipped his head towards

the musicians and said with teasing formality, 'May I have this dance?'

She nodded, her enchanting smile aglow. 'It would be my pleasure.' She knew, in that moment, a thousand handsome men could not compare to William. He was the one who owned her heart. She swallowed, her eyes drawn to his by some magnetic force.

The powerful volley of sensual persuasiveness that William Lancaster was capable of launching against her womanly being could reap devastating results. When his eyes delved into hers, he all but turned her heart inside out and nibbled at its tender core. Were he to continue such delectable assaults on her senses, it might well mean the collapse of her resistance and her ultimate doom.

While she had despaired of ever seeing him again, William was now holding her in his arms, making her feel euphoric and radiantly alive as he twirled her round the dance floor. He was a superb dancer. Their progress was an effortless glide over the floor.

Anna was aware of his closeness, the strength of his fingers holding hers and the warmth of his hand at her waist. She raised her eyes to his. He was watching her, his face expressionless, but there was something in his eyes that sent a shiver down her spine.

'You dance divinely, Anna. You must have spent many a time dancing the night away with handsome young soldiers in the cantonment in Bombay.'

Tipping her head back she met his gaze. 'A few— although I cannot remember many of them. They were always passing through to other parts of India. But I did enjoy the dancing.'

For a lengthy moment, William's eyes probed the amber depths of hers. 'I've missed you, Anna. Have you missed me?'

There was a low intimacy in his tone that made Anna feel as flustered and nervous as if she was a debutante and the *frisson* of awareness was disturbing. 'Yes, yes, I have,' she confessed, feeling his warm breath on her cheek, 'which is perfectly natural, I suppose—after spending so much time together on board the ship. But I have missed you, terribly. When we parted I thought...'

'What? What did you think, Anna?'

'That you didn't want to see me again.'

'And that hurt you?'

'Yes—a great deal, in fact.'

'I'm sorry. I would never hurt you intentionally. I want you to know that.'

Content to let the music carry them along, they fell silent, unaware of the passing moments. Anna stared up at William's achingly handsome face and into his bold, hypnotic eyes, lost in her own thoughts, before she realised that his gaze had dropped to her lips and his arm had tightened around her waist, drawing her even closer against the hard rack of his chest.

'Your cheeks are pink,' he murmured, spinning her round.

'It's the heat. It does get warm when one is dancing and the floor is as crowded as this.'

'As I recall,' he said softly, a spark of laughter in his eyes, 'the temperature was definitely heated on that occasion when we were alone together on the night of the storm.'

Anna's cheeks burned and her heart began to throb

in deep, aching beats. The reminder of what they had done, his touch, had been branded on her memory with a clarity that set her body aflame. She raised her eyes to his, seeing them darken and his expression gentle.

'You, my dear Anna, are still blushing.'

'Any female would blush when you say the things you do and look at them like that. Please stop it, William. People are watching.

'Then let's go somewhere more private.'

Impatient to be alone with her, William danced her towards the French windows which gave access to the balcony. Opening one, then taking her hand, he drew her outside, closing the door behind them, which lessened the sound of the music. Thankfully they were the only ones to have sought the solitude of the balcony, which was hardly surprising since the evening was cold.

Chapter Eight

'Do you find it too cold?' he asked. 'If so, we can go back inside.'

'No. It was stuffy in there. It's a relief to get some air—although I suppose it's most improper to be out here alone with you.'

'To hell with proprieties. I will not stand by and watch every male here tonight ogle you.'

'Why, William—are you jealous, by any chance?'

Taking her hand, he drew her close, his voice husky and warm when he spoke. 'I am jealous of your every word, thought and feeling that is not about me. I want you. It is my dearest wish to make you mine. Don't waste your time on the likes of those young beaus in there. They're not worth it.'

Anna's heart flipped over at his words, the intimacy and possession of their meaning not lost on her, and wondered what had brought about this change in him. Trying to ignore what she saw in his eyes, she tried to still her rapidly beating heart. 'And what of you, William?' she asked. 'Are you worth it? You say you want me—which has come as something of a surprise, I must say. If I were to yield myself to you, would you honour me?'

'Until death,' he breathed, raising her hand and placing his lips on her fingers. 'Since we parted you have been for ever in my thoughts, plaguing me, torturing me. Dear Lord, Anna, you sorely test my restraint. Don't you know how much of a temptation you are to me?'

Her mind reeling over the shock of what he was saying, Anna could only stare at him as a torrent of emotions overwhelmed her.

'I want you, Anna,' he murmured, tracing the gentle curve of her cheek with his fingertip. 'There is a chemistry between us—has been from the start.'

She shook her head in an attempt to regain her sanity. 'What I am afraid of is how long will the chemistry last.'

'For ever.'

'And you are certain of that, are you?'

The eagerness of her reply and the soft look in her eyes were almost William's undoing. 'I've never been more certain of anything in my life.'

He was mesmerised by the feelings unfolding inside him, his gaze locking on hers. Drinking in the tranquillity, for a moment he felt as if she had reached into his chest and squeezed his heart. A slow smile of admiration swept across his face as he beheld the lovely young woman. Her golden hair, reflecting the light through the doors, was a cap of shining curls. The dark liquid of his eyes deepened as he became caught in the warmth of her presence.

Anna read in his face such evident desire that heat flamed for a moment in her cheeks and she moved closer to him. Though the light was dim, William could perceive her lovely face, more serene than he had ever seen it.

'Do you ever think of what happened between us on board ship—on the night of the storm.'

'All the time. And you?'

'Often. I suppose we could blame the storm for creating circumstances that threw us together.'

'We could, but it wasn't the storm. What happened between us had nothing to do with that. It was down to me. I should have known better. My passions were in grave danger of running out of control. But nothing I can say or do will change what happened between us. It was a pleasant interlude, one I would like to repeat.'

'You would?' She swallowed nervously and stared at him, memories of what he had done to her, memories of his passion, his gentleness and restraint filling her mind—and added to that were memories of her own urgent desire.

A lazy smile swept over his handsome face and the force of that white smile did treacherous things to Anna's heart rate. 'Admit it, Anna,' he said, raising his hand and casually coiling a loose strand of her hair round his finger. 'Admit that you are here with me now because you want to be. Because you find yourself irresistibly drawn to me—as I am to you. Is that not so?'

'Yes…yes, I am, but you make me feel uneasy when you speak to me like this—and look at me the way you are doing now. After the storm, we each agreed that there could never be anything between us. We both understood that.'

'That was when I was your guardian and I was duty-bound to hold to my promise to Johnathan. Everything is different now. I am no longer your guardian.'

Anna was too innocent and naive not to let her emotions show on her face and for a long moment William's gaze held hers with penetrating intensity. The clear blue eyes were as enigmatic as they were silently challenging and, unexpectedly, Anna felt an answering thrill of excitement. The darkening in his eyes warned her he was aware of that brief response.

'I want you, Anna. I want you in my life and I know you feel the same.'

'Yes, I do want you,' she said fiercely. 'But can you not understand that there is a part of me that does not want to want you?'

'Then I think you should give me the chance to persuade that part of you to want me, too.'

Anna felt herself tremble with the need that he always invoked in her when he was close. He placed his hands on her shoulders, his eyes feasting on the delicate creaminess of her face. The sweet fragrance of her perfume drifted through his senses. For a moment he thought she was going to try and escape him, to return to the ball. But then she looked at him and became still, and, while the strains of the music wove its spell around them, she allowed him to draw her against his chest.

'A kiss, Anna? Do you mind?'

Shaking her head, she swallowed nervously, wanting him to kiss her quite badly. 'No,' she whispered. 'I don't mind.'

She kept her eyes wide open as he bent his head and placed his mouth over her own, plucking the breath from between her parted lips. Her kiss was tentative at first, as if she wanted time to reconsider what she was doing, but when his arms snaked around her, she began to relax and followed his lead, instinctively yielding her mouth to his.

She was too young and inexperienced to conceal her feelings, too genuine to want to try. The moment William felt her response his arms tightened around her, circling and possessive, desire primitive and potent, pouring through his veins.

Seduced by his kiss, what he was doing to her was like being trapped in a cocoon of dangerous, pleasurable sensuality where she had no control over anything. She shivered, pressing herself to the hard muscles of his chest.

Parting her lips, she welcomed the continued invasion of his tongue, sliding silken arms tightly about his neck and pressing herself to the hard contours of his virile form, little realising the devastating effect her body pressed to his was having on him as her lips blended with his with an impatient urgency. She threw back her head and arched her back when his lips left hers to draw a molten trail down the slender column of her throat.

William was physically shaken and unable to believe the desire that pounded through him when he felt her body coming into intimate contact with his own. Everything around them seemed to vanish in a haze as he kissed her. He wanted to crush her in his arms and drown in her sweetness. The days of being around her on board ship, of wanting her, of self-denial and frustration had finally driven him beyond restraint on seeing her again.

When he at last pulled his mouth from hers he drew a long, shuddering breath, meeting her gaze and seeing that her eyes were naked and defenceless. His features were hard with desire, and, aware that someone could appear at any moment, he knew that he must keep their passion under control.

'It is my dearest wish to go on kissing you, but I fear we will be missed and your aunt may appear at any moment. How do you feel now? Did you enjoy kissing me?'

She laughed softly, unable to ignore the warmth, the pull of his eyes. 'You should know better than to ask that, but since you did—yes, yes, I did—although I'm beginning to think you are something of a rake—enticing me on to the balcony so you could have your way with me,' she teased.

'A rake? Good Lord! I've never been accused of being a rake—in the past, maybe—but not now. Although there is a saying that reformed rakes make the best husbands.'

'Who said it?'

'I did.'

Anna turned towards the balcony doors, feeling it was time to return to the ball. Suddenly, something he'd said had her turning back and her eyes snapped to his. 'Why did you say that?'

'What?'

She swallowed. 'About husbands.'

'Because, my love, I want to marry you—to make you my wife. To have you by my side always.'

Understanding dawned with his meaningful gaze. In the deafening silence that engulfed them, neither of them moved. Anna breathed at last, staring at him in confused shock as she understood the truth of what he was asking of her.

'I want to marry you,' he repeated, watching her closely.

'I heard you, but—I cannot believe you want this.'

'You are wrong. Since our parting you have never been far from my deepest thoughts. I've known many women, Anna, but it is to you that I offer marriage. No other woman has been able to get that close. So, what do you say? Will you do me the honour of accepting my proposal—and become my wife?'

Anna hesitated. 'It—it is all so sudden. You—seem very determined.'

'It is in my nature to be so. Do you mind?'

'No, of course not. You have given me much to think about. I will consider it. Give me a little time—and not a word to Aunt Constance. She would have the guest list and the wedding arranged before we leave the ball.'

William smiled at her. 'While you consider such a momentous matter, I will keep my silence. But I am not a patient man, Anna, so don't take too long. Are you ready to go back inside?'

She nodded, running her hands down the front of her dress and patting any stray curls back in place.

William took Anna's arm and escorted her inside. There were no further exchanges between them because as soon as they emerged through the French doors, Constance, fanning herself, saw them and waved them over. She'd remarked to Anna as they entered the house and the music assailed them that she could already feel one of her headaches coming on. Apparently, it had become worse and she insisted that they went home.

As she was marched away, Anna turned and looked back at William. The sweet urgency of their kiss and his proposal of marriage had made Anna lose touch with reality. It filled her soul. The embers that had glowed and heated any rebellion inside her now burned with passion. It was a kiss so exquisite that whatever conscience she had left died, as she had become imprisoned in a haze of dangerous, terrifying sensuality over which she had no control.

And he wanted her to be his wife. Her heart soared at the very thought, but common sense brought her back down to earth. She had told him she would consider it. And she would, for he had given her a great deal to think about.

With the sun shining out of a blue, if somewhat cold, sky, the day after the ball found a small, isolated knot of boisterous young people gathered beneath the trees in Hyde Park to enjoy themselves. They were a friendly group and made Anna welcome. The conversation was daring, witty and immensely stimulating. They also laughed a lot and recounted provocative, funny jokes. Anna, somewhat shy among these strangers, held back a little, sitting close to Alice and speaking only when spoken to, but she was thrilled to be among young people again.

She had met James at her mother's house. He had arrived in his carriage and one of his father's grooms had turned up with the horses, which was fortunate because Anna, having worried about riding off with James alone, had commandeered Alice for the afternoon to act as chaperon. She had accompanied her in the carriage.

Now, as Anna looked at the horses grazing beneath the trees, she had the urge for a good gallop. As if reading her mind, James got to his feet.

'Are you glad you came? You don't find my friends offensive?'

'They're friendly—different to what I am used to, but, no, I'm not offended.'

'Then I think you should marry me, Anna. You and I would be so happy together.'

Anna laughed, hoping he was joking. 'That will soon change when your father disinherits you. It's one thing to take my mother as his mistress, but he would not countenance a marriage between us.'

He sighed. 'That won't matter. You are rich enough to keep us both.'

Anna glanced at him sharply. 'And you know that for a fact, do you, James?'

He shrugged. 'Everyone knows your brother made his money in India. You really should marry me, you know.'

'No, I don't know, James. Besides, you don't love me.'

'I do. Desperately.'

'No, you don't.' She got to her feet. 'Now come along. You promised me a ride. I'll race you to that post on the edge of the park. See if you can beat me.'

He gave her a leg up into the side saddle and, with a gentle kick at the horse's flank and her skirts ballooning behind her, she was off, with James tearing after her.

Their horses' hooves thundered over the soft turf. All the way to the post they were neck and neck and not until they turned for home did Anna pull ahead, finish-

ing a length ahead of James. Unfortunately, her horse
was going so fast she had to pull up sharply when she
almost collided with another rider, causing the animal
to stumble and throw her from the saddle in a tangle
of flounces and furbelows. To exuberant cheering from
the group, who had watched the race from beginning
to end, unhurt and laughing happily, despite the loss
of her dignity—for she had won the race after all—she
scrambled to her feet. Taking a moment to compose
herself and smooth out her skirts and straighten her
bonnet, only then did she spare a glance at a familiar
face of fury.

'For God's sake!' the owner of that face exclaimed
in a furious voice, his temper roused at being almost
knocked off his horse, 'Why don't you look where
you're going? You might have caused a serious acci-
dent.'

Anna turned and looked at the large, looming figure
bearing down on them. She stared in horror, her heart
beginning to pound in genuine terror as recognition
flashed into her eyes. His clenched jaw was as hard as
granite and he was emanating wrath so forcefully that
she began to tremble.

'William!'

William raked her with an insultingly condescending
glance from the top of her gloriously tousled hair to the
tips of her feet. 'Of all the brazen, outrageous stunts I
have ever seen, yours beats the lot. You are not in India
now, Anna. In London, young ladies do not go around
flaunting themselves as you have just done.'

Her mirth having disappeared, she threw back her
shoulders, lifted her head and met his eyes with a fiercely

direct stare, unafraid and absolutely uncowed, the action telling him quite clearly that she was neither sorry nor ashamed of her behaviour.

'I was not flaunting myself. I was doing no wrong. I took a tumble and you managed to get in my way, that is all.'

'And almost knocked me off my horse. Do you go out of your way to court danger? I suppose it's pointless me asking if your uncle knows you are here?'

Anna shook her head. 'I am sorry. I can say no more than that.'

James glanced at the newcomer who had dismounted when he was almost knocked from the saddle. 'Why, Lord Lancaster. I didn't expect to see you here today. Care to join us?' He bared his teeth in what might have been politeness, but wasn't.

'Like hell I will,' William ground out with withering scorn.

Glancing at James, Anna saw that he had paled, though he remained otherwise unruffled, but it occurred to her that he might possibly be as unnerved as she was by William's arrival and to find himself confronted by his wrath.

William ignored James, giving Anna the full force of his fury. 'What the hell do you think you're doing?' he bit out savagely, his glittering eyes alive with rage.

'We were doing no harm. Sorry you got in the way—but you look unharmed,' James said, his face taut with anger on being confronted by the man responsible for his dismissal from the Company.

William spun round with an expression of contempt. 'Be quiet, damn you.'

His voice curled round Anna like a whiplash. So unnerved and disorientated was she that she made no protest when he took her arm.

'Let her go,' James demanded. 'Leave her alone.' His face had gone an unhealthy shade of red. At this point he seemed to notice that those around them were staring at them. 'Come with me, Anna. He can't force you to go with him.'

'Yes, I can. She's going nowhere with you, Ryder,' William said in a voice iced with loathing. 'And I want a word with you.'

James faced up to him, hands fisted against his sides. He was struggling to control his temper. 'A word, is it? And what have you to say to me that you haven't said already?' He smirked in the face of William's rage.

'Just this. I think your father would like to hear of a certain young woman known to you, a young woman who has good reason to despise you.'

The words hung in the air in an oasis of stillness.

'It would be advisable for you to leave now, Ryder. I'll escort Miss Harris home.'

There was no hiding the dangerous, highly charged antagonism between the two men. The wariness in Ryder's eyes told William that there would be no hiding place should he decide to do his worst.

James paled visibly. 'Go to hell, Lancaster.'

'It's all right, James.' Anna spoke, her voice low and trembling, but loud enough to be heard.

James turned from them and mounted his horse. He looked at Anna. 'Take the horse and carriage back to the house. I'll have someone collect them later.' With that he rode away.

Anna turned to William. Her features, no longer fearful, were defiant. 'How dare you?' she flared, angry and embarrassed at being so openly reprimanded and so ignominiously hauled away from James. 'What are you doing here, William?'

His face was expressionless, but his lips were white. 'Looking for you. Where the hell should I be with you taking it into your head to go riding with Ryder without a care to your reputation. It's fortunate that I saw you when I rode into the park.'

'Fortunate? I would not say that.'

'No, you wouldn't.' In exasperation his hand closed round her arm like a manacle as he led towards where her horse had wandered. He walked so fast she had to almost run to keep up with him. 'Now get on that horse. The sooner we're out of here the better.'

Sending Alice on ahead to Curzon Street in James's carriage, William had no intention of letting Anna out of his sight while Ryder was at large. They left the park together and did not speak until they reached William's house in Mayfair.

William was thoroughly enraged. For Anna to be visiting the house paid for by the Earl of Brinkley—which he had found out without much difficulty from an acquaintance—was one thing, but that she was seeing his son was another matter. Dear God! Was he never to be rid of James Ryder?

Something shattered inside William, splintering his emotions from all rational control. A million thoughts and feelings spun in chaotic turbulence and he was scarcely able to contemplate the enormous debacle. Had she been with any other man it wouldn't have been so bad. But this wasn't just any other man. This was James Ryder—a charlatan, a man of no substance, cruel, slothful and hedonistic.

The Lancaster town house was startlingly spacious, luxurious, essentially masculine and tastefully furnished. At any other time, Anna would have been awed by what was the most sumptuous house she had ever seen, but she was too angry and upset to give it more than a passing notice.

As it was, beneath the raised eyebrows of an astonished footman, with her in tow, William strode to the entrance of his study. He pulled her inside and slammed the door. Anna was conscious of nothing but disaster and felt very much like Mary Queen of Scots must have felt when she'd put her head on the block and was waiting for the axe to fall.

'Sit down,' William snapped, striding to the sideboard and pouring two snifters of brandy, one that he gave to Anna, the other that he drank straight down.

Anna sat in a chair, sipping her brandy, and glared at her executioner. William—clever William, who was well experienced in the art of wielding power—remained standing. He looked very tall, very authoritative and very menacing. The brandy coursing through her veins warmed her, but did nothing to stop her trembling limbs as she waited in tense silence for what she was certain was going to be an explosion of verbal blasting. She didn't have long to wait. He twisted round, his gaze narrowing on her face. Nervously she averted her eyes.

'Now,' he said briskly, 'we can talk. Are you listening?'

She nodded mutely.

'Then look at me.'

Anna somehow brought her eyes to his.

'That's better. Have you any idea of the recklessness of your actions today? You should know better than to be seen anywhere with James Ryder. That man is perpetual trouble. After all I have told you, how could you have done something so stupid?'

'Very easily,' Anna replied, her courage rising as always when she was cornered. She considered William's treatment of her and the severe reprimand for her behaviour totally undeserved. She met his gaze at last. 'What James did when he was at Oxford with your brother was a long time ago. He behaves towards me with respect and is always considerate to my needs. I also find him amusing.'

'No doubt—and degenerate and decadent and an opium addict.' His scathing sarcasm sliced into Anna's highly sensitised emotions like a razor.

Anna knew there was no point defending James, but she couldn't help being angered by William's harsh attitude. 'Despite what you say about James, I have found no trace of the corrupting force you speak of.' William came to her and braced his hands on the arms of the chair, putting his face close to hers, his eyes glittering like shards of ice, impaling hers. She could feel the warmth of his breath on her face, feel the rage in him.

'Can you not? Then he has influenced you more than I realised. God knows I have no interest in Ryder, but I don't like to see you with him. I don't like it one bit and I will not endure it.'

Anna felt a new, violent rage herself. '*You* will not

endure it! Whom I associate with has nothing to do with you. I am no longer your problem. It is none of your business.'

'I'm making it my business. For God's sake, I asked you to be my wife. Either you distance yourself from Ryder now or you will find yourself sucked in and ruined and ousted by society.'

Anna shifted uncomfortably and turned her head away from his penetrating gaze. 'I have no desire to enter the kind of society you speak of—you know this. I have not forgotten that you proposed marriage—but I have my own ideas about what I will do with my life and it doesn't involve fluttering about aimlessly in society—and will you please not speak to me as if I were a mentally deficient schoolgirl?'

'I will tell you exactly why I do, Anna. It is because I consider it my absolute moral duty to make you see sense. As Johnathan's friend and your friend—'

'Please stop it,' she cried, her colour gloriously high, her eyes stormy with hurt indignation, 'and do not bring Johnathan into this. You are not behaving like my friend. If you care about me at all, you will treat me as an adult—as an adult woman ought to be treated. I don't want to talk about James any more.'

'That's too bad,' he bit back, unwilling to let her off the hook. 'I haven't finished and you're going to listen. He's under pressure from his father to marry—preferably a wealthy woman whose money will keep him for years to come. Has he propositioned you in any way?'

Anna shifted uncomfortably. 'Yes, but I think he was speaking in jest.'

'Don't you believe it,' William bit back. 'He has actually asked you to marry him?'

She nodded. 'Yes. My mother has suggested that he would make me an ideal husband.'

'At last we have it. Does he know you have inherited Johnathan's money?'

Anna stared at him. 'Yes—although I have not told him.'

'What about your mother? Will she have told his father?'

Anna thought for a moment. 'That's highly likely.'

'I would lay bets that she has. If it's marriage he has in mind where you are concerned, then it's your money he wants.'

Anna was astonished then outraged. 'Are you suggesting that he only proposed because he wants—?'

'Yes, Anna, that is exactly what I'm saying. He wants your money and you're too blind to see it.'

The implication stung. Pushing his hands off the arms of her chair, she stood up, her hands clenched tightly. 'Thank you, William. Thank you so much,' she raged, deeply hurt by his insulting remark. 'Has it not occurred to you that James might be attracted to me as a person and not my inheritance?'

'No,' he replied coldly. 'Not for one minute. Ryder is heading for a fall—a big one—and I don't want him to take you down with him.'

'Stop it, William,' she cried, her battered nerves crying out for relief. 'I've done nothing to deserve this. Do you have to be so cruel?'

'It's a cruel world, Anna. One has to be hard to be realistic.'

'All the anger you feel because of what James did to your brother is understandable, but it was a long time ago and people change. Maybe you should try to do the same.'

'Is that what you think?' His voice was quiet and controlled. 'Next you will be saying I should feel pity for him, for he is a pitiful figure, but I don't. I could never forgive him for trying to corrupt Charles.' Thoughts of Johnathan flashed into his mind, of the guilt and the shame that continued to eat away at him. He knew the time was fast approaching when he would have to tell Anna, and in doing so he might lose her for ever. When Anna opened her mouth to argue, he interrupted sharply. 'Anna, James Ryder is a topic we have exhausted. It would be a relief to me if I never heard his name mentioned again.'

'No one gets a second chance from you, is that it?'

William's mouth tightened. 'Certainly not James Ryder. Only those I consider deserve one.'

'I see. Then I suppose there is nothing further to be said. Now if you don't mind, I prefer not to continue this conversation. The horse James brought for me to ride has to be returned. I will ride the short distance to my mother's house. Uncle Robert is sending his carriage to collect me shortly and I don't want to keep it waiting.'

'I'll accompany you.'

'No, you will not,' she flared, facing him like a termagant. 'Leave me be, William. It's a two-minute ride, if that. I will go alone.'

In the tearing agonising hurt that enfolded her, with her head held high she strode to the door. She was ashamed at how easy it had been for him, following

all her harsh words, to expose the proof of her vulnerability.

William followed her from the room. Mac was in the
hall.

'Go after her, will you, Mac. She's going to her mother's house in Curzon Street. I'm worried about her. Bring
her back here.'

Left alone, deep in thought, William poured himself another snifter of brandy. What was he to do about
Anna? He had known a jealousy and fury on coming
across her in the park with Ryder that was beyond anything he had ever experienced. He couldn't keep his
mind off her. He could hardly contain his jealousy at
the thought of any other man touching her.

An image of her sunburnt face as she'd taken in the
beauty of the Cape flashed across his mind, as vivid
now as it had been then, so vivid, in fact, that despite
his efforts since arriving in London, he'd failed more
often than he'd succeeded. Her image persistently invaded his dreams. Anna, he thought, beautiful, unpredictable Anna. Something hard and tight squeezed his
chest, like a hand around his heart.

How strange, he thought, that he was unable to put
her out of his mind, like a puckish sprite forever dancing and weaving a spell about him, pulling at him with
forces too strong to deny, and an awareness came slowly
like dawn breaking, and everything that had seemed in-
comprehensible before suddenly began to make perfect
sense. He knew he could not go on without her. Of all
the women he could think of, no one suited him better
in every way than Anna.

* * *

Arriving at her mother's house, Anna felt her heart plummet when she saw James waiting in the hall. Having come straight from the park, he looked perfectly composed, his moody eyes appraising. To avoid any awkwardness she would have liked to go straight up to her mother's room, but now they had come face to face she couldn't ignore him.

'Hello, Anna. I hope you don't mind, but I thought I would wait for you. I knew the carriage was coming here to take you home.' His words were slightly slurred with the excess of too much alcohol he'd consumed while waiting for her.

'Then you've just caught me. The carriage will be here any moment and I must see my mother before I leave.'

'I hope you enjoyed your ride. It was unfortunate that Lord Lancaster came upon us.'

'Yes, wasn't it,' she replied coolly.

'He was angry.'

'That's an understatement. He was furious.'

'There never was anything quiet about His Lordship. He always did let his temper get the better of him.'

She smiled. 'You can't be accused of being quiet either, can you, James? You're the opposite, self-confident, and you love being the centre of attention.'

He grinned. 'That's where you're wrong. It's just a camouflage. I'm quite nervous really underneath. That's why I like being with you. I can be myself.'

'Can you?' she asked, touched by his simple admission, sincere, she hoped, but following her angry confrontation with Williams she could not feel sure of him.

'I don't have to put on an act. That's why I was so put out when you went off with William Lancaster—and I must apologise for taking you there. It was a mistake. I do realise that now.'

'Yes, it was, but it was my fault. I should never have agreed to go there.'

'I imagine Lord Lancaster was angry with you.'

'As I said, he was furious.'

'By the way, do you like him?'

Embarrassed by his question, which had come out of the blue, she looked away, sure, somehow, that James knew perfectly well how deeply she felt for William. The mere mention of his name made her relax her guard. 'William? Why—yes, he—he's a good friend. I—I'm fond of him.'

'Fond in the way you're fond of me?'

'No—it's different.' Seeing a light in his eyes she mistook for humour, she said, 'James. Stop it. Don't tease.'

'I'm not teasing. I am deadly serious. You might as well know I'm fond of you—more than fond—and I should hate it to be one-sided.' He grinned boyishly, but there was a sly gleam in his eyes. 'I meant it when I asked you to marry me. I would like to talk about us.'

'There is no us, James.'

'I'm damned jealous of William Lancaster—I admit it. You say you're fond of him—and you really shouldn't be. He's such a dark horse—he's ruined me. I get really angry when I think about you and him.'

'Stop it, James. What makes you think I should be interested in William?'

'Don't play with me, Anna. I know women and I

watched you together on the ship. I can see his attraction—the looks and his money, and his title—and how noble he must have seemed when he showed his knightly qualities and escorted you to England. He must have seemed a better proposition than I.'

'Stop it, James. This is not the time for this conversation.' She was beginning to feel extremely uncomfortable in his presence.

Suddenly he stopped and caught her arm, pulling her closer. He turned her to face him. 'I want us to be more than friends. You're so beautiful, Anna.' His voice was coercing. 'I'm obsessed with you. I can't get you out of my mind. You're still angry because I took you to the park.'

'Now you're being ridiculous. This has nothing to do with the park and I went of my own free will. Please don't say any more.'

Her rejection triggered his anger. His face twisted with cruelty and when he spoke there was an underlying violence in his tone. 'Damn you for a tease, Anna. Every time we've been together the invitation in your eyes has enticed me. You led me on—admit it.'

That he should deliberately misinterpret her actions made Anna furious. She tried to wrench her arm free, but his grip tightened viciously. He came so close to her that his face was almost touching hers. For the first time she was seeing something that William had warned her about. There was a coldness, a meanness about James's features she had never seen before. She was seeing a different version, someone angry, let down, hurt, how he might retaliate by hurting her.

'It's William Lancaster who's responsible for this,'

he hissed. 'I can well imagine what he's said to you. No doubt he listed all my evil traits—told you how that sour-faced shrew called Lucy did for me—and warned you to keep clear.'

Anna felt the colour drain from her face. She couldn't believe what was happening, what she was hearing. As James dissolved into a taut, violent stranger, she felt as if she were witnessing the opening of a door to reveal unspeakable horrors beyond. She glimpsed a dark side to his personality she had never seen before.

But then he looked away as if he knew his eyes were betraying him, pulling down the shutters of that dark side. But too late, for Anna had seen how strong he was, disciplining his violent emotions and thoughts, but beyond that she sensed other, harnessed emotions—guilt, pain, misery and despair.

'As a matter of fact, he has never spoken to me of anyone called Lucy. I think I have a great deal to learn about you, James, and I feel that when I do, I won't like it. Perhaps you should begin by telling me about Lucy. Who was she?'

James' face became shuttered. 'Just a woman we both knew. She means nothing. Will you heed William Lancaster's warning to keep away from me?'

Anna heard something like desperation in his voice. 'I am able to make my own decisions. And since you want more from me than I care to give, I think it would be for the best if you don't come here while I am visiting my mother.'

'You don't mean that.'

'I do. We don't want the same things from life, James. I don't love you. I never will.'

'I don't believe you. I don't want to lose you.'

Anna drew herself up straight and faced him, her expression resolute. 'How can you lose something that was never yours in the first place? I may be younger than you and inexperienced in the ways of the world, but I am no fool. When you asked me to marry you it was my money that attracted you to me, not myself. I do know that.'

She walked to the door, wanting this to end. 'The carriage has arrived to take me home. I'm going to say goodbye to my mother and when I come down, I would like to see you gone, James.'

'This isn't over, Anna.'

'Yes, it is. Goodbye, James.'

Climbing the stairs to her mother's room, she felt exhausted and shaken. William had told her James was no good, that he was a dangerous man. She should have listened to him after all. In his anger James had mentioned a girl called Lucy. Was she the reason why there was so much enmity between him and William? Had she rejected him in favour of William? No, she thought. There was more to it than that.

Chapter Nine

Taking leave of her mother, Anna was relieved to find James had gone when she returned to the hall. She was surprised to see a carriage containing Iain Mac waiting outside the house. She went to speak to him.

'Mac, what are you doing here?'

'His Lordship insisted I follow you to make sure you come to no harm.'

'Harm? What could possibly happen to me visiting my mother?'

'He wanted to make sure.'

'Well, that's considerate of him, I suppose.' She was surprised not to see her uncle's carriage waiting for her. 'My uncle was supposed to send the carriage for me. It should have been here half an hour ago.'

'I know. Forgive me, but I took the liberty of sending it back. The driver will explain to your uncle that there is nothing to worry about and that I will take you back later. Lord Lancaster wants to see you. You were upset when you left. He wants to talk to you.'

'I see.' Anna was confused. What could William possible want? Hadn't everything they had to say been said between them? She was tempted to tell Mac to take her straight to Kensington, but didn't. Clearly William had something else he wanted to say to her and, following her conversation with James, there were questions she wanted answers to.

Climbing into the carriage, she looked at Mac seated across from her. 'Then I suppose you'd better take me to His Lordship. You spent a great deal of time with William when you were in India, didn't you, Mac?'

He nodded. 'I became his valet—batman—call it what you like when my old employer died. I shall be eternally grateful to His Lordship for taking me on. I serve him as best I can.'

'I am sure you do and you are deep in his confidence.'

His expression became grave. 'I am—but I do not speak of them.'

'You are very loyal, Mac. We—had words before I left—which I am sure you are aware of. It stems from my acquaintance with James Ryder. Why is William against him? I know he and William have had their differences in the past, but there is something else, something concerning a woman called Lucy.'

Mac looked at her steadily. His mouth, which could harden in a second, hardened now. 'His Lordship is right not to like James Ryder. He's no good, but it's up to His Lordship to warn you against forming any kind of relationship with Ryder. He has a past. He—he is evil. There is no other word for it.

'Evil? That is a strong word to use.'

'It fits.'

'He must have done something very bad.'

'He did.'

Anna was filled with confused frustration. 'I cannot make sense of it. What did James do?'

'It's not for me to say. His Lordship guards his privacy. He has my trust. I will not betray that.'

Anna knew there was no further point in defending James or trying to get anything out of Mac. As William's loyal servant, his lips were well and truly sealed.

William was where Anna had left him an hour ago. His eyes locked on hers with a piercing, questioning intensity.

'Mac tells me you want to see me, William. I thought everything had been said between us.' Her voice was flat and emotionless.

'Not quite.' He studied her. Her stillness was like a positive force.

Taking a deep, fortifying breath, she intended to remain distinctly detached, erecting a wall between them to achieve that end. It had been an affront to her pride, her outraged, abused pride, to have him speak to her as he had earlier, without explanation of why he hated James so much and what she had done that was so wrong.

'Then what else is there?'

'The Earl of Brinkley, James Ryder's father, is your mother's keeper. Why did you keep it from me?'

'Because I knew exactly how you would react. Besides, it has nothing to do with you—or me, for that matter.'

'Have you met the Earl?'

'Yes, although I make a point of not visiting my mother if I know he's to be there... It may surprise you to know that my mother and Lord Brinkley are extremely fond of each other.'

'I don't doubt it—otherwise he would not keep the house on. That the man has a wife and sons obviously doesn't appear to bother him. Does he know that you travelled to England on the *Bengal*—the same ship as James?'

'Yes. It would appear my mother tells him most things. He also knows that I was in your care when I left India. I've just seen James. He was waiting for me at the house.'

'And? How was he?'

'Different. For the first time I saw a side to him I didn't like.'

Anna walked across the room, her arms wrapped around her waist. After a moment she perched on the edge of one of the sofas. Suddenly feeling very sad and weary, feeling tears come to her eyes, she let them fall, too exhausted emotionally and physically to stop them. She was sick with remorse and regretful of her behaviour, the arrival of William in the park and his fury robbing her of all sense of reality.

Studying her in frozen silence, all at once William felt his heart fill with empathy. The anger he'd felt earlier melted, greatly alleviated by what he assumed to be her capitulation where Ryder was concerned. She seemed so young and so vulnerable. He went to her, towering over her, his broad shoulders blocking out anything but him. Gently placing his hand beneath her chin, he tilted her tear-drenched face to his.

'Forget you ever met James Ryder, Anna. He can do you nothing but harm. Don't you see?'

She shook her head, thrown off balance by what sounded like gentleness in his voice.

'How long have you been seeing him?'

'I haven't—at least, not in the way you mean,' she said, dabbing her eyes. 'We met at the ball and he challenged me to a ride. I should have said no. There really is nothing between us, you know. It's terribly important to me that you of all people believe that.'

'I do. More importantly, do you believe me when I tell you the man is no good?'

'Yes,' she whispered. 'I do now.' She didn't want to argue about James any more. She didn't want to talk about him. In the safe silence of her heart, she realised just how much she wanted William. She wanted to make him happy. She wanted his trust, but more than anything else she wanted his love.

William heard the break in her tearful voice. Raising his hand, he placed it against her cheek, his thumb arresting a rogue tear. 'No more tears, Anna. You've cried enough for one day,' he murmured. 'I can withstand anything, but not your tears.'

For a moment they didn't move. William studied her with heavy-lidded, speculative eyes. Suddenly Anna saw something exciting and welcoming kindle in those eyes and her heart soared. 'I intend to put James Ryder behind me. After today I don't like him very much.'

'It isn't going to be that simple. At least, not while you visit your mother on a regular basis. You are bound to come into contact with Ryder. So, what is to be done to keep you out of his clutches?'

Anna pulled a face and walked to the window where she stood looking out. 'I don't think I want to talk about him any more.'

'I do,' he said, his voice low and husky, pain and

guilt in his eyes as he prepared to open his heart to Anna, to open the wounds that had been caused by guilt and shame. 'I've got something to say that you should know. Come and sit down. There is so much to tell—which I confess will be difficult for me. It's knowing where to begin.'

Anna crossed the room and seated herself on the sofa. William came and sat beside her. 'Very well. If you must. The last thing I want is for you to rake over some repellent, painful past, but you are right. I want to know everything—you must be open with me. I am listening.'

'I had hoped to spare you hearing the ugly and very tragic story, but I think in the light of this new development you should be told and, since I was very much involved, then it is only right that I tell you myself. It is something I should have told you before I asked you to marry me.' He looked at her hard. 'When you know the awful, sordid truth of what really happened to Johnathan, you may never want to see me again. And I have to say that I would not blame you.'

Anna frowned. 'You're beginning to worry me now, William.'

'James Ryder's father has got a special reason for hating me—for several reasons. When Ryder worked for the Company in India he was buying and selling commodities. I was due to sail for home and had stopped off in Bhopal to see Johnathan—which was where Ryder was stationed at the time. Already there was gossip about his illicit dealings with others, which Johnathan picked up on. He saw what Ryder was up to—reporting a lower amount in the books and pocketing the remainder. But what Johnathan objected to the most was his total disrespect for those beneath him—in particular the Indian people themselves. But that is not all. You remember I told you about my brother.'

'When he was a student at Oxford with James?'

He nodded. 'It didn't end there. When I met up with young Ryder in India he was having a jolly old time of it. He thought the world was his stage and he could do what he liked without impunity. Already addicted to opium, of which there is a good supply in India, he developed a love of gambling and women—one in particular.'

'Was her name Lucy?'

He frowned. 'Yes. How did you know?'

'He mentioned her name, that was all. Who was she?'

'She was the daughter of a respected Company worker—a quiet man, devoted to his family. Lucy was young, naive, very pretty—and she and Johnathan had become close. He was in love with her and wanted to marry her.'

Anna frowned. 'Johnathan? He never mentioned her in any of his letters to me."

'No. He was due to travel to Bombay to see you. I believe he wanted to tell you in person that he was to marry Lucy.'

'But—what has this to do with James?'

'Johnathan and myself were responsible for getting him dismissed from the Company.'

'Oh, I see.' When William fell silent, as if reluctant to tell her more, she prompted, 'What happened to Lucy? She must have been very upset when Johnathan died.'

'Yes. She was devastated. But before that…one day she disappeared. Johnathan and I took part in the search. We found her wandering in a less than respectable district.' Averting his eyes, he swallowed, finding it hard to go on, but he had to. 'She was disorientated, with no idea where she was or exactly what had happened to her—which was probably a mercy. She'd been drugged and violated. The poor girl was in quite a state. I found Ryder in a stupor in an opium den.'

Anna stared at him, shocked and appalled by what he had told her. 'But—that is dreadful. Poor Lucy…for something like that to happen to her. How truly shocking—and how devastated Johnathan must have been. And it was definitely James who…?'

'Yes. Lucy was sure of that. He wasn't convicted—it was hushed up, but nothing could excuse his brutal, heartless actions. Lucy wouldn't let anyone near her—definitely not Johnathan. After what had happened to her, she felt unclean, no longer innocent. It was a thoroughly unpleasant business. I dare say what Ryder did to that poor young woman was done under the influence of narcotics—I couldn't say for certain. But he was determined to avenge himself on Johnathan and myself for his dismissal from the Company—hence his attack on Lucy.'

Anna stared at him in disbelief. The colour had drained from her face. 'And Johnathan?' she whispered, sensing that what he would tell her next would be devastating. 'Knowing my brother, he would retaliate against the man who had wronged Lucy.'

William nodded. 'He did. He went looking for Ryder—he wanted me to go with him, but I couldn't,' he said, avoiding her eyes as he said this. 'Ryder was waiting for him—Ryder and several of his associates. There was a fight. Johnathan was badly injured. It was never proved who wielded the knife, but there is no doubt in my mind that it was Ryder.'

A heavy silence replaced William's strangely calm, slow voice, broken only by the sound of the fire as it flared in the hearth. A lump in her throat, Anna struggled to find words which were neither meaningless nor hurtful, for she sensed in William a raw and quivering sensitivity.

Her expression was one of confusion. 'But—why didn't you tell me this before now? Why keep it from me? I would never have befriended James had I known any of this—that he had killed my brother. You had no right, William. No right at all.'

Agitated, William got to his feet, raking his fingers through his hair, deeply troubled about what he was about to tell her next. 'I know that, Anna, but there are times when the truth is hard to face—hard to bear. How could I tell *you* when I couldn't even bear to think of what I had done myself?'

Anna's throat went dry as she witnessed his anguish. 'What is it? What did you do?' A light blazed briefly in his eyes, then was extinguished. 'Tell me.'

A sudden shadow fell across his face. His voice hardened. 'I swore to put it behind me…'

'And now your conscience has smote you and you have decided to do the right thing and tell me what really happened when Johnathan died.'

He nodded. 'I wanted to tell you—God knows how much I wanted to tell you, but I was too ridden with guilt—too ashamed.'

'But—why?'

'Because on the night he was attacked I could have

prevented it—but I was otherwise engaged. It was an ill-fated wind that blew that night and cost Johnathan his life. It was a troubled district we were in—people were often set upon and robbed. We always went about in groups...'

'But that night you let Johnathan go off alone,' Anna said quietly when he fell silent.

He nodded. 'Johnathan had been drinking—drowning his sorrows over Lucy. Drink emboldened him. When he left, I had no idea he was going to go looking for Ryder otherwise, the state he was in, I would have tried to prevent him. Unfortunately, Ryder and his friends got to him first.'

'Why did you do that—let him go off alone? What were you doing?' The look he gave her answered her question. Her lips twisted with cynicism. 'I hope she was worth it.'

'I am ashamed. I wanted to tell you—I couldn't. I wanted to spare you the sordidness of it all—and Johnathan wanted the manner of his death kept from you.' He sighed deeply. 'When he died, I had my own demons to battle with. I chided myself relentlessly for what I did— or didn't do—that night. Remembering, I hated myself with a hatred and contempt that were absolutely bottomless. Telling you would force me to recognise and reflect on things I had locked away in my mind. When Johnathan died, I vowed never, ever, to look back, to wonder how my life might have been if only I'd done things differently that night.'

'It's too late for regrets, William.'

Anna was caught between torment and understanding over what she had seen in William's face when he had told her of his failure to stop Johnathan going after James that night. His guilt was acute.'

'Johnathan died because of me.'

Anna looked at him. His suffering was there for her to see. Her heart went out to him. Beneath his stiff façade was something dark and savage kept on a tight leash. 'And who is to say Johnathan would not have died anyway? Falling off a horse or contracting some infernal disease like cholera. You do not have the power over life and death.'

'He died because I failed to protect him.'

Anna stared at him, as if seeing him for the first time. There was no anger in her, only an immense sadness and pity which welled up from the bottom of her heart towards this man whose sufferings must have been great indeed. She preferred not to think of what agonies he had been through. A lump in her throat, she struggled to find words which were not hurtful. She wanted to help him get over the guilt that still ate at him, but in a vulnerable state herself, where this man was concerned, she must proceed with caution.

'The memories of that time still pain you,' she whispered. 'It's a heavy burden you have been carrying, William, but it is over now. I do not blame you—not at all. Nothing you do will change anything.'

But, she thought as she fell silent, seeing the raw pain in his eyes, *the consequences linger on.*

'How full of hate you must have been for James Ryder.'

'Yes, I hated him. I still do.'

Anna was stirred by the depth of passion in his voice. Silence fell inside the room. In the hearth a log split asunder and collapsed in a pool of red embers. William stood very still, but it seemed to Anna that his broad shoulders bowed, as though under the force of some strong feeling as he grappled with his thoughts.

'James died from his wounds a week later.' William looked at her. 'Can you understand now why I couldn't tell you?'

'Yes...yes, I can. The truth is never easy. But it is over, William. You must put it behind you. You cannot let it go on eating away at you. Johnathan wouldn't want you to do that. Why was James not sent to prison for what he did—not only for embezzlement?'

'It could not be proved who had wielded the knife that killed Johnathan. Ryder's father was all powerful—and the Company didn't want a scandal—so he was dismissed.'

'And his father blamed you along with Johnathan for his son's dismissal. Did he know what he had done to Lucy?'

'No. He was told that James was embezzling Company money—which became the main and only reason, for his dismissal where his father was concerned.'

'Did Lucy recover from her ordeal?'

He shook his head. 'I'm not certain. My time was taken up with other matters. Her family was devastated. To protect his daughter, her father wanted the whole affair covered up—the Company, also. It was a sensitive issue. Gossip can be vicious and because there had already been so much gossip associated with James Ryder, his violation of Lucy would only fuel the vicious tongues and tarnish the family name for ever. She had suffered enough. Besides, something like that was bad for the Company. Ryder had to go—there was nothing else for it.'

'Poor Johnathan. James robbed him of his life—of his love for the woman he would have married. I cannot forgive him for that. I can't believe he asked me to marry him—especially after what he had done.' Anna looked at him solemnly. 'The truth is hard to take, but I'm glad you've told me.'

William heard the depth of her emotions, saw the expressive face go through a range of changes and how her eyes glistened with tears, and he finally understood the inexplicable anguish she had needlessly been through. A look of sympathy softened his grim features. 'I'm sorry, Anna. None of this has been easy for you.'

Anna saw that he was looking at her openly and with a passionate warmth. Getting up, she went to him. 'No, it hasn't. I always felt there was more to James Ryder. Thank you for finding the courage to tell me.'

Her sincere thanks after all he had put her through since he had found her with Ryder earlier demolished what was left of William's reserve. His throat constricted around an unfamiliar knot of emotion as he looked at her lovely face, her tear-drenched eyes looking like warm amber. At this moment of raw emotion, he had never been more moved by her loveliness, her tenderness. In an attempt to comfort her and savour the sweet feelings swelling inside him, with aching gentleness he wrapped her in his arms.

'I'm sorry, Anna. I'm a thoughtless brute. I didn't mean to make you cry.' Without a word she turned her face to his chest. Alex held her, stroking the soft silk of her hair, cursing Ryder for preying on her innocence and cursing himself with equal savagery for making her cry.

Looking down at her and having to resist the urge to kiss her damp cheeks and soft, trembling lips, he drew a long fortifying breath and tenderly kissed her brow instead. 'From the moment I saw you riding hell for leather with Ryder through Hyde Park, I haven't been sure of anything.'

Anna drew back in his arms. She felt absolutely exhausted, limp and bedraggled. 'I'm sorry, William. I must look a sight. What must you think? I don't suppose my ride through the park will have gone unnoticed,' she said on a jocular note in an attempt to lessen the tension, 'which was the case during the storm on the ship—and again when you waltzed me on to the balcony at the ball, thank goodness—but if I carry on like that my reputation will be completely ruined.'

'Not if you marry me. When I asked you to be my wife at the ball, you said you would consider it. Have you?'

'You haven't changed your mind?'

'I am perfectly serious, Anna. I want to marry you—to make you my wife.' William's features softened and his eyes warmed, as if he understood how confused she felt. 'Have you any objections to me as a husband?'

'No—of course not. Quite the opposite.' She spoke with measured care, not because she was unsure of herself, but because she felt the need to be cautious.

'I know you have plans of your own, Anna, that you want independence and to achieve a more meaningful future than flitting uselessly through society. But if you marry me, you can do whatever your heart desires—be it a school or an orphanage for destitute children—or nothing at all.'

She stared at him in amazement. 'You would do that for me?'

'Anything, my love.'

'But—what about my mother? We are not of the same social class.'

'And that matters to you?'

Anna looked away. She wished she wasn't so aware of him, of the strength and the power of that long lean body and handsome face—and her own silly emotions that seemed to be all over the place following his proposal. 'No. There is nothing I can do about it—but it will certainly concern your grandfather.'

'I am not asking you to marry my grandfather.' His face shuttered, William regarded her sombrely. She looked so young, so defenceless, so in need of protection. Something tightened in his chest and he was aware of a feeling of tenderness for her.

'You and I did not meet under normal circumstances, Anna, and because we spent so much time together on board the *Bengal*, where we were not hemmed in by the dictates of society, in the months it took for us to reach London, we learned more about each other than any man and woman would learn in a year about their intended spouses.'

'I know—but—marriage? All I know is that I had not thought… There may come a day when you will resent my background.'

Placing his hand under her chin, he tilted her face to his, wanting more than anything else to eradicate any doubts she might have.

'I confess that I know nothing of what our marriage will be like, but what I do know is that after I left you with your Uncle Robert that day we arrived in England you were never far from my deepest thoughts. I missed you like hell when you were no longer there. That was when I knew I wanted you to be my wife. You suit me better than any other woman I have known or am likely to. You anger, amuse, delight and frustrate me to the point where I don't know whether to throttle you or kiss you. And yet, despite all this, I still want you for my wife—and I did give you my protection, too, when you needed it on board ship,' he reminded her with an impudent grin.

'Now you're trying to make me beholden to you.'

'Because I'm trying to persuade you to consider my suit.'

Anna looked directly into his face just above her own, feeling herself respond to the dark intimacy of his voice. His expression was gentle, understanding, soft as she had never before seen it. And there, plain for her to see, was the sincerity of his words.

'Have you spoken to Uncle Robert about your intentions?'

'Not yet, but I doubt he will have any objections.'

'No, I don't expect he will. We haven't always seen eye to eye but I am grateful for all he has done for me. At a time when I had nothing, he gave me a home and his protection. Marriage is important and serious and not something to be undertaken lightly—especially for me. It's true. I'm not indifferent to you—and you must believe me when I say I was never attracted to James—

it might have looked that way to you sometimes, but I could never love him.'

'Can you know yourself as well as that? You are certain?'

'Yes, I am.' Her eyes darkened with a love she wasn't trying to conceal from him any more and she managed to hold his gaze as she quietly and shyly admitted the truth. 'Because I love you, you see—quite desperately, in fact. Oh, it's all right,' she said quickly when she saw his eyes widen with astonishment, 'you don't have to say anything—make any declarations of love and things like that. But please don't say I'll get over it because I won't. I shall love you all the days of my life. I fell in love with you on the *Bengal*. That hasn't changed. It's a fact. There it is.'

She was looking at William with eyes as large as her soul and as dark as midnight. The emptiness that had been in her heart since leaving the *Bengal* began to fill with something disturbing, something strong and dangerous, and as his fingers tenderly touched her temple, it became a desire so strong it was like an intense pain— urgent, a need to be fulfilled.

She moved closer to him, facing him, then took his face between her hands and beyond all rational thought kissed his mouth. Her lips were as soft and gentle as butterfly wings and as sweet as extracted honey. She kissed him with a strange combination of naive expertise and instinctive sensuality that almost drove William wild.

William's face remained strangely expressionless, but his eyes told her he felt the same. Dozens of feelings raced through her mind, among them doubts and uncertainty that she was doing the right thing, but over it all was a joyous feeling that he wasn't going to reject her.

Drawing back a little from his face, she sighed. 'I can't believe I did that.'

William was stunned by the feelings unfolding inside him, at the tenderness and desire throbbing through every nerve ending in his body. An unbearable sense of joy leaped in his heart. The yielding softness in her eyes, the gentle flush that bespoke her untainted innocence and youth, brought faint stirrings of an emotion he thought long since dead. They sat without moving, their gazes arrested, magnetised by the silent communication of sexual attraction.

'That was some kiss, Anna,' he said in a thickened voice. 'However, I can't let you have it all your own way. I think it's about time I kissed you—to show you how it's done.'

'But it is not the first time we've kissed. How can it be different?' she whispered, her warm breath caressing his skin. Moistening her lips with the tip of her tongue, she was unaware of the sensual invitation of her action.

'I'll show you.'

Anna watched his gaze drop to her mouth and in a state of anticipation that was reaching dizzying heights she waited. After what seemed to her like an eternity, he shoved his fingers into her luxuriant mass of hair and drew her face close to his. His hands were gentle and controlled, yet unyielding, and then he found her generous mouth with his own. It was warm and exciting, his kiss devastating. As his tongue probed for entrance, she opened to him, wanting his possession. She pressed herself against him, answering his passion with the same wild, exquisitely provocative ardour, feeling a burgeoning pleasure and immense joy that was almost beyond bearing.

When William released her lips and raised his head, her mouth curved in a smile. 'So you do feel something,' Anna said softly. His eyes mesmerised her, held him to her.

'Dear Lord, you're incredible. Have you any idea how lovely you are—and how rare?' he whispered hoarsely, touching the smooth cheek of this unpredictable, artless young woman with unconscious reverence. Desire, potent and primitive, poured through his veins.

The touch of his fingertips against her cheek, and the deep, compelling timbre of his voice, had the seductive impact Anna had always dreamed of. She could not believe the pulsing happiness that glowed inside her, or the exquisite sensations speeding through her veins. For a long moment they gazed at each other, each feeling more exposed to the other than ever before.

'Then perhaps you should kiss me again—just to make sure.'

Lowering his head, he placed his lips on the soft curve of her lips once more, moving gently, exquisitely, assaulting her defences.

'I never knew I could feel this—this wonderful wanting,' Anna breathed, when he raised his head, gently placing her lips at the corner of his mouth. 'I want you to love me, William—properly. This is as far as my knowledge goes. What lies beyond a kiss I cannot imagine. I want you to tell me what to do—to show me.'

His senses drugged with the scent of her, the feel of her lips on his flesh, with the last shred of rationality he possessed, William looked at her. He was accustomed to having women desire him and his love making always followed a familiar pattern. But with Anna it would be different. She was not like any of them—she was sensual, a virgin and inexperienced, urgent and unschooled.

'It will be my pleasure—when you are my wife.' He arched a brow. 'You are going to marry me?'

'Are you really sure that this is what you want?'

'I've never been more sure of anything in my life.'

Her eyes were drawn to his, for no matter how a man looked, stern and firm, the eyes had a will of their own and could not be fixed. There was a light in them now. Warm and compelling. 'And if I insist on having more time to think about it?' she teased. 'Would that suit?'

'Absolutely not.'

'You should learn to be more patient.'

'And you would enjoy seeing me suffer,' he said, pulling her against his chest. 'You're a sadist, Anna Harris. I knew you were going to be difficult the minute I laid eyes on you.'

She laughed lightly. 'My tutors at the academy were always scolding me for being so, but I can only hope that I will improve with age.'

'Do you always intend being rebellious towards me?'

'Always, for I don't think you would approve of a new me.' She smiled serenely and placed a featherlight kiss at the corner of his mouth, her eyes warm with laughter. 'You're not cross with me, are you?'

'No.' He laughed. 'It's good to see you gaining in confidence.' He returned her kiss lightly, then added in mock threat, 'But don't let it get out of hand or...'

'Or what?' she whispered, placing another kiss on his lips.

'I'll think of something,' he said, capturing her lips and kissing her long and deep.

When he raised his head Anna met his gaze, her eyes slumberous. 'Then I think I will *have* to marry you.' Even if he had not mentioned anything about love, he had proven himself to be a considerate and honourable man. If she didn't have his whole heart now, she would win him.

Something in her flushed face brought an instant response from William. Brushing her hair from her face, he smiled. 'Thank you. You have no idea how much this means to me.'

'I know,' she said, searching his eyes. I can't believe this is real—that it is really happening.'

He took her hand and pressed her palm to his cheek. 'It is—it will—as soon as the ceremony can be arranged.'

'I would like that.' She closed her eyes and kissed his lips. When she moved back, his eyes were dark, solemn. She laid her hand against his cheek. 'What is it? Does something trouble you?'

He shook his head. 'Now you have agreed to be my wife, I'm reluctant to let you go.'

She wrapped her arms around his broad shoulders. 'Then let me stay with you.'

Desire stirred within him at her whispered words, but he captured her face gently between his hands and searched her eyes. He would like nothing more than to have her stay the entire night—in his arms, in his bed, but with admirable restraint, he said, 'You can't do that, my love. In no time at all I would have your uncle knocking on my door demanding you return home. Have patience. We will soon be together. Now it is settled that you are to be my wife, I will leave for Cranford. I need to speak with my grandfather.'

Anna looked anxious. 'Please try not to argue with him. Give him time to get used to our marriage—to me. It will come as a great shock to him. I hate to think you will be at daggers drawn because of me.'

'We have been at daggers drawn for years, my love. It has nothing to do with you. My grandfather's grudges, both in magnitude and longevity, are legendary. If he takes a dislike to anyone or they cross him in any way, then he doesn't forgive. That I can guarantee.'

His words only rekindled a deepening of Anna's unease. 'Perhaps, given time and having you back at Cranford, will soften his attitude to our marriage.'

William sighed, wondering if by some miracle Anna was right and he should be more understanding. Would time soften his grandfather's hostility to his marriage and accept the inevitable?

William lost no time in asking Robert for permission to marry Anna. Robert gave it gladly. Had the circumstances been different, William would have approached her mother, but as matters stood it was Robert who was her guardian.

They were to be married at St George's Church in Hanover Square, Mayfair's most fashionable church, as soon as the banns had been called for the ritual three weeks. In a flap for the first time in her life and already planning a grand affair for the wedding of her niece to the illustrious Lord Lancaster, heir to a marquessate, when Aunt Constance declared that it was too soon, that there was so much to be arranged—the invitations, the flowers, Anna's wedding dress, they would never be ready in time—Anna quietly but firmly told her it would be a quiet affair, with just close family. Never having been to a wedding before, when Anna asked them to be bridesmaids, Mary and Dorothy were so excited they could talk of nothing else.

Later, alone in her room, Anna had time to reflect on this sudden change to her life. She found it hard to get used to the idea that she was to marry William Lancaster, who was as deep and complex as the seas over which they had sailed together from India. She went through a great deal of deliberation and heart searching. She could hardly believe how deep her feelings were running and the joy coursing through her whole body melted the very core of her heart. She loved William. She knew that and that perfect certainty filled her heart and stilled any anxiety she might otherwise have had.

Chapter Ten

As William approached the gargantuan Cranford Park, presided over by his grandfather, Stephen Lancaster, the Marquess of Elvington, he experienced a feeling of unreality closing in on him and his grandfather was an essential part of it. Gazing out of the carriage window, he felt a lump of nostalgia in his throat when his eyes settled on the exquisite splendour of Cranford Park in the heart of the Berkshire countryside. It was surrounded by parkland, timeless, gracious and brooding, its elegant façade expressing power and pride.

What surprised him was the realisation of how much he had missed it. His thoughts turned to Anna and he knew she would be happy living there. They would make their marriage work. He was sure of it. He wanted his family name and the title to continue and to do that he must start producing heirs. He wanted his life to have meaning, to have a real marriage—meaningful and lasting, a wife and children and love—not the empty relationships that passed for most marriages in society.

He wanted Anna more than he'd wanted anyone in

his life. At twenty-nine years of age and after more affairs than he cared to remember, he had fallen victim to an outrageously spirited, beautiful girl who blithely incurred his displeasure, amused and infuriated him as no other woman had ever done.

When the carriage drew to a halt in front of the house and gold-liveried footmen appeared and descended to strip the coach of the mountain of baggage, accompanied by Mac, William stepped into the familiar environment that was to be his world from now on.

He was met at the door by Horton, clad in his usual black. Horton had been the butler of Cranford Park from time immemorial. William smiled at this old retainer.

'Good afternoon, My Lord,' he intoned formally. 'And may I say how good it is to have you home at Cranford.'

'Good afternoon, Horton,' he said with a smile as he handed over his gloves and hat to the footman by Horton's side and he could have sworn there was a look of genuine pleasure in the butler's eyes. 'It's been a while, but you haven't changed, I see. It's good to see you. From my observation as I approached, nothing appears to have changed.'

'Indeed it has not, My Lord. The fabric of Cranford is as it was before you went away.'

William entered the large hall. It was an impressive room with ten columns supporting the weight of those in the magnificent marble hall immediately above. It was opulent, with beautiful artefacts reposing on gleaming tables, and on the walls were portraits of long-dead family members in gilded frames, while shadows from the dark corners whispered wealth.

The house exuded an indefinable quality—a sense

of order, centuries of happiness and disappointments, memories of men and women who had lived and breathed within these walls, all folded into the fabric. The house was living, breathing, but devoid of life.

A small contingent of footmen and housemaids seemed to be lurking about, ostensibly going about their work. As William looked around him the maids stole long, lingering looks at him, then turned to exchange swift, gratified smiles. With his mind set on getting cleaned up before his meeting with his grandfather, he was oblivious to the searching scrutiny he was receiving.

'How is my grandfather, Horton?' William enquired. 'Better in temper, I hope.'

Horton smiled. 'He has mellowed a bit with age, but he's not been well—spends most of his time in his rooms. Arthritis, the doctor says. He has good days and bad days and there is an inconsistency in his behaviour. His mind wanders and he sits staring at nothing for long periods.'

William nodded. 'I'll go and see him as soon as I've cleaned up.'

It was late afternoon when William made his way to his grandfather's suite of rooms. Chester, his valet, met him in the anteroom to his grandfather's bedchamber.

'Welcome home, My Lord.'

'Thank you, Chester. I've come to see my grandfather. Is he awake?'

'On the doctor's orders I gave him a draught earlier. It has relaxed him. In fact, I was about to get him into bed.'

'Then I won't keep him long. I am not here to cause him distress,' William stated.

William was admitted into the bedchamber. It was dominated by a huge bed hung with blue silk damask. It was a comfortable spacious room, but there was an air of tension about it which manifested itself in the old man seated in a chair by the window and the slow metronome ticking on the clock, which seemed to herald the coming of something the Marquess might not care for.

He sat there in his chair, where he spent most of his time when not in bed, looking out over his domain. William saw that his grandfather's body had wasted, that his shoulders were thin and unnaturally hunched. His distinguishing features were his bushy eyebrows over deep-set, piercing grey eyes and the thrust of his jaw line. His hair was almost gone and his flesh was furrowed with age.

William went to him. They had parted on bad terms—two men possessed of the same proud arrogance and indomitable will that marked all the Lancaster men—and as far as he was concerned nothing had changed. He had not come to be reunited with his grandfather, but to accept what was his right. He wanted to get this ordeal over with as quickly as possible.

'Grandfather?' William drew in his breath, old angers stirring within.

The Marquess lifted his head then and saw William. He studied him for a moment, taking in the tough lines of the man he had become. William thought he detected a flicker of pain in the depths of his eyes. When he spoke, he was coherent, his voice low and thread like.

'William! So, the prodigal is back.'

'As you see, Grandfather, but I beg you not to think of killing the fatted calf.' He reminded himself to hold his temper as the old man looked him over as he would a horse at an auction.

'I won't. You're disappointed to find me still alive, I expect.' His mouth curled in a mocking, world-weary smile that for some obscure reason struck a pain in William's heart. 'Are you staying?'

So, William thought, nothing was changed. It wasn't much of a welcome, but then he had not expected one. His grandfather would be hoping he had returned to heal the breach and, if so, he was to be disappointed. The pretence was gone between them. They were alike in many ways and his grandfather had known when he left that he would not willingly disclaim the title that would be rightfully his when his grandfather died. That he would return.

'It is my intention,' he replied, his voice cold and resolute, devoid of affection or forgiveness.

'You are heir to the marquessate. Despite your determination to stand against it when you left for India, I always knew you'd return some day to claim your heritage. I expected you to return some time—to accept what is rightfully yours. I know you take no more joy than I did when I had no choice but to take it on when my brother died, but one can't avoid their responsibilities, can they, William? But why have you come now? There has to be a reason—and I very much doubt it's to see me.'

'My mother died while I was in India. I am here to see my siblings.'

'*Half*-siblings,' his grandfather was quick to emphasise. 'They're no blood of mine.'

'They are my family.'

'Aye, well, be that as it may,' he grumbled.

'There is something I must tell you—something that affects me deeply. It is my intention to bring Charles and Tilly to live here—at Cranford.' His declaration caused his grandfather to rear up in his chair.

'No, you will not. I forbid it. I will not have that woman's offspring in this house—not while there is breath in my body. I forbid it. Your mother chose her path when she left.'

'She was still my mother and I loved her dearly.'

Surprisingly his grandfather nodded. 'I expect you did.'

'I loved both my parents. It was sad they were taken so soon.'

His grandfather merely grunted. William's outright declaration of love was too much for the old man to deal with. Any such term of endearment was not in his vocabulary. But when he remembered his father and how he had died of some incurable sickness, he recalled how his grandfather had retired to his rooms to grieve in private. He had been unable to forgive his son's wife for leaving Cranford to marry a man who worked for the government just one year after his only son had died.

'Did their father not leave them provided for?'

'Unfortunately, that was not the case. Charles is of an age to map out his own future, but Tilly is just seventeen years old and I have a responsibility to her. It will benefit them both if they come to live here—the house is large enough for them to get lost in, so I doubt you will even know they are here. Tilly has finished her education and Charles has joined the Company. He spends his time at East India House in London.'

'Will he go to India?'

'He's not yet certain.' William knew his grandfather would not argue about them coming to live at Cranford, particularly not when he could see it was useless. He was an old man, not long for this earth, and the strength of will and determination that marked William put him out of his grandfather's reach.

'You liked India, did you?' his grandfather asked suddenly.

'Yes, as a matter of fact I did. Why do you ask?'

'Because there were times when I thought you would not be coming back.'

'I always intended coming back at some point. I believe you always knew that.'

'That's all very well for you to say,' said his grandfather, his face showing the strain he'd been under—for the first time William felt a twinge of regret that he was the cause. 'You haven't been the one sitting here wondering if you were still alive. Are you to return to India?'

'No. I'm home to stay.'

'To live here—at Cranford?'

'Cranford is my home.'

'Are you married?'

'No.'

'Then it's time you were—married, with heirs to come after you.'

'I intend to.'

'Now you're home, doubtless you'll find someone to marry—wealth and a marquessate will tempt any woman.'

'I should tell you that I have already met the lady I

will marry. Her name is Anna Harris. I was in India with her brother, who met an unfortunate death. I accompanied Anna on the voyage from India.'

His grandfather pinned his hard gaze on him. 'She is suitable?'

'Eminently suitable.'

'Her family? She has connections, I hope.'

'No. I will tell you about her family some time. For now, be content that I have found the woman I am to marry. I do not judge a person by their birth.'

'From your tone I can tell she is not suitable.'

'She is to me. Anna is a lovely young woman—and she has a sizable dowry.'

'I don't care how much money she has. You must stop this travesty at once.' He was so angry a vein in his forehead was bulging.

'No. I'm a grown man, Grandfather. You cannot tell me who I should marry—or forbid me to marry the woman I love. There was a time when I thought I would never marry a woman who wasn't eminently suitable to be the Marchioness of Elvington—until I met Anna. I will not end up like you and Grandmother, disliking each other for the entirety of your marriage—lonely and miserable, because you married someone from the *right* family. I'd rather be married to a woman from a less noble family than the wrong woman, which is what you did.'

'And I'm telling you that you will live to regret it— and my marriage to your grandmother and the reasons for it are none of your business.'

'Maybe not, but as a boy, when I watched you and Grandmother avoid each other, leaving the room when either of you entered, loathing each other—which was probably why my father was the only product of that miserable union—I do not want that for myself.'

They both knew he was right, but his grandfather was not giving in without a fight.'

'I will not receive her in this house.'

'Her name is Anna—and you will. You will accept her, or I will marry her anyway and you can disinherit me.'

On that final word, supremely confident that his grandfather wouldn't disinherit him, he turned and left the room. He felt a stirring of sympathy for his grandfather, who had not been allowed to follow his heart as he was doing. Abiding by his family's wishes, he had set aside the love of his life and married a respectable woman from one of the finest families in England.

These were different times, but back then, met with the same circumstances, would he have made a different choice? he wondered. He liked to think he would have allowed nothing to come between himself and Anna.

Back in London, when their betrothal was officially announced in the *Post*, it was received with considerable surprise and raised many curious eyebrows. Since returning to London from India, Lord Lancaster was already known as one of London's most eligible bachelors, but nothing whatsoever was known about the woman who had accompanied him from that far-away country and speculation about her background was rife.

William was determined that Anna should enjoy herself before the wedding, so there followed an intense round of social functions. Escorted to several stylish events by William, more often than not with Aunt Constance or a maid in attendance, there were visits to a play at the theatre at Covent Garden or Drury Lane or the opera at the King's Theatre in the Haymarket.

Anna lived in a kind of dream. This new experience of being in love was a constant wonder to her. Like a bird set free, she was surprised to find herself revelling in the fun of it, and most of all she was happy because William was nearly always present, attentive, considerate—conspicuously so. She never failed to look stunning. Their forthcoming wedding was uppermost in both their minds. Afterwards they were to leave for Cranford in time for Christmas.

Anna was delighted to meet William's half-brother, Charles. He was dark like William. Tall and lean, he carried an indisputable air of certainty. He was attractive with dark blue eyes and a ready smile on his lips. Anna liked him and felt at ease with him immediately.

Anna's mother, who had changed her opinion of William the more Anna told her about him, was happy they were to marry.

'I wish I could be there to see you wed, Anna. I'd be as proud as a peacock to witness your marriage to Lord Lancaster—knowing you are to be the future Marchioness of Elvington. I wish your father was alive to see it—to walk his precious daughter down the aisle. He would be so proud.'

Anna was happy that her mother wished her well and at the same time saddened, for when she looked into that gaunt face, she knew her mother wasn't long for this world.

The wedding day arrived and took place with as little fuss as possible. With no more than thirty guests and with Mary and Dorothy as Anna's bridesmaids, escorted by Uncle Robert, scarcely able to believe it was happening, on this, the happiest day of her life, Anna walked down the aisle that was illuminated by candles to marry William, to join her life with his.

Carrying a small posy of pink and white flowers, radiant with happiness, she was a vision in a simple gown of cream satin delicately embroidered in matching silk and tiny seed-pearls that matched to perfection the glorious creamy pearls around her throat. They were a gift from her mother to wear on this special day. She took her place beside William—he was handsome and impressive, his dark blue frock coat hugging his broad shoulders and narrow waist with not a crease anywhere. His dark good looks were a striking contrast to her delicate beauty.

He turned and looked at her and his throat constricted at the vision she presented. It snatched his breath away and pride exploded throughout his entire body until he ached with it, for no bride had ever looked as lovely. This was Anna, as dashing and audaciously bold as when she had ridden her horse on the day he had first met her. Anna—defiant and brave and generous and loving. Pray God, he thought, let me be worthy of her. Before she had been lovely, but today, as his bride, she was exquisitely perfect.

He stretched out his hand and offered it to her. She lifted her own and placed it in his much larger, much warmer one. William felt the trembling of her fingers and saw the anxiety in her large eyes. With a smile he gave her hand a little squeeze in an attempt to reassure her. He drew her the rest of the way to the altar steps, where he would make her his for all eternity.

Time stood still as they were swept into the ceremony. After the ritual sacred vows had been said and the Reverend had pronounced the final blessing, not about to forgo the custom of kissing his young bride, William placed his long fingers beneath the delicate bones of her jaw and tilted her face to his. His head lowered and his parted lips moved gently over hers. At last he slackened his grip and stepped back. Offering her his arm, through which she slipped her hand, he led her back down the aisle.

It was with relief that Anna, now enveloped in a warm velvet cloak, with a hail of good wishes, left the church with her husband. Charles, assured and confident, waved them off. He looked as if he was accustomed to acting as best man. Anna had already made up her mind that William's younger brother would go far. Some things were learned quickly by those who wished to learn them.

Travelling to his house in Mayfair in a closed carriage, Anna felt that the whole day had taken on an air of unreality and she found it almost impossible to believe that the man sitting next to her was now her husband. She was Anna Lancaster now—Lady Lancaster, future Marchioness of Elvington, William's love, to love and to cherish, as he had promised to do before God. She could have floated, she felt so light. The future was as blue as the skies over the Indian Ocean.

Looking across at her husband, telling herself how fortunate she was when she gazed at his clean-cut profile and proud features, she realised, not for the first time, how incredibly handsome he was and began to think of the physical side of their marriage, of her duty, and all that would come later. She experienced a curious mixture of apprehension and excitement and prayed she would not disappoint him.

She thought of the kisses they had shared and how William made her feel alive, rekindling desires she had tried to suppress in the days leading up to the wedding, desires she would later experience in full when they were alone later.

The mere thought of the intimacies they would share brought a rush of colour to her cheeks and she looked away, but too late, for at that moment William looked at her and laughed softly. Coming to sit beside her, he took her cold hand in his own and lightly touched the golden ring on her finger—the ring that bound her to him for ever—before raising it to his lips.

This simple act of reassurance released her from her anxiety and she began to relax. The icy numbness that had gripped her from the moment she had left home for the church began to melt and the feel of his lips on her fingers sent a strange thrill soaring through her.

From beneath hooded lids, William watched her with brooding attentiveness. The winter sun shining in through the windows spread a halo around her. At that moment he thought she was the most magnificent creature he had ever seen—and she belonged to him. This delectable, golden-haired woman was his wife, to preside at his side, at his table, and to bear his children. She would never bore him, this he knew.

'Tell me what you were thinking—that caused you to blush and look away?'

As Anna met his gaze, her lips curved in a little smile. 'Oh, nothing in particular—only how lucky I am.'

'How does it feel to be my wife—Lady Lancaster, the future Marchioness of Elvington?'

'If you must know, I don't feel anything at the moment. It's difficult to take it all in. I feel no different to what I did before the ceremony.' She arched her brows in question. 'Should I?'

'I can think of plenty of females who would. Are you happy?'

She nodded. 'Very happy.'

'No regrets?'

'No—none that I can think of.'

He contemplated her for a moment and Anna was riveted by his gaze. 'Did I tell you that you look adorable?'

'Yes, before we left the church.'

'Then I shall tell you again. You are beautiful, Anna—like some perfect work of art.'

She laughed. 'I'm sure every groom says that to his bride on their wedding day. I am no more beautiful than any other.'

His eyebrows rose. 'I think I should be the judge of that and perhaps they don't all mean it as sincerely as I.' His eyes darkened as they fastened on her soft pink lips, moist and slightly parted, revealing her small white teeth.

His voice was husky when he spoke, which sent a tremor through Anna. 'Would you mind if I kissed my wife now we are alone? For I fear that when we arrive back at the house I shall not have you to myself for— let me see—at least eight hours.'

Anna's eyes widened in mock amazement and her

mouth formed a silent *Oh*. 'That long?' She smiled softly. 'Then in that case I think you should.'

William's gaze was intent and he was looking at her in a way he had never done before lest he betray how he really felt. He prayed by all he held sacred that he would be able to bring her all the joy and happiness she was meant for.

Sliding his hand beneath her cloak and around her waist, he drew her towards him, his eyes dark and full of tenderness. He did not kiss her at once, but studied her face, close to his, with a kind of wonder, his eyes gazing intently into hers before settling on her parted lips, which he had at last covered with his own, his arm about her waist tightening, drawing her closer, until their bodies were moulded together and Anna could feel the hardness of his muscular body. Her heart was beating so hard that she was sure he must feel it.

His lips, moist and warm, caressed hers, becoming firm and insistent as he felt her respond, kindling a fire inside her with such exquisite slowness, a whole new world exploding inside her. She raised her arms, fastening them around his neck, returning his kiss, her lips soft and clinging, moving upon his in a caress that seemed to last for an eternity.

William's lips left hers and he buried them in the soft hollow of her throat. He heard the sharp intake of her breath, but she did not pull away from him and, when he lifted his head and looked at her, his eyes burned with naked desire. Anna trembled inside, feeling as if she was on the threshold of something unknown, which caused unease to course through her and also something else, a longing so strong that she wanted to pull him towards her, for him to kiss her with all the savage intensity of his desire.

Seeing the hunger in her eyes, William sighed deeply. 'So—I was right.'

'Right?' she murmured. 'What do you mean?'

'That first time I saw you, to me, as a stranger, you epitomised everything that was youth and beauty, yet you seemed so remote. You were something of an enigma to me, Anna, and I was glad to get to know you better, to find that behind your lovely façade there beat the heart of a warm and passionate woman. I hope you will never regret your decision to marry me.'

'How could I? You have given me everything I could possibly want.'

'Everything?'

Just for a moment her eyes clouded, but quickly they became clear. 'Yes—everything.' Smiling, she leaned forward and kissed him gently on the lips, just as the carriage came to a halt outside his house.

A splendid luncheon was served at the house, followed by a beautifully decorated bride cake, for which William's cook took the credit. Everyone was in good spirits, including Uncle Robert, which, Anna thought, had a great deal to do with good wine and getting her off his hands with a satisfactory conclusion. The food was exquisite, the wine cold and delicious, the toasts numerous. William was at his most charming, regaling everyone with fascinating stories of his time in India, smiling softly when he caught Anna's eye, silently reminding her of the night to come.

'You'll be going away for a honeymoon very soon,

I expect,' Aunt Constance said, more amiable and relaxed than Anna had ever seen her.

With his arm placed possessively about Anna's waist, William shook his head. 'We have nothing like that in mind at present, is that not so, Anna?'

'It is. I think we've both done enough travelling for the time being.'

'India must have been exciting,' Mary remarked, looking extremely pretty in her pink bridesmaid dress, her face flushed to the same colour. Neither Mary nor her sister had experienced so much excitement in their young lives. They were thrilled with the silver bracelets William had presented them with before the ceremony.

'You must come and visit us, Mary.'

'Of course you must,' William said, turning to Robert. 'If you have nothing arranged for Christmas, you and your family will be most welcome at Cranford.'

'No, we have nothing planned,' Constance was quick to say, unable to believe her family's good fortune and the advantages that would benefit them all because of Anna's prestigious marriage to the future Marquess of Elvington. 'Thank you for your generous offer. I think I speak for Robert and our daughters when I say we would love to accept.'

'Then that's settled.'

Replete and exhausted, the time came for the guests to leave, leaving the bride and groom alone. Charles was staying in the house, but, tactfully, he informed them that he had a prior engagement to meet with an acquaintance and took his leave.

Inwardly relaxed and cloaked in the comforting

warmth of the wine she had consumed, Anna turned to her husband, feeling the warmth of his gaze. There was nowhere she would rather be at that moment and yet she suddenly felt extremely vulnerable and strangely apprehensive about being alone with him.

William moved to stand close to her. 'Alone at last. You look extremely beautiful, Anna,' he said softly, his voice oddly ragged and his eyes brilliant with what he felt for her. 'I don't think I've ever seen your eyes sparkle so bright.'

Emotions swept over Anna as she remembered the kisses they had shared up until this moment and the intense passion he always managed to rouse in her. 'I think that must be because I'm slightly foxed. I must have drunk too much champagne,' she declared with a happy smile. She sighed, sinking down on to a sofa and gazing up at him. 'I cannot believe that I am your wife. I keep having to pinch myself to make sure. I wonder how I will feel when you take me to Cranford.'

William sat beside her, taking her hand in his. A peculiar inner excitement touched her cheeks with a flush of delicate pink. 'I think you will adjust very well. Are you missing India?'

She smiled ruefully. 'India is a long way away. I do miss it, but not as much as I thought I would.'

'You never cease to amaze me,' William said, his voice soft and warm. 'Your life has not been easy, I know that, and I salute your courage and your boldness to deal with the emotional disruption that turned your well-ordered world upside down when Johnathan took you to India. You are undeniably brave and very lovely.'

Anna looked at him steadily. How well he knew her.

His powerful masculinity was an assault on her senses. 'Life touches everyone with a hard hand at times, I am no different, only some are able to deal with it better than others. I've done my best.'

'And now you are about to enter a new phase of your life, Anna.' Taking her hand, he drew her to her feet. 'Come, we will continue this conversation in the bedroom.'

They had connecting rooms. Anna's suite was opulent, with heavy green velvet curtains edged with gold, rich oriental carpets and a huge bed fit for a king. William disappeared into his own while Anna's maid helped her remove her wedding finery. The girl was noticeably quiet as she proceeded with the ritual, which Anna welcomed. After she slipped the white satin nightdress over her mistress's head and let it fall in a swirl about her feet, Anna watched as she snuffed out the candles, leaving just one burning close to the bed, its covers turned down.

Alone, for what seemed an eternity she stood perfectly still, her eyes fixed on the connecting door. She saw a silver light beneath it and a shadow passing to and fro. When at last it opened her heart slammed into her ribs.

William paused in the doorway, looking at her in a way he had never looked at her before. Her nightdress gleamed, outlining the womanly shape of her—the soft swell of her breasts, her tiny waist, rounded hips and long, slender legs. In that strange pattern of candlelight, she looked almost ethereal.

William was implacably calm. Anna watched him close the door and move slowly further into the room, his robe falling open to the waist, revealing his firm, well-muscled chest covered with a mat of dark hair. She stood in silent fascination, watching him as he walked towards her. He stopped in front of her and she could feel the warmth of his body close to hers as he stood looking down at her. Her whole being reached out to him, yearning for him to draw her into his arms.

'You were gone a while,' she said softly. 'I was beginning to think you had deserted me.'

He laughed. 'Desert you? I could never do that. Not when I have yearned for this moment for so long.'

With her heavy mane of hair falling down her spine, she reached up to brush his lips with a kiss, her hands sliding up his chest. He returned her kiss while slowly slipping her nightdress down over one shoulder, so that one breast appeared from beneath the concealing garment, and, a little at a time, the rest of her tender flesh was revealed to him.

The candlelight washed over her and his wonderful eyes caressed every curve of her body. His obvious delight in her sent the blood singing through her veins. Impatient to possess her, he swung her up into his arms and carried her to the canopied bed, placing her gently on the sheets and leaning over her to place his mouth on hers in a long, lingering kiss before raising his head and looking deep into her eyes.

'You are indeed beautiful, Anna. Nothing matters at this moment but that we have each other.' He saw apprehension darken her eyes and touched her cheek. 'Don't be afraid. I'll be as gentle as I can. If you feel pain, it will only be for this one time. We have the whole night

ahead of us, so let us take advantage of it and enjoy it
to its fullest.'

No more words were said. None was needed. Shrug-
ging out of his robe and stretching out alongside her, he
drew her to him, his mouth meeting hers again, at first
demanding, then sweet and achingly tender.

Anna was unable to think of anything but him, her
husband, whose clever fingers teased and fondled and
caressed her with the ease of long practice and as if he
had all the time in the world, whose mouth claimed
her for his own. The play of his fingers over her naked
flesh was agonisingly subtle and delicious, teasing her
desire to the limits of her endurance.

One brief flash of pain escaped her lips when he pen-
etrated her completely. William waited until the moment
had passed and then, smothering her with kisses, he
moved slowly, taking her with him in this erotic dance.

Anna was amazed that her body so easily accom-
modated him, her hips moving with unconscious seduction as she arched up against him, unable to believe
the intense pleasure that suddenly erupted through her
body. The absolute power of it, the sweetness, left her
dazed beneath his driving body as the two of them were
plunged into a sensual world inhabited only by lovers.
Opening her eyes, she watched his face, his changing
expressions making him unbelievably beautiful and
sending her emotions soaring even higher.

Abandoning herself completely, she revelled in the
joy, the pleasure he was giving her. Her responses were
spontaneous and all enveloping. It was an experience
surpassing anything that had gone before. It rose above
her memories of how she had felt when he had kissed

her on the night of the storm on the *Bengal*. It was supreme fulfilment, as she responded to him not as a girl, but as a woman.

She was surprised how easily he had brought her body to life, and then bliss as a wonderful aura burst around them, combining their bodies, their minds and their souls in physical release and the act of love. That was the moment she knew what it was to be a woman, the hard, powerful body of a man pressed against hers, for she had found such pleasure, a pagan pleasure, in his arms. How could she explain how she felt? Everything was changed now. Nothing was the same. She wasn't the same. She wanted nothing more than to revel in this new discovery of herself and the fullness of the moment.

All night long they made love and slept with the exhaustion of two sated lovers, then waking when they loved again, kissing and caressing until Anna's flesh cried out for fulfilment once more.

With the flickering candlelight dancing on the walls of the room, it was some time later before either of them drifted back to reality.

Wallowing in the aftermath of the most erotic, tender night of love imaginable, William was amazed by what had happened between them, how he had been unable to resist her. He had been unable to think of anything except the heat of her body, the exquisite softness of her flesh as he drove himself time and again deep within her. Her kisses and the sound of her low moans had fed his desire and intensified his pleasure. Her responses, the way her body had accepted him, was the most sensual feeling he had ever experienced. How satiny soft her skin was, how it had quivered beneath his inquisitive touch, and how the throbbing ache in his loins had found solace in the pulsating softness of her body.

Something had snapped inside him, something he had never felt before with any other woman. When the mist of fulfilment cleared from his brain, at that precise moment he had felt an ecstasy that was something extremely rare and very precious.

Anna's body was filled with a languid heat, her body tingling from his touch. She made no attempt to escape his arms. She wanted never to move again. All the memories came flooding back and her heart almost burst with love for the man in whose arms she lay—her husband and her lover in every sense. It was wonderful to feel safe and protected, to listen to his steady breathing as she rested her head on his chest.

'Good morning, My Lady. Did I hurt you?' William asked, kissing the top of her head.

'Only a little at first. On the whole it was a physical delight—a joy—an experience I'll never forget.

'To be repeated tonight. Did you sleep well?'

Tilting her head back, she looked at him. The sun wrinkles around his mouth and eyes deepened when he gave her a lazy smile. 'Not as much as I usually sleep. You allowed me little time for such luxury.'

He laughed. 'As I recall, you gave me little chance of sleeping myself.'

'Are you complaining?'

'Not a bit of it. It shows promise for all the years ahead of us.'

Having learned the meaning of passion and fulfilment, Anna wanted to be carried away with it for evermore. 'I don't think I'll ever get used to being called Lady Lancaster...'

'The future Marchioness of Elvington.'

'It sounds very grand,' she said on a sigh, shuffling to make herself more comfortable against his naked body.

'Titles are only superficial. It's what's behind them that counts.' He gathered her more closely to him. 'For God's sake, Anna, don't ever change. I want you to remain just as you are—to stay yourself. There's nothing false or conventional about you. That's as I want you to stay.'

'I'll try—although I must confess that I'm apprehensive about going to Cranford and meeting your grandfather.'

His arms tightened about her. 'Don't be. I can't guarantee how he will welcome you—just remember that I'll be with you. I'm eager to take you to Cranford, to show you your new home. You will be happy there—we will be happy together.'

Chapter Eleven

There followed a round of social occasions as Anna and William prepared to leave for Cranford. It was a happy time for Anna, but her happiness was to be short lived. It was early evening. William had gone to his club and Anna was alone in the house when a message arrived from Alice informing her that her mother had taken a turn for the worse and was not expected to last the night. Anna's heart wrenched.

Leaving a note for William, she hurried to Curzon Street. The physician was just leaving. He confirmed what Alice had said and that he was very sorry, but there was nothing further he could do for her mother. She hurried to her mother's room. She was unconscious, her head sunk into the pillows, her face very pale.

Anna sat beside the bed. There was nothing else she could do. It was both strange and comforting to think that on the death of her father, the only man she had truly loved, her mother had continued to hope and dream of a better life.

Anna didn't want to think about the wantonness of

her mother's actions. All she knew was that she was the one person she had trusted to give her love without reserve and she had not. If only she had shown her that she cared, she could have forgiven her everything. But it was too late now. And yet, despite the love she had withheld as a mother, Anna could not fault her for anything, nor could she blame her or judge her. She did not have the right to do that.

Her father's face came to mind and she remembered his merry eyes and his ready laugh. It had been a happy, spontaneous laugh that was so contagious it made the most restrained of people smile. He had made her feel comfortable and nurtured and she had loved him dearly.

Her mother died just before midnight. Having kept vigil since the physician had left, Anna closed her eyes, her chest seized with the pain of her loss.

Later, having sent a note to inform the Earl of Brinkley of her mother's passing, with the feeling of death and the oppressive weight of the house and a terrible sadness pressing in on her, she left to go home.

Entering the house, never had she been more relieved to see William crossing the hall towards her. Handing her cloak to a footman, she met him halfway. His expression was serious, anxious even. She was oddly moved.

'My mother is dead, William. She died about an hour ago.'

'I'm so very sorry for your loss,' he said, his voice low with compassion. He scrutinised her face, feeling her despair. She looked up at him with her great amber eyes smudged with weariness and grief. 'How are you?'

Her face contracted in pain and her eyes were lost and lonely, those of a child who finds itself among strangers. She stepped a little closer to him, her gaze held by his, and there was something in them. It was as though he had put out a hand and taken hers, held it close and was telling her to relax and confide in him.

William saw the great wash of tears spring from her eyes and flow down her face. His heart jolted for her pain and he strained to give her something, anything which might ease her hurt. Holding his arms out to her, he said gently, 'Come here.' She walked into them and placed her face against his chest. His arms closed round her and he held her. He was surprised to realise the urge to comfort her came from a place of authentic compassion, not simply desire.

'Cry, Anna. Let it go.'

Anna wept, her face pressed into his chest. He felt her body shudder with the force of her anguish and her voice was muffled as she cried out the words of love and loss of her mother. His heart contracted with pain and pity, for never had he seen or heard so much desolation in anyone before.

When the weeping was done, she stood back. He saw her eyes soften gratefully as her mind dwelled wonderingly on the compassion she had seen in his eyes and the consolation she had found in his arms. He had been so tender, so infinitely soothing, comforting her in her grief at a time when she was at her most vulnerable and emotionally insecure.

He had just returned from his club and Anna could smell cigars and brandy on him. She smiled wanly, wiping her face with the back of her hand.

'Here, have my handkerchief.'

'Thank you.' She dried her face and blew her nose. 'I didn't mean to cry on your shoulder. I didn't mean to cry at all. It's just that—well, I can't seem to help it.'

'It's natural that you should cry. Feel free to cry whenever I'm around. I have a strong shoulder.'

'And an incredibly comforting one,' she added, her lips trembling in a wobbly smile. 'I shall have to think about what to do next. I shall have to tell Uncle Robert. He will arrange the funeral—I can't think. I'm floundering, I'm afraid.'

'It's hardly surprising. Come into the study. There's a fire to warm you and I think a brandy would not go amiss before we go upstairs.'

Anna smiled up at him. 'Thank you, William. I would appreciate that. What would I do without you?'

According to Uncle Robert who, as the brother of the deceased, took over the arrangements for the funeral, the Earl of Brinkley was deeply saddened by his lover's death. The funeral which took place at the church in Covent Garden—which she would have approved of, being in the heart of the London she had loved—was a quiet affair with few mourners. The Earl was not present.

Now Anna had come to Curzon Street to dispose of the trappings of her mother's life. She looked at the house, reluctant to enter, but knowing she must.

William looked at her with concern. 'Would you like me to come in with you?'

She shook her head. 'No—I'll be all right.'

Reaching out, he squeezed her hand. 'This is hard for you, Anna. I know that.'

She nodded. 'I mourn a woman I didn't really know. I wish I'd known her better. Since coming back from India time has been too short for me to get to know her. I feel cheated. There's an ache in my heart, a lonely ache, and when I weep, I suppose they are selfish tears, angry, unforgiving tears. To me she was always a beautiful, radiant, yet vague personality. There were so many things I wanted to know about her—about her life with my father.' On a sigh she shook her head and looked at William. 'What I have to do shouldn't take long. Go and take care of your business, William.'

'I'll be back in an hour or so.'

Alice let her into the house. That was the moment that she realised with suddenly heartbreaking clarity that her mother was gone for ever. The house was strangely silent, almost like a tomb. Anna shuddered, keen to get on and be gone.

'I'll be in the kitchen it you want me. The Earl is arranging for the house to be sold, so everything has to be packed away.'

'I'll try not to be long.'

Anna went up the stairs, entering the room where her mother had spent the last few months of her life. The sombre atmosphere preyed on Anna more than she cared to admit. Everywhere she looked was a painful reminder of her mother. Pulling herself together and feeling a need for haste, she sorted through her mother's clothes—lovely gowns in the finest fabrics and cloaks trimmed with soft fur. Her mother's scent hung in the air and Anna could almost feel her eyes watching her.

Alice would arrange for the garments to be given to charities and anything of value given to her by the Earl he would claim.

She was surprised to find things that had been her own as a child—pictures she had drawn, hair ribbons and a likeness of her drawn on a miniature. These she put into a bag she had brought with her, along with other items that had belonged to Johnathan which she would look at later.

When she was done, about to leave the room and go downstairs she hesitated on hearing slow and measured footsteps climbing the stairs.

'Alice,' she called, 'is that you?'

It wasn't Alice, it was James, sporting a gold-knobbed cane and looking dapper in a purple jacket and breeches. Seeing him and remembering all that William had told her he was guilty of made her skin turn to ice.

'James! What are you doing here? This is no place for you.'

He saw her fear and his mouth turned up at the corners. It was a complaisant look—the look of a man who knew he was in control. This was the man who had no qualms about violating a young woman in India in retaliation for Johnathan reporting him to the East India Company for embezzlement—the woman Johnathan was to have married. The same man who had in all probability wielded the knife that had killed him.

This thought caused the chill to evaporate suddenly, driven out by the blood that coursed red-hot through her veins, as anger took its place. Ryder's viciousness had destroyed two lives and now he was here with a superior look on his face as though nothing had happened.

Anna had never hated anyone as much as she hated James Ryder at that moment. She was ashamed. At one time she'd thought him charming, kind, pleasant and funny. How could she have been so blind, so wrong? She'd done a foolish thing encouraging what she had mistaken as friendship on board the *Bengal*.

His eyes pinned to her face. 'I disagree,' he said in answer to her question. 'Is this not where my father spent a good deal of his time, pandering to your whore of a mother?' He smiled when he saw her flinch at his callous description of her mother. 'Don't look so shocked, Anna. You cannot deny what she was. You look surprised to see me. I knew you'd come some time. I waited.'

Anna watched him warily as he came further into the room, closing the door behind him. The charismatic façade that had once attracted her was now arrogant, saturnine, cruel, even, and the cocksure smile had acquired a malevolent twist. She sensed something purposeful and intent about him which troubled her and made her feel uneasy. 'Why would you do that? We have nothing to say to each other. I am here to sort through my mother's possessions so I would appreciate it if you left me alone to get on with it.'

Shaking his head, he laughed softly. 'I congratulate you on your marriage to Lord Lancaster. I wish you a happy life together at Cranford—while it lasts.'

'Our lives together will be a long and happy one.'

His eyes narrowed as they locked on hers. 'What has happened, Anna? Unlike the time when we went riding in the park, you do not seem happy to see me.'

She glared at him, contempt written broadly in her eyes. 'I think we both know the reason for that.'

James laughed, the sound an unnerving rumble deep in his chest. 'I can see Lord Lancaster has changed your opinion of me.'

'Yes, I'm afraid he has and I think you are still the same blackhearted villain who molested a young woman in India—Lucy.'

'So—he told you that, too. And you believed him?'

'Every word. Lucy was a young woman my brother would have married—a man I believe you killed.'

'Did I? Well—I don't suppose you will ever know the truth of what happened that day.'

'No, I don't suppose I will, but what I do know, what I believe, is that my brother would have been alive today had you not worked your mischief. Now will you please go? I have nothing to say to you.' She made to turn away, but his arm shot out, his fingers closing round her arm like a steel band.'

'Ah, but that is where you're wrong.' His smile left no doubt about his meaning.

'Take your hand off my arm. At once.'

He chuckled. 'Nay, Anna, I am not your husband to order about—and don't even think of calling for that maid—Alice. I have sent her on an errand—she won't be back in a hurry. You are beautiful in a temper—beautiful like your mother was beautiful to my father. Like mother, like daughter—beautiful, promiscuous, wanton—eager to fall into a pair of masculine arms just as she was.'

Anna paled. The meaning of the words and the force with which they were delivered hit home. 'How dare you? I am nothing like my mother.'

James's veneer of sham politeness crumbled and the

smile on his face disappeared as he thrust his face close
to hers. 'You still think you will be happy with Lancaster? For years he has thwarted me at every turn. Now
it is my turn. I will leave him with nothing as I left your
brother with nothing. How will he feel when he knows
that I have taken you myself?'

'I don't know what warped memories you harbour
against William, but it would seem that every rebuff he
has given you has festered inside you.' Anna knew in
that moment that he was dangerous. The house and the
street outside suddenly seemed alarmingly quiet. 'And
now,' she said, breathing deeply, seeing the fire in his
eyes, that she knew spelt danger, 'please move out of
my way. I would like to leave.'

'Then I will tell you that this, maybe the last time we
will be together, will be one to remember.'

He moved closer to her and she could feel his breath
hot on her face and the smell of spirits, which made
her stomach churn. She stepped back, her face showing revulsion.

'Do not touch me. Do you intend to hold me here by
force?'

'Only if I have to. It's a cosy room, Anna. Your mother
always found it so.'

Panic and fear overcame Anna and she began to
tremble. He noticed and smiled with smug satisfaction.

'Why, you're trembling. Come, Anna,' he drawled,
his voice thick with passion, placing his hands on her
shoulders and looking deeply into her eyes. At his touch
she struggled, trying to free herself from his grip, but
they tightened, refusing to relinquish their hold. 'So,'

he hissed, 'you want to fight me—well, all the better. I like a woman with spirit—one to match my own.'

Anna was suddenly filled with fear, but it was a different kind of fear from any she had ever known. Never, in all the time she had known him, had he been anything other than charming. But now, as she faced him, his expression dark and ruthless, she knew that at last something had touched him enough to bring about this ill-mannered stranger. She had no doubt that it was William who had brought about this change.

She was gripped by panic. James saw her fear, feeling her quivering body beneath his hands, but he only laughed, a deep, horrible, mocking sound that curled his lips, and a look of madness filled and dilated his eyes, which told her that his mere triumph over her, her very resistance, excited him much more than all her passive docility. He wanted her whatever the odds and the very fact that she belonged to William made him more determined to possess her wholly. He would settle for nothing less than that she surrender herself to him completely—absolutely.

Brutally he pushed her back towards the bed. She cried out and stumbled, but he caught her, throwing her on to the neatly arranged pile of her mother's gowns on the bed. She was enveloped in their softness and an icy terror gripped her. She tried to get up, but he fell upon her, crushing her with his weight, his face close to hers, contorted with passion as he began tearing at her clothes. A fierce, merciless struggle began between them. Now that she was faced with the terrible prospect of being raped, renewed strength surged through Anna and she fought as if her life depended on it, like a wildcat turning on its tormentor, and in her blind fury her nails raked his face, his eyes, anywhere she could see his flesh, feeling an immense, unholy satisfaction when she drew blood.

He laughed, a fierce, demonical sound that sent a chill through her. 'That's it—fight, my beauty,' he hissed. 'Fight all you want. I shall soon have you crying and pleading for mercy.'

By some miracle Anna somehow managed to tear herself away and scramble to the edge of the bed, but he grasped a handful of her thick hair, which had come loose, pulling her back with such force that she cried out, tears of helpless rage filling her eyes.

And then, abruptly, something happened and his weight left her. There was a dull thud and she ceased struggling, trembling in what remained of her clothes, the taste of blood in her mouth from a cut on her lip.

Through a mist she looked up and discerned a terrifying, faceless figure looming over her. Instinct made her draw her defiled body into a ball and shove herself back, quivering like a terrified child, clutching her torn bodice. In the wild tangle of her hair, her eyes were enormous and full of fear, accentuated by the transparent whiteness of her face, streaked with blood.

She peered up at William, who was in a towering rage, his face contorted out of all recognition as he glared down at her, beside himself with fury. The spectacle of the vile and contemptible James Ryder forcing his attentions on Anna and the pitiful state he had brutally reduced her to made him feel physically sick. He thanked God he had come in time. Tenderly he helped feet, as pale as death and shaking from ... thy hide, Ryder,' spat William, his ... ade. 'Your methods of seduction ... way, to the man who had ac- ... irs, while not taking his eyes ... on the floor. 'Behold,' he ... Your rapist, murdering ... d the truth of why ... and may ...

...now you will comprehen... he was kicked out of the Company in India— God forgive you if you condone his disgraceful action.

'By God, I will not,' Lord Brinkley remarked, barely able to contain his fury. 'Get to your feet, man,' he ordered his son.

James staggered to his feet, his clothes dishevelled and his expression deadly. He stood and faced his father, who was slightly taller than himself and was making a visible effort to control his anger.

'This is not your affair, Father,' he grumbled, 'and I resent your interference.'

'Really?' he thundered. 'But you are bothering the young lady and I am making it my affair.'

'Young lady?' James sneered. 'She is nothing but a common trull.'

'The young lady you have just tried to rape is my wife,' William said, his eyes deadly as they settled on James Ryder.'

'What were you trying to do?' Anna demanded. 'Violate me as you did Lucy—or kill me as you did my brother?'

There was a long silence as the suggestion hung in the

air between them, and s
couldn't explain, she k.. re were sev-
'You did, didn't yo ..at night. It could
Johnathan for having y
for embezzlement.'
'You'll never prove i
eral people involved in
have been any one of u...
'I expect you covere...
know how you ha...
ever had ...

...a your traces well enough. But I
...ad your revenge on Johnathan for what-
...turn you think he did you.' She looked at the
..arl, who had listened, stony faced. 'What about the
reputation and respectability of your family?' she continued. 'Rumours have a habit of getting out of control.
People will shun not just you, but your entire family.'

'Lady Lancaster is quite right. You are a disgrace,
James,' Lord Brinkley said, 'and I will not tolerate it.
Do you hear? I was prepared to give you the benefit of
the doubt when I heard of your fraudulent actions with
the Company in India. I see I should have listened to
Lord Lancaster.'

He looked at Anna, modesty causing her to pull her
torn skirts together. 'I'm sorry, my dear,' he said, stepping towards her. 'It's hard enough to have lost your
dear mother—but to suffer this, at the hands of my own
son—I cannot apologise enough.'

'Just—just get him away from me,' she said, no longer able to look at the man who had just tried to violate
her. 'I never want to set eyes on him again.'

'Touch her again and I'll break your neck,' drawled
William.

The threatening quality in his voice caused James

to look at him again, anger blazing from his eyes, and suddenly, unable to restrain himself, he sprang at William with clenched fists. Perhaps, if his brain had been fogged with drink, he might not have missed his target, but as he raised them to strike, William deftly sidestepped and struck out, hitting James on the side of his face. His eyes rolled in his head and he staggered and fell to the floor, his face bleeding from a cut caused by the blow. All vestige of pride was stripped from James, who was enraged to find himself so humiliated by William. His body shook with the intensity of his anger and sheer hatred blazed from his eyes.

'You deserved that and more,' his father thundered. 'Now get out and wait for me downstairs.' Without another word James stumbled out and down the stairs. Lord Brinkley turned to William. 'You have my word that he won't trouble you again. I have a brother in America— South Carolina. He owns a plantation in the south—a hard man, stands no nonsense. I think some time over there making himself useful will do him good.'

Moving towards Anna, he felt inside his jacket and removed a box. 'I knew you were coming here today to sort through your mother's things. I wanted to give you this. It's a necklace—sapphires. I gave it to your mother when we—when we first met. Of all the gifts I gave her this was her favourite by far. I thought you might like it.'

No longer trembling and with William's arm supporting her, she took the box and opened it. The sapphire necklace lay on a bed of black velvet, the precious stones winking in the light. 'Oh—they—they're beautiful.' Tears filled her eyes when she thought of her mother wearing them. They were exactly what she would have loved to wear. She looked at William.

'Take them,' he murmured. 'I'm sure your mother would have wanted you to have them.'

Closing the box, Anna smiled at Lord Brinkley. 'Yes, thank you. They—they're beautiful.'

He smiled and nodded. 'Good.' With nothing left to say, he walked to the door where he turned and looked back. 'Your mother was very dear to me. I shall miss her.'

When he'd gone Anna pressed her body close to William. What James had tried to do to her had shocked her to the very core of her being. Her body felt bruised and defiled and weighted down with a terrible misery and despair. The thought that she would have to go on living after this was almost inconceivable.

'Come,' William said, wrapping one of her mother's cloaks about her shoulders, concealing her tattered dress. 'Let's get out of here. The maid will be back, I'm sure, to sort everything out.'

In the coach taking them home, William laid an arm about his wife's shoulders and drew her to his side. 'Tell me, my love, are you hurt?'

'No, just shaken. Thank goodness you came when you did. I shudder to think what James would have done to me had you not…'

'Hush. Don't even think about it.' William's arms tightened about her. 'It's over now,' he said thickly and then hurriedly cleared his throat, trying to force back the emotion that welled up inside him. It threatened to choke him when he thought of what Ryder had put her through. He knew if he had succeeded, it would be too hard to bear. He kissed the top of her head as she nestled against him. 'Are you sure you're all right?'

'Yes. I'm just tired. The last few days have been—difficult.'

'I know.'

'I can well imagine what must have gone through your mind when you came into the room—how it must have brought back memories of what James had done to Lucy.'

'Listen to me, my beautiful, tempestuous wife. I love you. I love you so much I couldn't bear the thought of anyone causing you harm or of losing you. I love you more than my own life and when I walked into the house and saw what Ryder was subjecting you to, what he might have done to you, I could not bear it. I love you and have done so for a long time. Of all the women I have known, none can hold a candle to you.'

Later, in the privacy of their bed, William held his wife for longer than usual, Then took her face between his hands. They looked at each other for the length of several heartbeats. His features were less guarded than Anna had ever seen them and there was something so tender in his eyes that all she could do was stare.

'I love you so much, Anna.'

'I know,' she murmured,

He never wanted to let go of her. He was content to let his eyes dwell on the softness of her lovely face, to gaze into the depths of her half-closed eyes, to glory in the gentle sweep of her long dark lashes which dusted her cheeks.

Almost unconscious of what he was doing, he lowered his head closer to hers, overcome by a strong desire to draw her mouth to his and taste the sweetness of her quivering lips, which he did, succumbing to the impulse that had been tormenting him from the moment he had rescued her from Ryder's clutches.

The moment he placed his mouth on hers Anna parted her lips to receive his longed-for kiss, her heart soaring with bliss. He kissed her slowly and deliberately and Anna felt a familiar melting sweetness flowing through her bones and her heart pouring into his, depriving her of strength.

With a deep sigh William drew back and gave her a searching look, his gaze and his crooked smile drenching her in its sexuality.

'There are times, Anna, when you confound me,' he murmured, placing his warm lips on her forehead. 'You are a Lancaster now. You belong to me—to Cranford. Will you be sorry to leave London?'

'No, of course not. It will be a relief. I'm looking forward to seeing your home—and meeting your grandfather,' she added, with a look that didn't convince William. 'From what you have told me, when you left Cranford all those years ago, you were deeply angry with him. Would you say you made peace with your grandfather when you saw him recently?'

'Peace? Of a sort.'

'And he will accept me as your wife?'

They stared at each other for a long moment. Anna watched him warring with himself. His eyes turned bitter with resentment when he recalled his meeting with his grandfather.

'As to that I must be honest with you. When I told him I was to marry you, it didn't go down well—but he knows I will walk away should he start throwing insults.'

Anna looked at him with understanding and dread at meeting the Marquess. 'Then it is up to me to try to win him over.'

'It is up to us, Anna. You won't have to face him alone,' he said softly, taking her hand and giving it an encouraging squeeze. 'Together. We will do it together.'

It was a beautiful day when they left for Cranford—not too cold, considering it was mid-December, causing Anna's spirits to lift. Nothing had prepared her for the exquisite splendour that was Cranford Park. When she saw the enormous edifice of William's ancestral home, which was an outstanding example of opulence on a grand scale, she was more than a little daunted.

'Oh, my!' she gasped. 'What a beautiful house.'

William smiled at the dazed expression of disbelief on her face, well satisfied with her reaction. 'I have to agree with you,' he replied, preferring to watch a myriad of expressions on Anna's face rather than the approaching house.

The four bay mounts pulling the crested coach danced to a stop in front of the house and William got out, gallantly extending his hand to help Anna. Scarlet-and-gold-liveried footmen appeared out of the house and descended on the coach to strip it of the baggage.

William led Anna into the house. She looked around her, in awe of everything she saw. Horton was there and offered her a warm welcome before William whisked her into the drawing room for refreshment. At a glance she became aware of the rich trappings of the interior, the sumptuous carpets and tasteful furniture.

William watched her, happy with her reaction. 'You like what you see, Anna?'

She nodded. 'It's a lovely house—and so big. I'm sure to get lost.'

William laughed. 'You'll soon get used to it. We'll have refreshments and then I'll show you around.'

'When shall I meet your grandfather?'

'He finds it difficult getting around and doesn't often leave his room. His temper often gets the better of him because his massive pride cannot bear for anyone to see him enfeebled. If we're fortunate, his disposition will have improved before I introduce you. I'll go and see him and let him know we've arrived. I'll take you to his apartment later.'

Anna was nervous about meeting the Marquess for the first time. In mourning for her mother, she wore a black but stylish gown, which enhanced the brightness of her golden hair. William's breath caught in his throat when he saw her. As she glided almost soundlessly over the thick-piled carpet towards him, slender and long-limbed, he was enchanted as he always was by her and gave a slight bow, his eyes making an instant appraisal.

His breath caught in his throat. Never had he seen a woman with so much beauty and it was as if he were seeing it for the first time in his life. From the moment she had boarded the ship in Bombay she had grown, phoenix-like, from the shell of a naive, vulnerable young girl.

When she was close there came to him the faint

heady scent of crushed rose petals, a scent he would for evermore associate with her. They looked at each other steadily for a long moment before Anna spoke, seeming ill at ease, which was to be expected on this, her first visit, to his grandfather, a daunting prospect for the strongest individual.

'Well, William?' she said softly. 'Will I do, do you think?'

'You are exquisite,' he said, taking her hand and raising it to his lips, feeling a slight tremble in her fingers. 'Don't be nervous. He was wealthy and powerful and a notable and admired figure about town in his day. He was also a man not to cross. I find it ironic that he outlived my father—his only offspring. I feel I must warn you that he has a despotic presence. Try not to let him intimidate or frighten you.'

She laughed. 'I won't. If I can withstand his grandson's wrath, then I can withstand anything.'

As Anna placed her hand on his arm and allowed him to escort her to her meeting with the Marquess of Elvington, she was not so sure. She had a strange sensation of helplessness and fatality that one sometimes has in a dream. In the surrounding haze she was aware of nothing but William by her side, offering her his support.

She was crushed by the weight of responsibility that descended on her, for not until that moment had she realised the importance of her position as the future Marchioness of Elvington. She prayed the man she was about to meet would set aside her background and accept her as William's wife.

William looked at her, noting her pallor. 'You look

terrified,' he murmured. 'Feel like running away? I couldn't blame you.'

Anna took a deep breath and squared her shoulders, knowing that if she turned back now she would never forgive herself. 'Yes, but I won't. I've never run away from anything in my life and I am not about to do so now.'

Chapter Twelve

The Marquess sat in a high-backed chair by the window, a rug tucked around his legs. Despite his great age he still possessed a commanding presence, along with the poise and regal bearing of a man who has lived a thoroughly privileged life. He watched Anna enter. Their eyes met across the distance of the room. He was still, alert and wary, watching as she crossed the room towards him beside William. The Marquess opened his mouth to speak, then closed it without taking his eyes off her and without uttering a word.

When they were close, Anna curtsied with deep respect.

'Grandfather, allow me to present Anna, my wife.' William was watching his grandfather closely. He was looking at Anna as if he had seen a ghost.

'Yes,' he said, continuing to stare at Anna with a bemused expression on his face. 'Welcome to Cranford,' he said. 'Please be seated.'

Anna did as he bade, sitting across from him, perching uneasily on the edge of the chair. It wasn't much of a welcome, but then she hadn't expected one. She had hoped he would hold out a hand to her, but she would not beg. Whether she was welcome at Cranford or not by the Marquess, she was here to stay. He spent his life in this room with his life behind him, brooding, ill. She might almost feel sorry for him, but no one felt sorry for the Marquess of Elvington.

'I am happy to meet you, Your Grace. William has told me so much about you.'

Immediately the old man's eyes flashed to his grandson. 'I imagine he has—none of it to my credit, I wager.'

Anna's eyes widened at his taunting remark, but William inhaled slowly, determined not to be drawn into an argument in front of his bride. 'You are too serious, Grandfather,' William said. 'I merely put Anna in the picture. It was daunting enough for her coming to Cranford for the first time. Meeting you was an added concern.'

'Yes—well—I'm sure we'll get on and she'll soon learn there's no need to concern herself with me. How do you like the house, Anna?'

'It's quite splendid—and so large.'

'You'll soon find your feet. William—and Mrs Coleman, the housekeeper, will show you how things are done.'

'Mrs Coleman informs me you have not been well,' William said, still standing. 'How are you faring now?'

'I've been better. I get tired and have difficulty getting around.'

'I'm sorry to hear that, Your Grace,' Anna said sympathetically. 'It must be a difficult time for you.'

Her compassionate words took the Marquess off guard. 'Thank you. It is.' He fell silent and looked at her hard, as if seeing her for the first time, yet it was as if he were looking at something, or someone, beyond her. 'William informs me your parents are both dead.'

'Yes, they are—my brother also.'

'Killed in India, William tells me. Bad job, that. Must have come as a shock.'

'Yes—although I do not shock easily, Your Grace.'

'I wouldn't think you did—considering your mother's profession.'

William's eyes blazed angrily. 'That will do, Grandfather. If it is your intention to insult and upset my wife, then we shall withdraw.'

Anna reached out her hand and placed it on William's to calm him. 'It's all right, William. I'm not upset—far from it. Better to get everything out in the open if we are to exist in the same house.' She looked back at the Marquess, her expression set in determined lines. 'You are quite right. My mother was a courtesan.'

'It must have shocked you.'

His gaze upon her was so frank that she wanted to turn away, but she would not give way before him. 'Shocked? Yes, but there was nothing I could do about it. My father was dead, my mother in dire straits. She had a living to earn.'

For some reason this defiance pleased him. He gave a chuckle of appreciation which was rich. 'You are no meek and mild miss. I can see that.'

'No, I'm not. You probably have no sympathy with the trials of women who fall on hard times through no fault of their own. My mother died two weeks ago, but that is neither here nor there to you. I was not ashamed of her. I loved both my parents.'

Surprisingly he nodded. 'That's as well. I like to see respect in a child.'

'My father was a good man, a proud man, if somewhat careless with his money, which resulted in him being imprisoned in the Fleet where he died. I was not ashamed of him either.'

The Marquess gave her a sceptical look. 'I see. You're forthright and speak your mind, which I like. I'll give you that, but it's plain that your father didn't leave his children decently provided for. However, that is in the past. No use fretting over it now. And you went out to India.'

'With my brother.'

He nodded. 'William and your brother were friends—both had the presence of mind to leave the Company and go their own way. It worked out well for him—and for you, William tells me.'

'Yes. Johnathan had no other family.'

'And you will not be daunted by Cranford—or my grandson, come to that?'

'No. I am William's wife. I love him and I will make him a good wife. We are equal. I will live in no man's shadow. You have to accept it—as I must accept so much about Cranford I do not yet understand.'

They talked, each picking their words with care. William noted that his grandfather had not congratulated them on their marriage, but he was thankful he had welcomed Anna to Cranford. He also noted that from the moment Anna had walked into the room he had not taken his eyes from her face. In fact, the aura of patriarchal control had slipped. It was as if her face evoked a memory.

* * *

While the two men talked of domestic matters, standing up, Anna sauntered over to one of the mullioned windows overlooking the gardens and the wooded park beyond. She spent a moment gazing out. *Beautiful*, she thought. That was the only way she could describe it. She would like living here.

After a while she turned and walked back, passing a small table with several miniature portraits of family members on its polished surface. Idly her gaze passed over them, men and women of various ages, wondering who they were, when her attention was caught by one in particular. The face had a dignified stillness, but the artist had captured a look in her eyes that was watchful, also knowing.

Without thinking, she said, 'Why have you got a portrait of my grandmother at the side of your bed?'

Both men stopped talking and stared at her in stunned surprise. In a flash, Anna knew what she had done—that her own grandmother was the woman William had told her about on the *Bengal*, that she had been the Marquess's forbidden love so long ago. For several moments the room was silent as they digested the enormous discovery that had been made.

Anna swallowed, her heart beating in thick, painful beats, wishing she had not blurted it out like that. The sensible thing would have been to hold it back until she knew more, to keep her discovery to herself in case it caused the Marquess pain—something Anna, with her innate soft heart, didn't want to do, but it was too late.

'Your grandmother?' the Marquess uttered softly.

'Yes,' she said softly, indicating the portrait she recognised. 'This is my grandmother.'

Suddenly his face looked worn and drawn, his eyes full of despair. 'Clarissa.' He uttered the name on a breath. 'You are Clarissa's granddaughter?'

'Her name was Clarissa Sharman before she married my grandfather.'

He nodded his silvery head, staring hard at Anna. 'I knew there was something familiar about you when you came in—in your face. I saw it from the first.'

'Everyone used to say I looked like her,' Anna said, sitting in the chair she had recently vacated across from him, 'and now, looking at the portrait, even I can see the resemblance between us.'

'I sensed it when I first laid eyes on you,' the Marquess said hoarsely. It's not just your hair and eyes—that strange colour of amber I've never seen in anyone else—it's something inside you—in your manner and the forthright way you have of speaking and looking at a person.'

'You—you knew her well?'

He sighed and nodded. 'I know my words may sound disloyal to my departed wife, but your grandmother was the love of my life. It broke my heart when we parted. The events that tore my life apart and took your grandmother from me happened a long time ago, but I remember. When my brother died and I was recalled to Cranford—which put an end to my military career—it was not what I wanted, far from it, but I had a duty to my forebears to continue the line.

'I should have married your grandmother. She was

the greatest love and the greatest tragedy of my life. I loved her very much—but I lost her to your grandfather because she did not have the right credentials to be the Marchioness of Elvington.'

'I'm so sorry. That must have hurt you terribly.' She saw his eyes go suddenly moist with remembering and she marvelled that an event that had taken place all those years ago could arouse such deep emotion. 'And now I suppose, by some uncanny twist of fate, it's like history repeating itself, that you could see the same thing happening to William.'

'I confess I did—at first—when I learned of your background, but he had the good sense to marry where his heart is and to hell with what people think—which was my failing. But tell me, Anna. Was your grandmother happy?'

'Yes, I believe so. She and my grandfather had a long and happy life together.'

Thinking of her paternal grandmother, her face softened. Her grandmother had loved her dearly and she had returned that love. Sadly, she had died when Anna was a child, but she had never forgotten her.

The Marquess closed his eyes, breathing deeply. He could not believe his good fortune, that his beloved Clarissa's granddaughter was William's wife, his granddaughter-in-law, that a part of Clarissa would be living at Cranford.

'Would you mind leaving me? I'm tired. I would like my valet to put me to bed.' Anna stood up and he looked at her. 'You will come and see me tomorrow—you can tell me about Clarissa.'

Anna smiled down at him softly. 'I would be happy to.'

Outside the room William paused, looking down at his wife directly, a look that searched her face with tenderness and with love. 'There you are, you see,' he said as he took her arm and escorted her down the stairs. 'It wasn't so bad after all.'

'No. Meeting your grandfather was something I dreaded and I'm surprised at how easily he accepted me—although it might have been a different matter had he not loved my grandmother in their day.'

'I'm finding it hard to believe that your grandmother and my grandfather were in love. I'm beginning to feel sorry for my grandmother. It must have been difficult for her knowing her husband was in love with another woman.'

'Yes, yes, it must.'

'Love is not something that can be picked up and put down.'

Anna knew what he was saying for was that not what she was feeling for William? 'No, it cannot. Love is for ever. What a pity your grandfather didn't have the strength of mind to marry her—although had they done so, then neither of us would be here now.'

'That is true.' Drawing her into his arms, he placed his cheek against her hair and held her close. 'My remembrance of my grandmother has become diminished by the passage of time. Only now, since meeting you, am I able to see myself in a whole new different light. Now I have you, Anna. In degrees of love, I have to admit that my feelings for you transcend anything I have ever felt before. It seems impossible and yet I know it is true, for here I am, totally enamoured with you, my love.'

William's heart was beating so hard Anna could feel it against her own. Raising her face to his, she whispered, 'Kiss me.'

His mouth consumed hers with a hunger that demanded more, rousing her sensations and persuading her heart to beat in a frantic rhythm.

Epilogue

Hearing wheels crunch the gravel in the drive, Anna looked out of the window. 'I see our guests have arrived.'

William came up behind her, sliding his arms about her and drawing her back to his chest. 'So they have. Tilly and Charles will be here tomorrow.'

'What a happy family we will be.'

Anna had fallen in love with Cranford. She could feel the great house wrapping itself around her. Christmas was upon them and she had busied herself to arranging for the comfort and entertainment of their guests.

Uncle Robert and his family were to remain until Twelfth Night. She watched Constance get out of the coach followed by Mary and Dorothy, their faces alight with excitement and wonderment as they gazed awestruck at Cranford. They'd never seen anything like it. Along with their mother's, their clothes were in the latest fashion—nothing but the best for Constance now she was closely attached to the future Marchioness of Elvington.

Anna and William went down to the hall to welcome them.

* * *

It proved to be a very merry Christmas. Everyone enjoyed the food and the warmth of good wine in the Cranford tradition of hospitality. The Marquess did not join in the festivities. He was content to remain in his room, more than happy when Anna would sit with him and he could remember and speak of his lost Clarissa.

After a stroll arm in arm through the gardens together, Anna and William stood in the doorway to the drawing room, the light from the chandelier shining fully on the happy scene. There was Charles, handing Uncle Robert another glass of brandy, and Constance, some of the starchiness having left her as she watched her daughters. Caught up in the excitement, they stood beside Tilly, watching in wonderment as her fingers danced over the piano keyboard playing a merry tune.

Tilly, bright and magical and strikingly pretty, always laughing and free, her violet eyes aglow, raised her head and looked across the room at her brother in the doorway with his wife. She seemed to open like a flower upturned to the sun when she smiled.

William returned her smile and looked down at his wife. His heart felt as if it would burst inside his chest from all the love he felt for her. Drawing her close, he placed a kiss full on her lips.

'Happy Christmas, my darling. You are happy?'

'Yes—ecstatically so. I see a fine future beckoning.' A smile of contentment curved her lips.

'What will be will be.'

* * * * *

COMING NEXT MONTH FROM

HARLEQUIN
HISTORICAL

All available in print and ebook via Reader Service and online

A ROGUE FOR THE DUTIFUL DUCHESS (Regency)
by Louise Allen
Sophie will do anything to protect her son and his inheritance. Even ask distractingly handsome rogue Lord Nicholas to retrieve her late husband's diaries before their contents bring down the monarchy!

HIS RUNAWAY MARCHIONESS RETURNS (Victorian)
by Marguerite Kaye
Oliver, Marquess of Rashfield, is society's most eligible bachelor. Except he's already married! Conveniently wed years ago, he and Lily have built separate lives. Only now she's returned...

SECRETS OF THE VISCOUNT'S BRIDE (Regency)
by Elizabeth Beacon
When her sister begs for help stopping her arranged marriage, Martha pretends to be Viscount Elderwood's bride-to-be. She soon discovers there's more to the viscount than she'd been led to believe...

A MANHATTAN HEIRESS IN PARIS (1920s)
by Amanda McCabe
New York darling Elizabeth Van Hoeven has everything...except freedom. But now Eliza's traveling to study piano in Paris and falling for jazz prodigy Jack Coleman in the process!

BOUND TO THE WARRIOR KNIGHT (Medieval)
The King's Knights • by Ella Matthews
As the new wife to stoic knight Benedictus, Adela finds herself in a whole new world. Their union is one of convenience, though her feelings for the warrior are anything but...

GAME OF COURTSHIP WITH THE EARL (Victorian)
by Paulia Belgado
American heiress Maddie enlists Cameron, Earl of Balfour, in a game of pretend courtship to win suitors. But now Cameron—who has sworn off love—is the only man she craves.

YOU CAN FIND MORE INFORMATION ON UPCOMING HARLEQUIN TITLES, FREE EXCERPTS AND MORE AT HARLEQUIN.COM.

HHCNM0223

Get 4 FREE REWARDS!

We'll send you 2 FREE Books plus 2 FREE Mystery Gifts.

FREE Value Over **$20**

Both the **Harlequin®** Historical and **Harlequin®** Romance series feature compelling novels filled with emotion and simmering romance.